Revisions, St

Florida Writers Association Collection, Volume 7

Featuring Person of Renown author

Marie Bostwick

Copyright © Florida Writers Association, 2015

All rights reserved.

Published by Black Oyster Publishing Company, Inc.

No part of this publication may be reproduced, stored in a retrieval system, or transmitted by any means, without prior written permission of the publisher and the author/illustrator.

For inquiries write to:

Black Oyster Publishing, 806 Dogwood Drive

Casselberry, Florida 32707

ISBN: 978-1-51464-277-1

ACKNOWLEDGMENTS

One hundred seventy-six entries poured in from one hundred thirty one FWA members, and forty-six of them submitted two stories. Entries were posted without author name to a specially designed website accessible only by our judges. The websites produced for viewing the stories and entering judges' votes were created and maintained by Karen Lieb, President of Florida Writers Foundation. Karen is also FWA's official photographer. Thank you, Butterfly.

Our anonymous judges read and scored the entries. FWA is deeply indebted to them, and thanks each for their time, dedication, and willingness to volunteer for this worthwhile project.

Each finalist's entry is presented as entered, with no editing. Many of the entrants took advantage of either attending one of FWA's many Critique Groups across the state, or using FWA's Editing Service, which offered special pricing. The quality of entries reflects the professionalism of our members. Thank you, Bobbie Christmas, for managing that special editing service.

Thank you to Leslie Salas for designing our cover this year. Her cover design expertise produced a wonderful cover for our collection book.

It is with heartfelt gratitude that FWA acknowledges Marie Bostwick's contribution to this publication. She had perhaps the hardest job of all . . . picking only ten to be her favorites out of the truly wonderful sixty winning stories.

This year our second annual Youth Writers Collection Contest, created to provide our youth members with an opportunity to become published authors, produced eight marvelous winners. FWA acknowledges and thanks our Youth Writers Groups, their Group Leaders and especially Serena Schreiber and Kristen Stieffel for their extraordinary efforts to accomplish this goal.

Finally, our congratulations and sincere thanks from FWA's Board of Directors to Tom Swartz of Black Oyster Publishing for becoming our official Collections publisher this year, and for graciously donating all publishing costs for the adult collection book, including our 2nd Annual Youth Collection Contest. Their patience and expertise throughout all aspects of publishing our Collection book has been invaluable.

Su Gerheim, Coordinator
Revisions, Stories of Starting Over: Florida Writers Association Collection, Volume 7
Starting Over: Florida Writers Association Youth Collection, Volume 2

Table of Contents

ACKNOWLEDGMENTS, *Su Gerheim* 3
INTRODUCTION, *Marie Bostwick* 7
Marie Bostwick, *Sunday Night Flight* 8

MARIE BOSTWICK'S TOP TEN PICKS

01 **Jason Bonderoff**, *The Cypress Tree's Apprentice* 11
02 **Kamesa Evette Carter**, *A Teen Mom Starts Over* 14
03 **Linda Kraus**, *Single* 17
04 **Frank T. Masi**, *Clopin Clopant* 19
05 **Phyllis McKinley**, *Your Mother Is No Longer Theresa* 22
06 **Al Perrin**, *The Human Singularity* 25
07 **Faun Joyce Senatro**, *The Molding of Rudy* 29
08 **J. H. Weis**, *Three Shades of Gray* 32
09 **Jeff Boyle**, *"Twenty-two"* 35
10 **Lynn E. Welsh**, *365 Beds* 37

Revisions, Stories of Starting Over:
Florida Writers Association Collection, Volume 7

Kelly Abell, *Broken* 40
Robert Alan, *The Sword and the Pen* 43
Ernie Audino, *The Ashes of the Martyrs* 47
Susan Bartlett, *Reshuffling* 50
Diane M. Boilard, *Mostly Blind* 54
Cindy Farrar Bryan, *The Replacements* 57
Bria Burton, *Empty Girl* 60
D. J. Cantillo, *Miranda Monday* 63
Patricia Crumpler, *A Perfect Companion* 66
Terri Hoffman Curtis, *The Plan* 70
Ian Darling, *Operation Fresh Start* 73
Vic DiGenti, *No Prom Like an Old Prom* 76

Karen Dillon, *What Happens in Vegas* ... 79
Allen Gorney, *The Son in the Telescope* ... 82
Patrick Guttery, *A Time to be Born* ... 84
Chris Hamilton, *My Bathroom Door* ... 87
Bob Hart, *Two* ... 90
Veronica Helen Hart, *Poisonberry Wine* ... 93
Robert Z. Hicks, *Career Revisions, Starting Over* ... 98
Christine Holmes, *The Smile* ... 101
John Hope, *The Drive* ... 104
Sharon E. Johnson, *Coming to America* ... 107
Beda Kantarjian, *Author* ... 110
Colleen Jeffery Kastner, *Catching My Breath* ... 113
Jade Kerrion, *Always Apart of You* ... 116
Bruce H. Kubec, *Melted Ice* ... 118
Peggy Lambert, *Help Wanted* ... 121
Stephen Leitschuh, *Ira's Bride* ... 124
Christopher Malinger, *Sweet Scent of Spring* ... 127
John Mallon, *Colonial Midwife* ... 129
Doris Manukian, *Coming to America* ... 132
Robert E. Marvin, *The Party* ... 135
Mark McWaters, *Reset* ... 138
John Charles Miller, *Taking the Bait* ... 142
Diane Mutolo, *Blossoming Popularity* ... 145
Bettie Nebergall, *Jumping the Fence* ... 148
Jean Axtell Nelson, *Marigolds* ... 152
Kate Newton, *Come to Papa* ... 155
Joan North, *Fresh Step* ... 158
Sheila Marie Palmer, *A Rose by Any Other Name* ... 161
Elaine Person, *Happy Dazed* ... 164
R. M. Prioleau, *When I Grow Up . . .* ... 167

Pat Rakowski, *Together* 170
Dale Simpson, *Seven-Eighths* 173
Kristen Stieffel, *Immolation* 176
Tom Swartz, *Twelve Steps Forward*.. 179
Aimee Taylor, *Let Him Go* 183
Dee Ann Waite, *A Soul Revised*.. 186
Sharon K. Weatherhead, *Kitchen Magic* 188
Judy Weber, *The Forgiveness Test* 191

Starting Over: Florida Writers Association Youth Collection, Volume 2

Age Group 10-13
1st Place: Sarina Patel, *Remembrance*.. 195
2nd Place: Jaina Hope, *The Wise Cherry* 197
3rd Place: Yasmin Vuong, *Emotion Chaos*.. 200

Age Group 14-17
1st Place: Mikaela Bender, *Terminated*.. 203
2nd Place: Tyler Vest, *Midnight* 206
3rd Place: Jade Browne, *Me, Myself and Time* 209
Honorable Mention: Kira Lieb, *Hope for a New Year* 212

Hide and Seek: Florida Writers Association Collection, Volume 8, and 214
Hide and Seek: Florida Writers Association Youth Collection, Volume 3

INTRODUCTION

Revisions, Stories of Starting Over:
Florida Writers Association Collection, Volume 7

As writers, we are well acquainted with the process of assessing our work with impartial eyes, searching for strengths and weaknesses, unearthing strategies to expand the former and eliminate the latter, before getting out a laptop, legal pad, or sharp-pointed red pencil to insert, delete, or trash entirely and face, yet again, the unnerving void of the blank page.

Many writers despise revisions. I'm one of them. I find revising to be least creative and most pedestrian part of the writing process – also the most necessary. As some smart person once said, "Good books are written. Great books are rewritten."

Indeed they are. Usually more than once.

As it is with writing, so it is with life. The life well lived is not a straight path. It requires constant course correction, a willingness to take a new road or retrace steps along an old one, to adjust thoughts, actions, and attitudes in response to or anticipation of changing circumstances, to take a deep breath start again, and again, and again.

The contributors to this collection displayed incredible imagination, creativity and skill as they examined the theme of revision and the challenges of starting over.

Within these pages you will encounter characters who, by choice or necessity, find themselves sailing through uncharted waters. You'll become acquainted with the newly single and the newly married, the ill, recovering, and recovered, the recently landed and the recently deceased, and some who have wished for death but chosen life. You'll meet men and women and the occasional robot, grownups and children, as well as one or two grownups who behave like children.

In short, as you read this collection you will encounter an enormous range of human experience – from birth to death and beyond – presented as stories, memoirs, and poems that will capture your imagination, spark your intellect, and engage your emotions.

So polish up your reading glasses, my friend. Find a comfortable chair, bring your favorite beverage, and prepare yourself for a wild and utterly enjoyable ride.

And when you're finished? Do what I did. Turn back to page one. The stories in the collection demand to be read again, and again, and again...

Marie Bostwick
2015

Sunday Night Flight

Boarding a Sunday night flight to Denver, I find row seven, quickly step out of the aisle, stow my stuff, and take the seat by the window, leaving the other for my husband, who settles in just as efficiently. We know the drill.

He's a consultant and I'm a writer, which means we eat what we kill and we travel a lot, but rarely to the same place at the same time. When people marvel at how we keep our commuter marriage from unraveling, we talk about quality time and our rule to never go more than two weeks without seeing each other. Lately though, the rule has become more of a guideline. We're overworked, overwhelmed, and on deadline. Always. Today is no exception. It's been nearly a month since we've seen each other and so it's nice even to sit together. But when the plane levels off and seatbelt sign is extinguished, we pull out our laptops and buckle down.

It's a two-hour flight. With luck, I can write another nine hundred words, perhaps a thousand. And if I can keep my heroine focused, prevent her from going off on tangents or making long speeches, as she tends to do – and who can blame her, poor thing, the situation looking so bleak, the dénouement so many hundreds of pages off, the happy ending further still – maybe I can finish the chapter before landing. If not now, maybe on the Denver to Seattle connection.

Opening my document, I hear the young voice of a young woman in the row behind, high and bright and nervous, as if she's spent the last fifteen minutes figuring out what she wants to say and how.

"I read that book. For a class. Do you like it?"

"Yeah," says her seatmate. His voice sounds young but not as young as hers. "Did you?"

"A lot. Are you reading it for school?"

"Just thought it sounded interesting. I'm into organics."

"Cool."

They talk about organic food, locavores, backcountry skiing. She still sounds nervous but keeps asking questions, one after the other, talking too fast, I think, her laughter too ready, her interest too obvious. It's distracting for me and upsetting my heroine, who is heading down a rabbit trail talking about a cousin she's never

SATURDAY NIGHT FLIGHT

mentioned previously and an incident with a dog that swam across a stream that was deeper and swifter than it looked from shore.

This isn't working.

Hopefully, the man sitting in row 8 will soon become bored, and say something about it being nice to talk to her but he'd better get back to his book, before withdrawing behind the invisible walls we erect for ourselves on airplanes, subway cars, and elevators, or while standing on line for lattes in the pre-caffeinated, preverbal hours of early morning.

But he doesn't. They keep talking and, thanks to some bizarre acoustical confluence of aerospace engineering, I can hear every word they say as clearly as if they were sitting in my row, in my lap. This really isn't working.

I look at my husband, hoping for a glance or an eye roll that will confirm my right to be annoyed but his eyes are fixed to the glowing screen, oblivious to my plight. I sigh, but only to myself, having too much respect for "the zone" to interrupt him when he's in it, feeling jealous.

I hit delete, excising the cousin and the dog. They were heading nowhere good.

Thirty-three minutes gone and my word count is a negative number. I won't finish the chapter now but... Maybe the scene? I take another run at it, training my eyes on the paragraphs, trying to discipline myself into deafness, and stop myself from narrating on the scene playing out in row 8, seats C and D.

I can't.

Sixty-five minutes gone, I delete a rambling and meaningless speech, raise the white flag, plug in my headphones and watch an episode of "The Office" on inflight TV. The story is pointless but still sort of funny. I start to feel less resentful about the time I've lost.

"The Office" ends. "Real Housewives of Atlanta" begins. Uninterested, I unplug the cord from the computer but leave the headphones on, open my outline, and stitch up a plot hole, the solution suddenly obvious.

One hundred minutes gone, I feel the slight increase in gravity that signals upcoming contact with the earth and save my document before powering off and removing the headphones. Husband does the same.

"Did you get some work done?" he asks.

"A little. Enough."

"Good."

The conversation in Row 8 continues, but the tone is altered, the interest more evenly weighted on both sides. Something happened while I was in "The Office." Now, he clearly finds her just as attractive as she found him from the first. Maybe he's just interested in a pickup or a hookup or whatever it is they call it now. But...what if there's more to it?

What if these were the minutes, these two hours suspended above the earth, when 8C and 8D met, and talked, and fell in love? What if this turns out to be the unscheduled and unlikely beginning to the tale they will relate to their children and grandchildren? The way 7C and I tell of our own meeting forty years past, at an employee picnic when my mother introduced me to a serious looking man who had hair as black as ink and trousers too carefully creased for a picnic in the park? What if this is where their story begins? What if I am the only witness?

I should have listened in. I should have taken notes. And I call myself a writer?

Touch down and taxi. The seatbelt sign goes off. The surge for the door begins. We deplane and we part, one hundred seventy-four strangers, traveling together on a Sunday night, continuing our journey alone or with another, as individuals, as acquaintances, as friends, as family, as lovers.

8C and D pass us, walking together. She wears a black sweater and carries a backpack, hair pulled back by a green bandana. He towers over her by a foot. His blond ponytail reaches to his shoulder blades. I try to keep sight of them we walk through the crowded terminal to our next gate.

"Let me carry that," says my beloved, reaching out for my heavy briefcase. We stop midstream while the river of humanity swirls and eddies around us. I hand my burden over to him with a grateful smile.

When I look up, 8C and D have disappeared, lost in the crowd. Where are they going from here? To bed? To heartbreak? To the rest of their lives?

Denver to Seattle. The plane levels off, the seatbelt sign goes dark. Beloved bends down for his briefcase, frowns curiously when he sees that I don't.

"You don't have work?"

"It'll wait. I'd rather talk to you."

He nudges the briefcase back under the seat with his foot. "Just talk?"

I reach for his hand. "Just talk."

Marie Bostwick

Marie Bostwick is an NYT bestselling author and master of warm, compelling fiction. Marie's eleven novels, published by Kensington, include The Second Sister, released in April 2015. Her 2012 title, Ties That Bind, was named Best Mainstream Novel of the Year in the RT Book Reviews Reader's Choice Awards. She also just received a Career Achievement Award in Mainstream Fiction from RT Book reviews.

The Cypress Tree's Apprentice

A hermit who lived in the woods and ate only mushrooms sent his collection of unpublished poems to Two Geese Books.

Two Geese Books rejected it.

Pompadour Press sent him a curt reply, telling him, "Your motifs are lyrically transcendent, but unfortunately not commercial. So few people live in the woods anymore."

The poetry/fantasy/sci-fi editor at Littlefinger, Bronn said no. But she did offer to revisit the project if substantial revisions were made. "Perhaps if your wilderness characters inhabited a dark, alternate reality..."

Pith, a biannual journal dedicated to the best in contemporary haiku, was willing to accept his work, with only "slight reformatting." They wanted him to turn his epic poem, Boiled Chickweed, into a 17-syllable verse.

Other poetry outlets weren't as kind. They called him a Luddite or dismissed him as lightweight. The Angry Foghorn, a San Francisco underground writers' collective, tweeted "too many shrooms, dude. #wheresthebeef."

The man who lived in the woods had no smart phone, so he never saw it.

The rejected poet sat under a lone cypress and considered his plight. The tree, withered by decades of pounding storms and grasshopper infestations, was no stranger to sorrow. It lowered its limbs to shelter him.

"I'll never get published," the poet cried. He buried his face in his hands.

The tree rustled its branches; the leaves fluttered, as if to comfort him.

"You need a platform, my friend," the tree said. "This is an age of ebooks, not tree books. Good for me. For you, not so much."

"What's a platform, and how do I build one?" the poet asked.

"Find your target reader, my friend. Connect with your niche audience."

"How?"

"Go on the Internet. Join Facebook. Embrace Twitter. Blog like the wind."

"It sounds scary," the poet said, "but I guess I'm willing to try."

"Don't try -- do. Change the wallpaper. Shift the paradigm."

"Wish me luck," the poet said.

"Yay!GoDaddy!" the tree answered.

The poet looked confused.

"No, I mean it," the cypress said. "Check out GoDaddy. They have great discounts on hosting and tech support."

***

The man who lived in the woods built his platform. He joined Facebook, embraced Twitter and blogged like the wind. He discovered social media. His clever hashtags enticed legions of followers. Tim Tebow friended him; Adam Levine retweeted his tweets.

He connected globally with millions of wilderness freaks and Henry David Thoreau groupies; he texted those who heard the call of the wild, linked in with Reese Witherspoon fans who loved the movie Wild, and chatted with detractors who thought Emile Hirsch did a better job in Into the Wild. His Instagram followers included Tibetan monks, Survivor finalists, and people who preferred not to bathe regularly.

And they all bought his books.

The poet no longer lived in the woods. He found the Internet service too spotty there. He moved to New York and rented a loft in Tribeca. When he felt homesick for the wilderness, he went to Central Park. His diet changed; he now ate legumes and certain dairy products. He developed a fondness for the BLT turkey avocado club at Panera Bread, sans bacon and turkey, of course.

His platform generated millions of dollars in sales. Boiled Chickweed stayed at the top of the Kindle ebook list for 47 weeks. Miramax optioned the screenplay rights. Two Geese published A Fungus Affection, a collection of the poet's favorite raw mushroom recipes. The coffee-table edition (cover price: $28.50) did well, but the trade paperback, A Fat-free Fungus Affection (cover price: $14.95), went viral.

Next, his publisher rolled out Soiled Garments, a patchwork of the poet's ramblings and scratchings on tree bark. It contained doodles of dismembered grasshoppers, daily to-do lists (i.e, "forage for mushrooms, check for toenail rot") and diatribes against the military industrial complex. When Soiled Garments took off, the editors began talking series. They tossed around phrases like "maximizing profits" and "vertical revenue streams." They quickly repurposed Soiled Garments into three separate volumes: Not Bathing, Not Flossing, and Not Caring.

The poet was hailed as the new Vijay Seshadri. He hung out at Jimmy's Corner, the popular West Side writer's bar. He wrote profiles for Vanity Fair and was profiled in The New Yorker. His editor kept pushing him to finish Soiled Garments IV: It All Comes Off. He missed one deadline after another.

The poet slept days and partied nights, while underlings managed social media for him. He hired an actor to impersonate him on book tours.

But, ultimately, he found his new life wanting. He grew to dislike the city: the morose crowds, the ghoulish street vendors, the grotesque carnival of it all. The stink of uncollected garbage in the streets bothered him. He smelled it everywhere, even when he stepped inside his apartment and shut the door.

One night, after enduring a terrible nightmare about bacon cheeseburgers and rabid dogs in Central Park, he awoke in a cold sweat, knowing exactly what he must do. He sublet the loft and bought a ramshackle cottage in Claverack, New York, a few miles off Route 82. It had an apple orchard.

On a whim, he returned to the wilderness and scoured the forest till he found the old cypress that had sheltered him. It looked more forlorn than ever. Still, when he poked among the branches, he saw signs of new growth among the brittle leaves. A week later, he came back with a tree surgeon to help him uproot the withered tree. They lifted it carefully roots and all, transported it to Claverack, and replanted it in the poet's apple orchard.

Day after day, the poet sat under the bony cypress, feeling the sap flow. Soon the branches turned green and leafy again. Man and tree, student and master, conversed for hours. After all, they were old friends. At night, the poet slumped against the tree's knobby trunk. He dreamed of Central Park.

"When I lived in New York," he told the tree, "I had nightmares all the time. Now thinking of the park gives me pleasant dreams."

"Parks are strange creatures," the cypress said. "You walk around, admiring the clipped precision of the lawns, the bright flowers in such neat rows. You can't help thinking, 'Is it real or artificial?'"

"Why did you tell me to go on the Internet?" the poet asked.

"It's what you needed to do. And it made you rich, didn't it?"

"It made me lonely."

"Do you remember what I said? I warned you. Good for me. For you, not so much. Besides, you were desperate to be published."

"I would have cut off my right arm."

"You did. Don't worry. It will probably grow back in time."

***

The poet never surfed the Internet again. When his boxer shorts got threadbare and the elastic bands unraveled, he didn't buy new ones. Eventually, he stopped wearing shorts entirely. He gave up most foods and the conversation of other human beings. Every fall he watched the apples ripen in his orchard, and every winter he saw the cypress tree outlast the killing snow. One day he wrote poetry again.

Jason Bonderoff

Jason Bonderoff has written fourteen books, including The Solid Gold Sandbox (Pinnacle),The Official Dallas Trivia Book (Signet), and biographies of Mary Tyler Moore and Sally Field (St. Martin's Press). He's penned articles for TV Guide and book reviews for The Philadelphia Inquirer. He lives in Boynton Beach, FL.

A Teen Mom Starts Over

As a kid, I was a fan of the Choose Your Own Adventure series of books. I liked choosing what direction the story took to its ultimate end. Once, I was eaten by a shark. Another time, I was betrayed by a friend and locked in a dungeon. Of course, I liked the ending where I found the treasure and became rich and famous.

While I didn't care very much for the boy-centric storylines of dragons, pirates, and space monsters, what I did like was that each book gave me the chance to start over and choose a different path, a different ending. I suppose if I had written a Choose Your Own Adventure book from my own life, a page would read like this:

You are a nineteen-year-old unwed mother in rural Mississippi. It's the late nineties. Your child's father is long gone. Your church has turned its back on you, people in your hometown give you dirty looks when you are out shopping, and random people tell you that no decent man would want to marry you. The men who do talk to you only do so because they think you're "easy." Forget the fact that you are in college and making very good grades. Forget the fact that you are working to support yourself and your child, because no one in Greenville, Mississippi will let you forget that you are nothing more than a whorish dreg on society. You are angry and tired of living this way. You want a fresh start.

Turn to page 15 to go online and meet a stranger.

Turn to page 20 to grit your teeth and bear it.

Continuing to live my life in Mississippi was not an option. I had few real friends to talk to because they did not have the same concerns. I wanted to move, but I had no money saved up to leave Greenville. In my boredom and desperation, I went online and began talking to a young man. After a few conversations, I visited him at his home in Michigan. A week later, he drove to Mississippi, and we got married in a hallway at the courthouse. The day after that, I packed up a few clothes and all of my books, and left town with my new husband. I wouldn't return for a decade.

I had married the first man who asked me. Who does that?

In my flawed logic at the time, I had to shed Kamesa Honour—she was a miserable loser. Kamesa Al-Rida was a wife and mother who lived in suburban Detroit, attended classes at one of the local universities, and had a great job at a popular bookstore. She didn't love her husband, but that didn't matter because the alternative was to live in rejection and isolation in Mississippi. It was a nice revision to my life story. I took a risk and started over. Who wouldn't love that story?

Another possible page:

Your ex-husband was a compulsive liar who was also emotionally and verbally abusive. He had the audacity to tell you that you owed him a child because he accepted another man's child. Screw him. You were only married for six months and now you're a divorcee. How glamourous! Surprisingly, you are not heartbroken. The world is your oyster and you have money and choices.

Turn to page 30 to stay in Detroit.

Turn to page 32 to move north to Saginaw and finish college there.

I loved Detroit, but I had no real desire to stay there. There was no way in hell I was going back to Mississippi. I had a taste of what it was like to live with respect and dignity, and I wasn't going to trade it for anything in the world. I enrolled at Saginaw Valley State University and graduated with a degree in social work. I made friends, had a job at a nonprofit, and lived in a nice neighborhood.

Now that I was a pro at starting over and changing myself, I wasn't afraid of what people would say about me. I was confident, I had a degree under my belt, and I loved the sense of adventure. It wasn't the Paris or London that I'd longed for most of my life, but it damn sure wasn't the backwoods of Mississippi.

Here's one more page:

It's time for a new adventure now that you're bored in Michigan. You've been contacted by a headhunter who has found two job offers for you. One is in Jacksonville, Florida, and the other is in Phoenix, Arizona. They both sound interesting and have NFL teams, bookstores, and lots of arts and culture.

Turn to page 40 to move to Phoenix.

Turn to page 41 to move to Jacksonville.

I packed up again and headed for Jacksonville. I knew no one, but within six months, my son and I had made plenty of friends. I enjoyed the beaches, the abundance of sunshine, and I fell in love with the Jaguars.

Ten years later, I'm still here. I've remarried and added another son to my family. He can't bear to miss a Sunday afternoon of football at EverBank Field. I'm proud to call Jacksonville my home and I could not see myself living anywhere else—unless it's London.

I always tell my middle school students that it's not how you start the race, it's how you finish. You might make some less-than-awesome choices along the way—like being a teen mother——but the decisions you make afterwards can either get you eaten by sharks or they can lead you to the treasure. You just have to be willing to get off that page, choose your adventure, and start over lest you end up in a dungeon.

Kamesa Evette Carter

Kamesa Evette Carter lives in Jacksonville. When she was in the third grade, she discovered that writing stories was a lot more fun than doing long division. Kamesa supports her reading and writing habits by working as a paraprofessional. She is a Jaguars fan and is currently in graduate school.

Single

When one has
previously been
seen as two,
a newly perceived
single woman
often suggests
the context of
a half-life,
an attempt
to double back
on her previous
secure identity.

I will never
accept the bromide
"my better half."
It implies that a
part of me
is not only missing
but is somehow
inherently preferable,
so that my oneness,
my uniqueness,
needs to be complemented
by an extension of myself
in order for me
to be considered whole.
Let me forge a
new identity,
remembering the

sweetness of
my love
to anchor
my new life lived
as one alone.
Some observers,
who can only
dream in coupledom,
will continue
to watch for my
counterpart to appear.

Linda Kraus

Linda Kraus has taught English Film Studies at the college and university levels. She has written film criticism, short fiction and poetry since adolescence and has published both poetry and film criticism.

Clopin Clopant

Colby Wynan always thought of himself as a man with three hearts—the one he showed to his loved ones, the one he showed to his friends, and the one he never showed to anyone. It was not that he was hiding anything; it was just that he didn't know himself what resided there. Was he saving it for a special purpose, or to protect himself in case the first heart was broken? It was a mystery, but Colby knew it was there, waiting.

His Greenwich Village neighbors considered him a fixture on their streets, as familiar as the high school basketball court that bordered West 4th Street or the firehouse that stood between the Perfect Bagel and the Serendipity Boutique. Day in and day out, from morning till evening, Colby painted cityscapes in soft warm watercolors—not harsh, bright oils, but blue, gray, and orange hues that seemed to bring out the friendly side of the city, make it a more comfortable place to live, like a familiar overstuffed chair. Living in a concrete jungle with glass and steel buildings tired the village residents. Colby's watercolor creations made the city a homestead, not just a home, but a place to hang your hat and bring up your family—a place to call your neighbors friends and not tenants. They loved his wide, toothy smile and the scrape of blue paint that seemed permanently fixed to his cheek. As his fellow villagers passed Colby, they waved and shouted, "Hello," adding, "We love you, Colby." And they bought his paintings.

Jessica, Colby's wife of thirty-one years, loved him from the very moment she set eyes on his watercolors. His pallet creations were a mirror image of his soul, and she loved his soul. Lovely Irish lass, straight from Ireland, Jessica was mesmerizing—her black hair glistened, and a fire burned in her eyes that no one, and nothing, could extinguish. She was determined and full of life. In quiet times, Colby could summon to his mind her lilting voice and contagious laugh. They married and settled in Greenwich Village; he painted, and she taught Irish dances at a local studio. On Sundays, they dropped all thoughts of work and worry and walked to Washington Square. Colby first picked a flower from the small patch of land behind their apartment, pinned it in Jessica's hair, then, hand in hand, they strolled to the Square and found an empty park bench where they sat and talked, sharing their love with heart-to-heart chatter and old memories.

On a Sunday, Valentine's Day, at the age of sixty-one, Jessica was hit by a car careening off another as it crashed into the park bench at Washington Square, killing her instantly. Sorrow darkened Colby's heart and crimped his hand. No longer were his cityscapes soft and inviting; instead they turned dark and foreboding? the buildings looked like giant headstones in a graveyard of streets and alleys. For Colby, the milk of life had turned sour. Neighbors expressed their sympathies, but Colby's deadened heart froze them out. The love in his heart for his wife, and the love in his heart for his friends, seemed to vaporize into the smoggy city air. He painted no more.

Each evening he walked the streets, head hung low, walking aimlessly just to keep his
body in motion. Andre Trousseau, a recently arrived French painter to the colony of village artists, described Colby's walk as "Clopin Clopant," the shuffle of a lover without his love. Trudging along, Colby wept silently, fighting off his pain with the shield of memories of Sundays in Washington Square with Jessica. For three years, Colby walked Clopin Clopant—his neighborhood now a graveyard of old friendships and days gone by.

The first time things changed was when Heidi came along. She was a twelve-year-old dachshund who became an orphan when her owner, Colby's next door neighbor for many years, was found dead in his apartment. It was three days until the body was discovered. During that time, Heidi had lain down, grieving next to her owner during that whole time, and she had not eaten. Colby fed her, and for lack of an alternative, put her up in his apartment for the night. He stroked her short fur and talked to her softly, telling her it was OK to grieve in her sorrow, that memories were real and would always be there to comfort her. Heidi seemed to understand. Small, with a long brown body, her belly just cleared the floor. They played chase-the-ball together and an oversized watercolor brush became her favorite chew toy. They slept together, dozing off and arising simultaneously each day. Heidi brought love back into Colby's life.

At first they both walked Clopin Clopant, but as their love grew, their steps grew faster and friskier. Friends waved hello again. Colby waved back, each time describing to Heidi who they were.

"That's Kevin, Heidi. He's the local policeman. Oh, that's Rita. She owns the corner beauty shop." Heidi seemed to understand as she welcomed each new friend with a lick and a hardy wag of her tail.

But fate intervened, and one evening life changed for Colby and Heidi. Out for their neighborhood walk, Heidi suddenly lapsed into spasms and collapsed. Colby picked her up and carried her home. A veterinarian's analysis was straightforward and concise. Heidi, he said, had suffered a stroke, and both back legs were paralyzed. But Colby transitioned quickly into caregiver mode. He was determined that Heidi would continue to be his partner. She had found that special place in his heart and nothing short of death could excise her out. He took his pants belt and wrapped it around her body in front of her back legs, effectively holding up her backside so her back legs never touched the floor. Heidi could now walk, but only on her front legs, as he supported the back legs by holding up the rear part of her body with his belt. They went walking every evening in that fashion. Neighbors smiled, shouting hello as he and Heidi took their stroll. Her eyes sparkled with love whenever she looked at Colby, sensing that she had found her place in his heart and letting him know that he had found a place in hers. Colby finally realized why he had protected that secret place all these years.

On a chilly, gray, autumn day in November, Colby wrapped Heidi in a newly-purchased dog sweater and walked to his old street corner facing the city skyline. He set up his tripod and mounted a fresh new canvas. He broke out his brushes and paint, and with loving strokes, brought the city back to life with his watercolors, the towering glass and steel buildings once again reaching out for the friendship of the villagers.

Heidi sat under his tripod, and looked up lovingly at Colby as he splashed warm hues of watercolor paint across the buildings and city sky. When a neighbor shouted, "We love you, Colby," he reached down, patted Heidi's head, and said, "They love you, too, Heidi." Heidi's tail wiggled and waggled. Colby's heart was finally at peace.

Frank T. Masi

Frank T Masi edited the nonfiction book, The Typewriter Legend, published articles in business publications, and won poetry awards from Maitland Public Library His stories are in FWA's short story collections 5 and 6 and Not Your Mother's Book...On Working for a Living. Frank is writing a horror-murder mystery.

Your Mother Is No Longer Theresa

The letter arrived. I was to appear in West Palm Beach at the Federal Courthouse on February 20, 2015. "This is a solemn occasion," it said, "appropriate dress required. No jeans, shorts or flip-flops." I took a deep breath. Solemn. No flip-flops. I agreed. I should not be taking this big a step in flip-flops!

So the following Friday, attired in an elegant suit, I waited, with forty-five others from twenty-seven countries, for the swearing in ceremony that would make me a new US citizen. All of us were there because in addition to becoming citizens, we had also opted to legally change our names. It had taken me ten years to arrive on this page.

***

First Draft: I grew up in a perfect home with a perfect family in a perfect town on a perfect street named after a noted Canadian tree famous for its sap.

Second Draft: My family was normal, as far as I knew. When you live cloistered and in a routine as predictable as the navy jumper and white blouse you wear to school every day, vocabulary adapts. "Dysfunctional" had not been coined yet. If the wringer washer did not work, it was simply "out of order".

Third Draft: Okay, so maybe we were a little dysfunctional by times. What nonsense to make a fuss over it. Grow up. Get over it. Get married. Have your own perfect family, the house with a white picket fence and potted geraniums.

Fourth Draft: Happily ever after. First step to finding truth is to recognize the fictions. Then address the expectations. It is not going to be a fairy tale after all. The potion is as apt to kill you as put you in a trance. You may have to fight, but for what? How hard and how long? Am I getting close to the story?

Revision One: It failed. Or I failed. It might all have been a dream had I not brought forth four beautiful, complex, lively little planets to circle my world forever, reminding me how two people fumbling in the dark and a fish and an egg can create a miracle so beyond the sum of the parts.

Revision Two: "Success" to outside observers looked like the bigger houses, the better neighborhoods and a move a year, every year for far too many years. I tried to keep things on an even keel, but like flimsy rafts they tilted and flipped when the weight accumulated too much on one side. An old battered house by the sea was my haven and my sanity. When you love the bones of a house, the cracked plaster doesn't matter. Like an old couple sitting holding hands on a park bench where you can tell she still sees him strong, doesn't notice his frail, stooped back and he still sees her dimples and smiling eyes, not everything that droops. Love is enough, isn't it?

Revision Three: After it all came undone I resumed living. I could still go to the old house alone, tend the roses, make bread, and feed apples to the deer that came at dusk. I could come home after work to the sea, unchanged, always changing. The bell buoy started to sound lonely. The fog seemed denser.

Revision Four: Solitude is fine when it's organic, nurturing new growth like lichen masticating the roots of old trees. It can also become a hat drawn too far down over the eyes. My brother and I had driven an hour along the coast, stopped at the Cape Enrage lighthouse. During the entire drive he had been sowing seeds of persuasion in me to consider leaving the area, to move on, get a new life elsewhere, like maybe near him in Alberta. The day before, we knelt side by side at the funeral of our older brother. But on that spectacularly beautiful cliff with the orchestral roar of the Bay of Fundy in our ears, I saw him tuck his chin deeper into his parka. His words were nearly vacuumed up by the brutal wind. "I don't know," he began thoughtfully, "but I'm not sure you could ever move away from here. " He went on. "Do you realize that on this fifty mile drive, you had a story every mile? You know who lives in every second house!" He didn't have to use the term "sense of community". That was ten years ago.

Let's Try This Again. I walked away from the shingled house that smelled of salty breeze and lilacs in spring, stewed crabapples in the autumn and in winter the fragrant incense of lavender smoke wafting into the crystal woods. I moved my earth two thousand miles away from those amazing planets I love and the sparkling stars of the miracles they had spawned who called me my favorite name, "Nana". I left the map where every house was a name and every tree a landmark.

I did not go to Alberta. My brother's kind offer was preempted by a marriage proposal, oddly enough, from one who knew the Canadian Maritime landscape as well as I did. "It's beautiful there," he acknowledged, " but there are other beautiful places… like Florida, for instance." "Caveat emptor" I'm thinking, but agreed to the possibility.

***

One More Time: The red tape was frustrating and time-consuming but we relied on the integrity of our immigration attorney to lead us through. After nine months, like the appearance of a new infant, we could announce: " It has arrived!" and I was allowed to enter this country through the vehicle of a fiancé's visa and get married here. Eventually, after more forms and rigmarole, I acquired "permanent resident" status.

I got lost. "They moved Publix!" I told my husband when he gave me directions using the grocery chain landmark. It's not as if there was just one of them like the old schoolhouse by the row of maple trees or my uncle's service station. Nobody anywhere knew my name. Nobody looked like me or my cousins or my friends. There were many different accents and I was addressed as "Ma'am".

I was here three years before I heard a friend call my name at CVS. Now, ten years later, I have friends from Siesta Key to Jacksonville. I know the shortcuts to town and where the best bookstores are. I make good guacamole.

I've made a new life here, letting soothing balm bathe old wounds. The day I was sworn in, I dropped Theresa, my middle name. I tell my children: "Your mother is no longer Theresa. I've flunked sainthood but enrolled in Healing-101." I reclaimed my maiden name as homage to the vibrant history of my family and homeland and the deep love-roots I've grown. When your roots burrow deep enough it gives you the confidence to let your branches spread where they will. When someone or somewhere welcomes you with open arms, you feel the liberty to return the embrace, knowing as every mother knows, there is always enough love to go around, or as every woman knows, you can love both snow boots and flip-flops.

Phyllis McKinley

Phyllis McKinley has won multiple awards for her poems and non-fiction writing. Author of four Poetry collections and one Children's book, her stories appeared in FWA Collections 1, 2 & 4. She recently became a US citizen and lives with her husband, Hanford Brace, in Avon Park, Florida. Contact: bracephyllis@gmail.com

The Human Singularity

"Good morning, Mr. Reynolds," she said. "My name is Dr. Linda Ullman. I'm a, Kinesthesiologist, which means I work a lot with muscles, and nerves, and movement. Are you ready for your new body this morning?"

"I guess so," I sighed. "Are you sure it'll work?"

"Positive, Mr. Reynolds," she smiled radiantly. "But, it'll be like nothing you've ever experienced before, so don't expect too much at first. You're not going to get right up off the table here, and walk." She gestured to a sheet covered form on the gurney next to me. "So, we'll take things very slowly at first. Small steps so to speak, but in this case literally as well."

"You'll have to pardon me," I sighed. "I'm just very nervous about this."

Dr. Ullman turned, and smiled sympathetically.

"Don't you worry about a thing, Mr. Reynolds," she said. "Although we're indeed breaking new ground with this, and you are the very first digitalized human being, this new body is state of the art. It's been tested, and retested over, and over again. Once we make the transfer, and you're residing in it, everything will work just fine. You'll see. There is a catch though. If you wait too long, and don't go in, the computer brain inside will self-destruct. This is a security measure for your own safety. This way, no one can hack into your own body, and gain control. It's a one of a kind thing, so please don't destroy it! I'd like to keep my job! The brain alone cost the university billions of dollars in research, and development."

"I understand."

"Okay, here we go," Dr. Ullman nodded, and the technician behind a translucent screen touched an icon.

Suddenly, like before, an envelope appeared in my field of vision.

"Okay, I got it."

"That's good," Dr. Ullman nodded. "Select it and a door should appear." The room was deathly silent, as I selected the envelope, and an ornate white door appeared.

"I got the door."

"Good. So, are you absolutely certain that you're going to do this before you open the door? If you're not, you should say so now, and we will all stand down, and wait until you are. Do you understand?"

"I understand."

"Do you want to make the transfer? Once you do, it is irreversible."

"I do."

"Okay," Dr. Ullman took a deep breath and nodded. "Go ahead."

I selected the door, and an "enter," button appeared just to the left of it. A timer appeared just above the button, counting down from thirty.

"Select enter," Dr. Ullman said quietly.

Suddenly, the whole concept hit me. Up until now, I'd had no choice in my uploading, and digitalization. Others had selected me, to come alive again, and live inside some giant supercomputer.

"Enter," Dr. Ullman repeated.

And now, I was actually choosing to be their science fair project, and placing my life, decisions into their hands.

"Fifteen seconds," a voice called out.

"Enter," Dr. Ullman repeated breathlessly.

The countdown stopwatch in my HUD went from green, to yellow.

"Select enter, Mr. Reynolds – please," Dr. Ullman said. "I know it's a difficult decision, but it means that you'll live forever. You really will. No more pain. No more illness. No more cancer. You'll be able to outperform Olympic athletes, and not even get out of breath! You have nothing to lose Mr. Reynolds, and everything to gain! Please, please, press enter?"

"Ten seconds!"

"Oh, Mr. Reynolds – please?" Dr. Ullman said her voice tremulous.

Then, it occurred to me, that I did indeed have nothing to lose. No matter what happened I would eventually outlive them all, and decide whatever I wanted to.

"Five seconds!"

The countdown stopwatch turned red, and began blinking.

I selected "enter," and the last thing I heard was: "He did it!"

***

All was darkness, and silence around me for really quite a while. It reminded me of what happens when your computer gets hung up, and goes blank, while you think seriously of throwing it out the window.

For some reason, the prospect of pretty Dr. Ullman losing her job, was a worse prospect for me than getting lost in some cyber netherworld Twilight Zone. I really saw, heard, and felt nothing at all. I was pure consciousness – pure thought. My philosophy professor would be proud, I thought. Surprisingly, I wasn't scared at all. I wasn't anything. I did exist, and I had thoughts. Somehow I knew I would surface somewhere. Maybe I'd reincarnate as a cat or something.

Suddenly, I did surface, and everything was bathed in a fuzzy white light. I could hear voices nearby. It was Dr. Ullman talking with project manager Dr. Murray. But, neither one of them sounded very happy.

"Are you sure, he hit the 'enter' button before the thirty second deadline?"

"Yes, yes. I'm sure," Dr. Ullman said.

"Then, why aren't we getting any reading on anything?"

"I – don't – know!"

Suddenly, the sheet covering my face was pulled back, and both Dr. Ullman, and Dr. Murray looked down at me. Dr. Ullman's eyes were red, and she looked very tired. Dr. Murray shined a pocket flashlight in my eyes.

"See?" he said angrily. "Nothing!"

"What do you mean, nothing?" I said, and both of them jumped backward, obviously startled. "What's wrong, Dr. Murray?"

"Oh!" Dr. Murray burst into a huge grin. "Mr. Reynolds! Why nothing! Nothing now!" He turned to Dr. Ullman, and shook her hand enthusiastically.

Dr. Ullman sniffed, rubbing her nose as the staff around her cheered.

"Oh, you don't know how glad we are to see you, Mr. Reynolds!" she laughed with joy. "Really!"

The cheering continued from around the room, as she reached down, and kissed my cheek.

"I-I felt that!" I said, sitting bolt upright. "I actually felt it!"

Everyone in the room gasped. I rubbed my cheek with my hand, and then suddenly realized I had a hand! I had two of them.

I examined them both in astonishment, as Dr. Murray, and Dr. Ullman rushed to either side, steadying me.

"Hold on now, easy," Dr. Ullman held on to my arm. "My God, Dan! Look at how his upper arm muscles are working in a coordinated fashion!"

"Astonishing Lynn. What do you make of it?"

"Way, way, beyond anything that was predicted!"

"Well, I'm going to stand, and walk, Dr. Ullman." I said.

"Oh, no, no, no." Dr. Murray said. "Not yet there tiger!"

"Why not?" Dr. Ullman breathed in excitement. "Let's see what he can do! Come on, slowly, steady."

Both stood beside of me, as I eased off the gurney, and onto the floor. The entire university staff gathered silently behind me in a semi-circle. No one made a sound, as I balanced myself on both feet, and took my first step. Dr. Ullman beamed at me, with tears in her eyes. They stood by like proud anxious parents, as I took my first unaided, unsteady steps.

I turned, and held my hands out.

"So, what you think?"

The applause was thunderous.

Al Perrin

Al Perrin lives in Ruskin, FL, and is a free-lance writer. His magazine articles have appeared in The Tampa Tribune, Grand Rapids Press, RN Magazine, and Grand Rapids Magazine. He's also written four books, The Movement, The Sloop John B, The Onion, and The Liberal Lie all published by Booklocker.com.

The Molding of Rudy

"What do you mean, you're not making fried chicken tonight?" Rudy had just walked into Stella's house which, this evening, lacked the usual Saturday night aroma of frying chicken. "You always do fried chicken on Saturdays."

"Watch my lips, Rudy. I am not making fried chicken tonight. In fact, I'm not cooking tonight at all. I'm going out to eat."

"Well, la-di-da. I suppose you think I'm buying dinner."

"'Course not. In our thirty years of—what has it been, Rudy—courtship? Friendship? Keeping company? Doesn't matter anyhow. Point is, in over thirty years, have I ever asked you to buy me anything?"

"I get it. You've been talking again to that nosy Jocelyn at work, right? The one who's always telling you that we should get married or we're not in a real relationship. Do you think we're not real, Stella? You know how I feel about you. Do you think in all these years I've ever been interested in another woman? Hell, no one could compare to you. Didn't we decide long ago that we don't need a license to be real? Why do you keep listening to those damn broads who've got nothing to do but mind other people's business? They need to get a life."

Stella nodded. "You're right, Rudy. They need to get a life. God knows, ours is one blast of excitement after another. Well, my new life starts with dinner at the café tonight. And no, I wasn't talking to anyone at work. I just didn't feel like making fried chicken today. I have my own money and my own car. You're welcome to come if you want, but don't feel obliged."

She turned her back on the bewildered looking Rudy, picked up her pocketbook and walked toward her car.

He followed.

***

The next Saturday evening, Rudy called ahead. "Okay if I bring a bucket of fried chicken and we eat in?"

"Sure, but we'll have to eat fast. You're welcome to stay and watch TV, but I'm catching the seven-fifteen movie at the Star."

"Stella, damn. You know how crowded Saturdays are at the movie."

"Uh-huh. I said I was going, Rudy."

"Well, I suppose it's a chick flick and you're meeting the girls?"

"No."

"Uh…going with another friend?"

"No."

"I guess I'll come with you then."

"If you want. You don't have to."

He went.

***

The following week, Rudy called three times, rather than his usual two. "Just checking to see how everything's going."

"Everything's fine," a chipper sounding Stella said.

He called again Saturday afternoon. "Do you want to eat in or out tonight?"

"I have plans for tonight with a friend, Rudy. You do whatever you want."

There was a moment of loud silence. "I suppose you're going out with the girls from work."

"No."

"Oh. Someone I know?"

"I'm pretty sure not. I have to go, Rudy, or I'll be late. I hope you have a nice evening." She hung up.

Stella pressed the message button on her answering machine before she climbed into bed that night.

"Hey, Stell, it's Rudy. Call me when you get home. Please."

She didn't.

***

He called Sunday. "Can I come over?"

"You never come on a Sunday. That's your fishing day."

"Today's not good fishing weather. Anyhow, I'd rather take you to dinner…if that's okay…if you don't have plans. I was thinking the buffet place down by the river. Good food and good views. Unless you'd like to go someplace else?"

"You're buying?"

"I'm asking you out, Stella. Of course I'm buying. I've got a good job, you know."

"Yes, I know. The river place sounds wonderful, Rudy."

She'd never seen him look so handsome, or so nervous. Their reserved table was on the covered porch, overlooking the water. The setting sun shimmered endlessly in the rippling river, which seemed to sway in rhythm with the passing leisure boats.

An attentive Rudy waited until they finished eating before rising from his chair and bending on one knee in front of Stella. He reached in his pocket for the ring. "I want us to be real, Stella...all the way real. We should have done this long ago. Please say it isn't too late. Say you'll marry me."

She smiled. "Yes, Rudy, yes. I'll marry you."

Clapping and cheering from fellow diners must have caused folks in the nearby sailing vessels to wonder what prompted the jubilation.

***

They arrived home from their honeymoon on a Saturday.

"Where would you like me to take you for dinner tonight?" Rudy asked.

Stella looked at him. "Did you forget—it's Saturday. I always make you fried chicken on Saturdays."

He smiled.

Faun Joyce Senatro

Faun Joyce, a retired Social Worker, lives in Port Orange with her husband and dog, Noli Priorities are her family, faith, friends, writing, reading, walking and traveling. She has been published in three Collections and was a finalist with her first novel, First Class to America, in 2013.

Three Shades of Gray

Alas, I failed to outline. I am at chapter fifteen and I don't know what comes next. The fair lady is definitely in distress, but how can my hero rescue her? I have written him into a box. Perhaps the fair lady should just be done in. Too bad for her! She shouldn't have made the mistakes resulting in her present pickle. In the end I lay down my pen, put the cover on the ink pot and go to bed.

The next morning I sit, looking for a way to make the plot come right. As I arrive at the end of what I remember writing, there are still more pages, not written by me. The writing is good and, what's more, the writer has discovered a new choice for my hero.

When I reread the new pages, I notice the handwriting differs from page to page. In all, it appears there is not one writer, but three. Three people, it would appear, have somehow snuck into my house in the dead of night, written about seventy-five pages and departed. This is certainly a puzzle.

The following morning, when I look for the last pages, they are once again not in my handwriting. In addition to the new pages, some of what I did write yesterday is missing. The net effect of all this is for the story to take on a whole new arc. My fair lady is no longer in distress. In fact, in chapter twenty she is about to rescue my hero, who has made a bumbling hash of things. What I thought I intended to write has been destroyed, but the current book is coming along just fine. In fact I rather like the story better than my original plot. But who is writing this new material, and will I have the right to claim to be the author?

In the evening I take up vigil in the loft. How much time passes, I do not know. Suddenly a match flares and someone lights the kerosene lamp on my writing table. In the flickering light I see three shapes gathered there. One is short and chubby, the next tall and very thin, and the third is old and bent over as though crippled.

They seem to be not dressed at all. They are transparent gray, a color which comes and goes in the light of the kerosene lamp. While they all have pens, they are sharing the ink pot. Each dips his pen and taps it on the rim of the pot to dislodge excess ink, making a clicking sound. Then there is a scritching sound as they write. I sit peering down on the scene as I listen to the click, click— scritch, scritch, scritch. I have no idea how they keep the story straight, as they say not a word to each other, clicking and scritching at a furious pace.

"Ahem," I clear my throat. "Might I have a word?"

The clicking and scritching cease abruptly as all eyes swivel in my direction. The old one speaks. "You may."

"Why are three ghosts helping me write my novel?"

"We are not ghosts," says the old one. "We are Shades—banished to the Underworld."

"I stand corrected," I say. "But you are here, not in the Underworld, and writing large bits of my novel."

"You were stuck," says the tall one.

"And headed in the wrong direction," adds the fat one.

"We were given this task as penance," says the old one in a solemn tone of voice.

"Penance?"

"For our sins," says the tall one.

"And just what were your sins?"

"Laziness," says the tall one.

"Plagiarism," says the old one.

"And excessive adverbs," says the fat one.

The old one gives him a look. "Anyway," he says, "when we show the finished copy to The Ruler, we may be allowed to leave the Underworld and rest in peace."

"But if you three are writing this, how can I call it my novel?"

"That will not be a problem. Bear with us. We are nearly finished helping you write. Then we will revise."

"Then we will edit," says the tall one.

"Yes, revise then edit," adds the fat one.

There is silence. The three sit at the table, and stare at me as though they expect a reaction. Finally I say, "Fair enough; I will bear with you."

The old one nods. "That will be all for now." He reaches over and turns off the lamp.

Although the windows are closed, I feel a breeze and suppose they are gone for now.

For the next week, the three Shades toil at night. At four hundred seventy-five hand-written pages the novel comes to an end and revision begins. Night by night, the pile of draft pages gradually diminishes and the number of revised pages grows. During this period, I never see the trio and they never see me. When they arrive at the last chapter in the draft, they cease revising, recopy the revised material and begin to edit.

They work through the revised pages, changing commas to dashes and happy to glad as it suits their mood at the moment. This is all well and good, but the novel still needs an ending. I wonder why the Shades didn't finish the last chapter.

Looking closely, I see the last chapter has become a poor fit for what leads up to it. We have the Countess besieged by the villain but her lover can't help her because he is stashed in a dungeon. To change that state of affairs, the previous two chapters need changing. That would create a domino effect, running backward. At present, the villain is chasing the Countess, who is in her carriage, roaring down a mountain, and her lover is starving in the dungeon. I can't think of any believable way her lover can escape and save her.

Then the light dawns. Applying the approach of chapter twenty, the lover doesn't save the Countess, and four quick, easily written scenes will get the story over the finish line. The Countess shoves the villain off a cliff, saves her lover from the dungeon and they return to the castle. She makes chicken noodle soup and they show signs of living happily ever after. I dash the scenes off and it's the end.

I'm up early the next morning to take the manuscript to my publisher. Imagine my surprise when I arrive at my writing table to find nothing there but one sheet of paper. It seems to be a short note from the Shades.

> We thank you for the lovely ending and bid you farewell. We are certain this manuscript will be our deliverance from the Underworld. You now know the story and can write a novel which will be truly yours, just as we promised.

J. H. Weis

James (JH) Weis is a retired college professor who writes Folk Tales as A. A. King. He is a member of the Society of Children's Book Writers and Illustrators, the Mystery Writers of America, the Florida Writers Association, the Ormond Writers League, and a graduate of the Institute of Children's Literature.

"Twenty-two"

The news said twenty-two veterans commit suicide each day, one self-inflicted casualty every sixty-five minutes. This is your day. Take back control and become one of them. Solve every problem. Say goodbye to the flashbacks, the nightmares, the failures. Write a love note apology to wife. Tell her she's better off. Leave the dress uniform on the bed. Get out the piece and load it. Bring a lawn chair to the back yard. Place gun in mouth, pull trigger, end all the pain in a split-second.

They'll hand her a flag as her husband is laid to rest, then process the survivor's benefits. No more waiting months for delayed disability claims. No more drinking the nights away and sleeping it off during the day when she's at work. No more avoiding her company and her hopes for a baby, this woman who still thinks the man who came home from the war is the same one who left, not the stranger who no longer sleeps in her bed.

Now she's stopped asking, instead dropping hints about her husband finding a job. No one would hire a guy running mental videos of dead Afghan kids and buddies blown to pieces, scenes they never talked about in training. Improvised explosions set off by an invisible enemy. Bad intelligence and not-so-smart bombs killing the wrong people. Discovering senseless death in heat, cold, fire, ice, lives ended or spared by chance. Videos that won't erase, looping replays of indelible horrors no eyes should ever see, no wife should ever know.

She says talk to a counselor. Her daily reminder sits by the phone in the kitchen, a symbolic quarter placed beside a card with the phone number for the veterans' crisis hotline. Make the call she says, failing to understand.

Only the weak ask for help.

The strong survive until their will is gone, battles won but souls lost. Nothing left but exhaustion, booze, and disconnected thoughts in a brain so mushed it can't return to active duty, immune to all prescriptions and those sleeping pills they gave out in the combat zone. Warriors deserve the ultimate sacrifice. A bullet allows no do-overs, no chance to reconsider. Mission accomplished, honor restored.

Her twenty-five cent piece on the counter begs otherwise, a plea for a miracle.

Washington's etched profile on the quarter frowns disapproval, a commander who cannot and will not lie. He knows some decisions offer choices so equal the decision comes down to a coin toss. Trust fate and go with it. Let George decide, heads for life, tails for death.

Flip the coin high, watch it bounce and come to rest beneath the table. Retrieve it, hoping to find George face down.

See him smile back with his order, a command to live, give life another chance, start over.

Put down the gun and pick up the phone.

Jeff Boyle

Jeff is a 2012 RPLA, Short Story Finalist for Euro Skyhop; a Mainstream Literary Third place winner for Unpublished Novel, Nam World, a 2013 FWA Collection winner for Guns, a 2014 RPLA Short Story Finalist for Miss Piano, a member of FWA, and the City Island Fiction Writers, Daytona Beach.

365 Beds

For the past 357 nights, I haven't slept in the same bed twice, not since the night Mama died.

It should have been raining, but the damn sun kept shining, day after day. In December, in Oregon, it's unnatural, possibly apocalyptic. Even in Corvallis it had been sun-shining like Vegas all month. When I came home to Portland to look after Mama, I had to sleep in her old bedroom upstairs. My room had long since been overcome by her abandoned projects, piles of fabric, half-stitched quilts.

Mama had been moved into the spare room downstairs, off the sun porch, the room where anything she could spare but couldn't part with wound up. Until she wound up there herself, too crippled with arthritis to climb the stairs, then too weak to climb out of bed, then dead in her sleep at the age of seventy-three.

She gave up too easy, didn't say goodbye. I brought her afternoon tea at three as always. Mama asked me to set it on the bedside table, thanked me and gave my hand an extra pat. When I went to check on her at suppertime, she'd checked out. Just like that.

***

I couldn't stay in the house after the funeral parlor took her away. Most people will never know how a house so full of stuff can leave you so empty inside. Or how someone as strong as my mama can say, "You shouldn't feel that way," and you feel like you shouldn't even exist.

I pulled weeds until dark, and then checked into the Lamplighter Motel, off Sandy, just a few blocks away. It had cable. It did not have any of Mama's things.

A soda from the machine, peanut butter-cheese crackers, and a bucket of ice. I watched Breakfast at Tiffany's and slept until ten. At eleven, I checked out, thinking I'd move right back in at Mama's for a night or two.

Instead, it took five days to schedule the funeral, what with the write-up in the paper, the memorial at the gallery and the ceremonial burial under one of her quilts. I stayed in a different room each night, a bit further from home every time. A trendy retro motel on East Burnside. A historic downtown hotel. Some funky place in Southwest Portland. Then way down the Willamette River at the Lake Oswego Inn.

The day they put Mama underground, I headed clean out of town.

***

I'm on the One Night Stand Plan—how to see America from a different motel room window every day, 365 days in one year. If I were Michael Moore, I'd be shooting a documentary. If I were Jack Kerouac, I'd be writing the next great roman à road. If I were a twenty-first century American with ambition, I'd be blogging and You Tubing daily, tweeting every 25 miles and uploading selfies from all the motel beds. I'd even have corporate sponsors—a tire manufacturer, coffee shop chain or an energy drink—with T-shirts and bumper stickers for sale at every stop and online 24/7.

Instead, I keep my receipts to myself. And make lists only for my own amusement. Like the Top Ten Bumper Stickers I Hate Most. Visualize Whirled Peas. Not All Who Wander Are Lost. My Child Is an Honor Student at Anywhere Elementary. Wherever You Go, There You Are. That one rings less and less true the longer I travel. Wherever I go, I am not there. I rub layers of myself off on motel towels and never look under the beds to see what's left behind. I have become one of the anonymous masters of diner chitchat, who talk about the weather and praise the apple pie.

***

When you leave no forwarding address, you never have to check your mail. Mama's cousin Tommy Leonard is a realtor. I told him, "Put the house on the market, estate sale the rest to hell and keep the change." Who'd have thought a craftsman bungalow hanging off the right side of Mt. Tabor could fetch so much these days. The money spits out of ATMs wherever I go, up to my own limits, $300 a day or $2,000 a week max, not counting the occasional truck repair. Insane? Quite likely.

I was always the kind of kid who made up special rules, believed in magic numbers. Read eleven pages a night and you'll ace all the answers on the test. Climb every other step so you won't have bad dreams. Walk around the house nine times for nine days, and Dad's car will be in the driveway. Sleep in a different motel room bed every night for a year and you're bound to bump into him.

He left us block-by-block and mile-by-mile. A gig painting murals downtown so he couldn't come home for lunch. Two summers teaching art at Oregon State University in Corvallis. A spring semester in Seattle. Then six months in Mexico. After that he only came back by mail, leaving me to guess his whereabouts from the postmarks on hand-painted postcards he sent for my birthdays until I turned fifteen. I saved all the postcards, even the envelopes from random money orders he sent Mama for child support, but there was never a return address.

It took me two months on the road to admit to myself what I've never said out loud: I'm following Dad's erratic mystery trail, zigzagging from postmark to postmark, motel to motel.

When most people think of driving coast to coast, they draw a line across the middle, slant the diagonal up or down to connect their dots. But those inside states give me the willies. I have to stick to the outer edges where the escape routes are, one if by land, two if by sea. Judging by the postcards, Dad liked the fringes, too; he be-bopped across the desert, made a beeline for the Gulf and then meandered his way up the Eastern Seaboard, but he never made it to Kansas.

***

Night 358. Only seven nights to go. If this storm lets up, maybe I'll cross the border by the time I meet myself in Room 365. A calm, no-nonsense Canadian motel sounds just right, as long as it's bare bones, stripped of anything that can't be nailed down.

I look forward to meeting myself there. I'll say, "What took you so long?" Then unpack my bag, fill up all the drawers, draw a hot bath and soak away the road. We have a lot of catching up to do—me, myself and I.

The only thing that worries me is what happens next. But I do have a plan. Once I'm settled in Room 365, I'll shuffle the stack of postcards saved from my favorite towns along the way—then draw my own future out of the deck. Or maybe I'll tape all the postcards to that last motel room wall and throw darts until one hits the spot, any spot.

Lynn Welsh

An award-winning advertising writer and Mississippi native, Lynn Welsh migrated to the Florida sun following decades on New York's Madison Avenue and in Portland, Oregon's gray drizzle. She's studied creative writing at the University of New Orleans, Prague; and Haystack and Flight of the Mind workshops, Oregon.

Broken

He knew better. He'd hiked this mountain a million times. He'd hunted and trapped here with his father, fished and rock climbed with his brothers, and spent many a night under the vast universe of stars. This time, though, was different. This time might be the last.

Glancing down at the offending bone protruding through his shin, he was reminded of just how stupid he was. Bright spots of pain swirled before his eyes, and he struggled to stay conscious. Past training as a SEAL gave John the discipline he needed for mind over body, but he struggled with it. It would be so easy to just surrender to the pain and go into that blessed darkness. Returning from Iraq was hell, not home. There were men left to protect, a country still in danger. But it wasn't his war any longer. Uncle Sam had given him the boot. Medical discharge for mental instability. Bullshit...that's all it was.

"Damn it!" He cursed at no one but the trees, and maybe a rabbit or two. His phone lie in a hundred pieces next to where he'd fallen. He smacked his fist on a nearby rock. "John, you're an idiot."

If he hadn't been so angry with her, he would have planned better. The only thing he'd grabbed, besides his phone, was his ever-ready backpack which contained enough food and water for three days, a change of clothes, and his pistol. Would Carol send someone to search for him in that time? He couldn't bet on it. If he planned to survive, he needed to reach the ranger's station he passed about two miles back before dark. He glanced at his watch. That gave him about three hours.

Rumors of a mountain lion were circulating through town. A few local farmers had lost some cattle to the big cat, and local hunters and trappers hadn't been able to track the illusive creature.

He'd only seen a cougar in the wild once, and that had been enough. John respected the awesome God-given power of those creatures. If this one was hunting cattle, then something was wrong. Cougars didn't come that close to people unless they were starving or rabid. Even with the ski resort that went up about two years ago, he knew there was still plenty of food in this wilderness to keep a big cat happy. The last thing he needed was to cross the path of a crazy cougar.

With tremendous effort, he hauled his body closer to a sturdy young pine. He snapped off three rigid branches. Removing his shirt, he mustered the strength to rip it into strips and tie the branches to each side of his leg. The mere thought of standing caused a wave of nausea. With shear willpower, he fought it. Rolling first to one knee, he used the third stick to hold his balance while he hopped to one foot. His other hand braced against the tree as black spots swirled in front of his eyes. He hooked his arm around the crook of the pine to stay upright if he fainted. John closed his eyes and focused, managing to hold the darkness at bay.

John knew if he could just make it to the ranger's station, he could make use of the radio and call for help. He'd have shelter and a place he could safely stay the night. But that two-mile hike might as well be fifty. He glanced back at the busted cell phone and cursed again.

Carol just didn't understand. She thought he was crazy too. He fingered the card in his pocket she'd given him for that veterans support group. Again…bullshit. He could start over without them. He'd do fine if she'd just stay off his ass. So what if it'd been ten months? It takes time to adjust.

He never heard the big cat approach. A low rumble in its throat was all that alerted John to its presence. Slowly, he glanced over his shoulder at the angry-looking mountain lion blocking his way to the trail. It was over. He'd never reach his gun before the cat sprung. He watched in horror as the animal's haunches bunched.

It sprung to the simultaneous crack of a rifle. The gigantic animal fell dead at John's feet. He lost his grip on the pine, and as the pain and relief claimed him, he caught sight of a man holding a sniper's rifle. Just like the one he'd used.

***

"John?"

He heard the mention of his name through a fog. His eyelids weighed heavily on his cheeks and the harder he tried to open them the heavier they seemed. He sensed pain at the edges of his consciousness and instinct told him to let go and head back into the darkness.

"John?" the voice said again. A woman's voice. His sister, Carol?

He struggled again to open his eyes, this time succeeding. Light penetrated the tiny slits and burned to the back of his skull. He shut his eyes tight. The blessed darkness swirled, always on the fringes of his mind. It would be so easy to given in. Not start over. Let it all go. Memory flooded through him. The anger, the night on the mountain, the cougar, the man who saved his life. He forced himself back to consciousness and the pain. At least it reminded him he was still alive, but for what purpose?

"Doctor, he's waking up."

A calloused hand roughly pulled one eyelid all the way open and shined a beam as bright as a spotlight into his eye. He jerked to the left.

"Damn it! Put that thing away," he croaked.

"That's my brother," Carol said. John caught a glimpse of her face when she leaned into his field of vision. "I was so worried about you."

"How long?" he managed.

Her soft hand smoothed the hair away from his forehead. He flinched. She drew her hand away. "About 24 hours. I've been so scared you wouldn't wake up at all."

"Why? Wouldn't it be better to be free of the crazy brother?"

"You were wrong to run away. Again."

"I got this, Carol," a male voice said, leaning into John's view. "Hi, there."

"Who the hell are you?"

"I'm the man who saved your ass from being cougar food."

John looked away, embarrassed. "I'm sorry, man. Thank you."

"Anything for a fellow brother at arms." The man reached out his hand and John shook it vigorously.

"You served?"

"Three tours with the SEALS. You?"... "Four."

"Haunts you, huh?" the man asked, his brown eyes full of understanding.

For some reason those words struck John in that deep place, where all the bad things were locked away. It started with one tear sliding down his cheek and then he erupted into sobs.

The man just held him until the storm had passed. When John's shuddering stopped, the veteran said, "When you're outta here, we'll deal with this. You can start over, John."

John nodded, and after one last tight hug, the man headed for the door.

"Hey, what's your name, bro?"

"Gabriel."

There really were such things as guardian angels.

Kelly Abell

Kelly is the author of eight published novels and short stories. She writes young adult thrillers as well as adult romance, romantic suspense and paranormal romance. Her aim is to write about gripping characters in tense situations that keep a reader turning the ages. Visit her at www.kellyabellbooks.com

The Sword and the Pen

Police Sergeant William Carter's retirement party was winding down. Carol, his wife of forty-six years, had rescued him from a group of young admirers, and pulled him to a table.

"Phew! Thanks. Feels good to sit down."

"Looked like you needed a break. You okay, Bill?"

"Hell, yes! Why not? I'm now a man of leisure! Go to bed late, get up late, do what I want. No more chasing robbers, rapists, murderers, and best of all," he added, putting a hand over the bullet scar below his left collarbone, "no more people shooting at me."

Carol looked knowingly at her husband. "I repeat. You okay, Bill?"

Bill smiled and responded in a softer voice. "Yeah, hon. I'm okay. No use fooling ourselves though, retirement will take some getting used to. But, thirty-five years on the force is enough. Honestly, I'm glad you talked me into it."

"Maybe now you'll have time to write that book you've always talked about?"

"Maybe. But first we should do those things we've always talked about; travel, visit the kids, maybe buy a boat, or a motorhome. We'll be happy, you'll see."

Carol reached across and squeezed her husband's hand. "I'm already happy. Always have been."

"Hey, hope I'm not intruding," Mark said, approaching the table. "Sally and I are getting ready to leave, and we just wanted to say goodbye."

"Are you kidding? My partner of twelve years is always welcome at our table. Carol and I were just discussing retirement plans."

"Great. Keep good notes. You find something that works, let us know. But seriously, Bill, I know you don't want to hear this, but I gotta say it; that bullet to your shoulder was meant for me. If you hadn't pushed me out of the way…"

"Okay, Mark. Enough. You know you'd have done the same."

"Listen, Bill, if there's anything you ever need…"

"You got it, partner. Now go home. You've got work tomorrow."

— One Year Later —

Retirement wasn't going exactly as Bill had expected. Why was it now harder to find time for those everyday jobs that were so easily done when he was still working? He pondered this question as he followed the lawnmower back and forth across the yard. Halfway down his last line of grass, Carol stepped out on the porch and yelled something at him. Bill silenced the mower, "What'd you say?"

"You've got a visitor! It's Mark! Says he needs to talk! Says it's important!"

***

"Jake Barce! How the hell did that happen?"

"He got beat-up in a prison brawl." Mark explained. "When they took him to the infirmary he somehow started a fire. In the commotion he managed to overpowered a guard, take his gun, and escape."

Bill shook his head. "Of all the people we helped put behind bars, that psycho is the worst; rape, murder, arson, burglary; sometimes all in the same night. My biggest mistake was not putting a bullet in him that night we caught him torching his girlfriend's house."

"Yes, and with his girlfriend still inside," Mark added.

"He blames us, you know."

"That's why I came here, Bill. He's probably hundreds of miles away by now, but like you said, he's a psycho. He may be looking for revenge."

Bill remained silent.

"Well, gotta get to work," Mark said, getting up from the table. "Just wanted to give you a heads-up."

"Thanks Mark. You take care. And watch your back."

"You too. If I hear anything I'll let you know."

"I'd appreciate that."

"Oh, by the way. How's that book coming?"

"Moving right along."

Marked grinned. "In other words, you haven't started yet."

"Been busy."

"I hear you — Later!"

— One Week Later —

Mark was right. Jake valued revenge more than freedom. By the time Mark and Sally returned from the late night movie, the fire department was already at their house battling the flames. The first thing Mark did was grab his cell-phone and speed-dial Bill Carter.

***

"Who was that, dear?" Carol asked.

Bill stared straight ahead as he slowly put down the phone, walked over to the gun cabinet, and withdrew his police revolver. "Carol, I want you to go to your sister's house and stay there until I call."

"Why? What's happened?"

"There's been a fire over at Mark's place."

"Oh dear God! Are they alright?"

"Yes, they weren't in the house."

"What does this have to do with going to my sister's?"

"Just being cautious."

"Just being evasive, you mean. What's going on?"

"Jake Barce — he's escaped."

"Bill! For God sake, you're not a cop anymore!"

"Please, Carol, not now. Just gather some things and…

When Carol screamed, Bill pivoted and raised the gun into firing position, but he was too late. The 'crack' of Jake's gun and the burning pain in his shoulder came simultaneously.

***

"Look, let my wife go," Bill pleaded. "Your beef is with me; she had nothing to do with your arrest."

"Collateral damage," Jake said indifferently, as he finished tying up Bill and Carol, and then started sprinkling gasoline around the room. "I spent ten years behind bars because of you."

"You're drunk, Jake. You're also stupid. You may have gotten away if you'd kept running. Your hunger for revenge is going to land you back behind bars before the smoke clears."

"Shut-up! You're just like the others. Begging for their lives. Well, it didn't help them, and ain'tgonna help you! I've already taken care of your partner. Waited until they turned off the lights, and went to bed. Then I torched their house."

"That's not exactly true," came Mark's voice from behind. "The lights were on a timer."

Gasoline splashed over the floor as Jake dropped the can, grabbed for his gun and spun around, but this time it was Jake who was too late.

— The Next Day —

"I can't believe it!" Bill said from his hospital bed. "Two times in the same shoulder; almost the same spot!"

Mark grinned. "Must be your lucky shoulder."

"What about the Jake? Was he also lucky?"

"He died in surgery, Bill. It's over. Jake was your last loose end. You've done your part. It's time for a revision. Time to get on with your life — How's that book coming?"

"I wish people would stop asking that!" Bill replied, irritably.

Mark laughed. "Okay partner. I've got to run; meeting with the home insurance adjuster at noon."

"Sorry about the house, Mark. You and Sally okay?"

"We'll manage. We're staying with Sally's folks for now. Anything I can get you before I leave?"

"No, no, — oh wait, yeah, if you could hand me that small briefcase Carol brought over."

"This one?"

"Yeah, thanks. Talk to you later."

Bill waited until Mark left the room before unzipping the briefcase and slipping out the laptop. Okay, he thought, Time to let go of the past; start anew. What's that saying? 'The pen is mightier than the sword'. For five minutes former police Sergeant William Carter stared blankly at the screen before finally extending a finger on his good right hand, and pecking out his first sentence: Grandpa was a cop, so was dad. I guess it's always been in my blood...

Robert Alan

Robert Alan, a native of Chicago, moved to Panama City, Florida after retiring from the Air Force. He is author o f the award winning suspense/thriller novel, This Way Madness Comes. Alan's short stories have appeared in FWA's Collection 5 & 6, and in Fireside Publication's Holiday Tales Anthology.

The Ashes of the Martyrs

It's Christmas Eve, and I am standing on the edge of a mass grave.
A thin, sad man joins me. He's the only survivor of a family of nineteen.
"They are all here, somewhere," he says.
We stand together for some time, but in contrast to what has become the norm for desperate peoples visited by Americans, he requests nothing of me. Not even, "Please, sir, help tell the world of our plight." He only stands quietly. I think he is simply tired of hoping.
The remains of his family members rest here in the Kurdish town of Halabja, the site of history's largest chemical weapons strike on a civilian population.
The main, formal cemetery lies nearby. A headstone and a footstone mark each grave and orient on Mecca. The rows are neat, quiet, and carefully arranged. Most striking, however, is a large, marble statue of a grief-stricken human form, hands turned in toward its chest as if to contain the unspeakable anguish that was the horrible reality of 16 March 1988. It cants its head skyward to offer a silent scream in warning to the world.
I hand my weapon to Kamal, my comrade-in-arms, and kneel below the statue to lay a wreath, but when it is time to stand, I cannot. Nothing seems adequate. The chemical graves of 5,000 martyrs demand something more. The many thousands left poisoned and disfigured demand more. The families of those who perished or were maimed, crushed by the great weight of history, demand more. So, I remain on my knees and pray. An Our Father.A Hail, Mary.But mainly a prayer for the survivors who somehow carry on despite their sacrifice to a very real Hell on Earth.

***

"This is the house I was in when the chemicals began falling from the sky."
Kamal is pointing to the typical, mud-brick home under a flat earthen roof on my right. It stands near the cemetery where concrete and stucco are everywhere stained an unnatural brown. Suffocating melancholy. Dismay and torment. A grossly disfigured man sits on a stone step near me staring into nothing through lidless eyes.

On the day of the attack, Kamal was a young peshmerga, one of the famed Kurdish fighters whose name means, "those who confront death."

"We had been conducting guerrilla operations against the Ba'athists," he explains. "They attacked Halabja with napalm, first, and the walls of flame forced the villagers to concentrate toward the center of town. Then strange, muffled bombs started landing." These were the chemical rounds.

The air soon thickened with a lethal rain of nerve agents, blister agents and, possibly, blood agents.

"We smelled apples and garlic. People were losing skin. Some twitched or laughed uncontrollably. Friends dropped dead before our eyes."

By day's end 5,000 Kurds were dead, and the man who orchestrated the attack, Saddam Hussein's cousin Ali Hassan Majid had earned his new name, Chemical Ali.

***

Kamal's wife, Nasrin, is half Hawrami, the name of the Kurdish tribe inhabiting the mysterious mountains that dominate the east side of Halabja. To many other Kurds none but hillbillies choose to live in those remote highlands.

"They are simple and speak a dialect few can understand," I'm told.

A very many of them also perished in Halabja.

But that is all mostly behind Nasrin, now. Today she maintains a beautiful, modern home in a bustling, pell-mell suburb of Sulaymaniya. She keeps it spotlessly clean with gleaming tile floors, a well-equipped kitchen and a living room ringed with couches and open day or night to any friendly visitor.

Aside from the typical, Middle Eastern rats-nest of overhead electrical wires running throughout her neighborhood, and the lack of lawns, it's much like happy, residential communities back home. Kids gleefully run loose outside while mothers gather to talk or plan their shopping. Soccer balls arc back and forth across the streets, and children play pranks on each other. No one has a care.

And any American soldier is welcomed like family.

Nasrin and Kamal are a wonderful couple, and their three young sons are bright, friendly, fun-loving boys. The five of them have become family to me, and their home has become a home away from home.

Shkar, the youngest, recently asked his dad to buy him a big, plastic Jeep he saw in the bazaar, because I showed him a photo of the one I drive back in the States. The middle boy, Sharo, presented me a drawing he made that shows his dad and me, Kurdish and US forces, fighting al Qaeda in Iraq.

"Look, colonel," he beamed, "no Americans or peshmerga are hit."

Rejwan, the oldest, wants to join the Kurdish security forces, like his dad.

And Kamal and Nasrin clearly love each other, as they should. She laughs at his endless supply of good-natured jokes about her Hawrami background, and he compliments her cooking.

"This," she tells me pointing to a TV show of an Iranian Julia Childs streamed to the satellite dish on their house, "is the next meal I'm going to cook. Tell my husband to bring you back tomorrow for dinner."

In a way, their family is an example of a much larger story, a story of triumph over atrocity, endurance under chemical weapons and freedom after genocide.

"The Kurds work every day to make today better than yesterday and tomorrow better than today," I tell Kamal.

"Yes," he responds, "that is because if we didn't, the blood of the peshmerga, the blood of the Americans, and the ashes of the martyrs will have been wasted."

"But don't worry, older brother," he continues, "If the Americans leave we will never let Kurdistan return to how it was. Never. We will continue fighting if we must, but we will fight even harder. We've learned lessons about how to govern, too, and we won't get it right immediately, but we will get it right."

**

"IT'S NOT ALLOWED FOR BA'ATHS TO ENTER."

These are the words painted on a large sign at the entrance to the Halabja Memorial. They are impossible to miss. The ground here glitters with hundreds of finned shells, residue from the actual chemical munitions that fell on the town.

Kamal and I step into the heart of the memorial. It is a dark, circular hall of vaulted ceilings and walls of black stone carved with the names of the 5,000 chemical martyrs. They stand patiently in columns of neat, golden characters reaching from waist-high to near the ceiling and whisper at me.

The small crowd of Kurds politely accumulating around us, now follow me as I prepare to depart. No one says a word, but somehow their presence respectfully guides me toward a large guest book, open, with an uncapped pen resting gently on a blank page. I pause, immensely conscious of my insignificance, and write:

Words cannot fully describe this atrocity. God bless the good people of Halabja. They will rise from these ashes and the world will understand.

As I turn to leave several Kurds converge on the page to snap photos. I feel very small.

Ernie Audino

Ernie Audino retired from the US Army in 2011 as brigadier general. He is an experienced combat operator with multiple assignments in armor, cavalry, infantry and Stryker units. He is especially grateful for his service commanding a team of combat advisors embed inside a Kurdish peshmerga brigade in Iraq.

Reshuffling

"Start over!"

"No." I know what is coming, a declaration that we have missing cards, she has one too many, or something like that.

Callie pauses and purses her lips. I ignore her. It's hard to do when your Canasta opponent is a bald-headed-ten-year-old wearing bright orange pajamas and Donald Duck slippers. Last year it was Goofy slippers, just like a pair I've had since I was a kid. I told her about them, and we've been friends ever since.

As I watch her face, I can see Callie picking her next words. She's eying me, waiting to see if I'll crack. I get more comfortable among the bunched up blankets and sort my cards.

"I don't think you shuffled well enough." Callie says in her naturally squeaky voice.

I give her my I'm not messing around look.

"It's Canasta sweetie. You're gonna have all sorts of matches no matter what. Now wrap your tiny paws around your cards, and lay your melds on the table here."

Callie gives me a harrumph and a bug-eyed look before redirecting her attention.

For Callie, I normally would reshuffle the deck, but I'm planning to meet friends after work, and if I want to get out on time, I can't dawdle. One person in the group is an old friend — to be more exact, a hot guy that I regret casting aside. I've been dateless for four long months.

Callie slaps the bedside table with her hand so the stacked cards tumble sideways. I can't help smiling. When Callie's trying to be obnoxious, she just gets cuter and cuter.

"Temper, Callie."

While she's straightening out the deck, I start to lay a row down, but I'm distracted by a flash of purple on the inside of Callie's right arm — the beginnings of a bruise right in the bend of her elbow. Around the edges it's pink and green.

"What the…?" I reach for her wrist, but she's already snaked her arm back under the blanket.

"Why didn't they use your port, Callie?"

I point to the spot below her collar bone where the quarter size implant protrudes from under her skin.

"My Chlorambucil was still running and they said they didn't have time to come back."

The way medical jargon tumbles out of her mouth — for a second I forget she's only ten.

"Call me next time, O.K?" I say it casually. I don't want to be overbearing. Callie's parents are major helicopters, hovering over every single staffer. Callie confided that she finds it embarrassing.

When I was twelve, I had Mono and was in the hospital for six weeks with my mother making everyone nervous.

I get it.

We resume playing.

Swish-swish.Thump-thump.

The speed of our card slaps gives our game a hip-hop rhythm. With each card I pull, Callie adds body moves by bending at the elbow and drawing her fanned out deck to her chin.

We pull and discard as fast as we can until there are two in the deck, Callie's got three, I've got four, and it's my turn to draw. She's wiggling around on her bottom and singing before I get the card in my hand.

"I'm gonna win. I'm gonnawin," Callie chants.

I drag one of the two remaining cards slowly toward me and hold it to my chest before looking. With a deliberate "hmm," then an "ah," I add it to the pair of fours in my hand and with a grin, lay the threesome on the table. "I win," I announce.

Callie responds by sticking her tongue out at me and scrunching up her nose. I'm thinking about what I want to wear tonight.

Then she leans over and grabs my forearms. My resolve crumbles.

"Please. One more round. Come on Aubrey. You've only been here, like, like, twenty minutes," she whines.

I resettle at the foot of her bed and deal new cards.

Soon the tempo of card slaps and swooshes returns until Callie's oversized Kidoozie clock alarms.

It's 3:00 pm.

I snap my head up and put my cards down. "Callie, I have to go."

"But the game?"

I think the crestfallen look on her face is a little much, a tactic she uses. Guilt creeps up from my subconscious but I push it away. Tonight is too important. Callie's too young to understand. Jumping up from the bed and walking towards the door, I talk fast. "I'll see you tomorrow. If I win again, I get your slippers!" I hike up my scrubs belligerently, mocking the threat. Callie smiles and I know we're okay. I run over, give her a quick hug, and leave.

A lab tech passes me in the doorway and I think about Callie's bruised arm, but I want to get ready. I'll leave it for tomorrow.

***

Everyone I pass is quiet. Not I haven't had my coffee quiet, but the kind of quiet that demands immediate pause. I quicken my pace and reach the unit just as housekeeping walks out of room 467.

Callie's room.

"…clot…pulmonary artery…," I hear, and then nothing but the ocean pounding in my ears. Thirty minutes later, I sit on the bathroom floor. My boss gives me the day off, but by the time I'm in my car, I've decided to transfer.

***

Adult Oncology. Three months. I do overtime in the radiation lab. If I learn the medicines, I'll fit in, I think. It's not working. When I'm in a patient's room and his grandchildren are there, I feel displaced, like an outsider.

I set up a meeting with my old manager.

***

"Hi, I'm Aubrey. I'll be your nurse today."

The twelve-year-old sitting cross-legged on the bed has a deck of cards in her hand. She has an Osteosarcoma and will have surgery in two days.

"Playing Solitaire, huh." The triggered memory shakes me.

"Yeah, but I'd like to have someone to play with. You could fix that." She says it to me matter-of-factly. I avoid eye contact. I don't want her to see my eyes getting red.

"Can I sit and talk to you while you play?"

"Sure. Wanna play Crazy Eights with me?"

"Sure." It's only one word, but it sticks in my throat.

I just stare. She probably thinks I'm nuts. "Yes" might be moving forward or back, I don't know which.

She cups the deck in her left hand, then grabbing a handful in her right, I watch her position her thumbs to fan out the cards. They fall with a dull thwack when she arches the piles back between her thumb and index finger.

"That wasn't very good." She lets out a sigh of exasperation and pushes the cards to where I sit gingerly at the edge of her bed. "Here. You do it."

I miss Callie.

"No, I think you should do it." I pick up the cards and place them back in front of her.

"Split the deck and try again."

Susan Bartlett
Susan Bartlett has taken classes on and off for the last six years, and while continuing to revise two novels enjoys submitting short stories inspired by her nursing work.

Mostly Blind

On my first day of school, I walked there with my cousin Denis. I held on to his hand because I couldn't see well enough to find the building.

Once at the school, Denis said, "Diane, follow me up the stairs, seven steps. Inside the building, follow me to the first door on the right and then all the way to the back of the room. We sit in the last seat on the right."

We sat in a double wooden seat with a small table in front of us. I knew there were other kids present, and I could hear the voice of an adult somewhere in the room.

My cousin was busy doing something. "What are you doing?" I asked him.

"I'm writing what the teacher said."

I memorized everything I heard and once in a while I answered to the adult's questions.

On my second day, I was bored and asked my cousin if I could write. He said, "Go to the front of the room and ask for a composition book."

I walked until I saw the shadow of someone sitting at the front of the room.

"I'd like a composition book, please."

The shadow gave me one. I smiled and said, "Thank you."

I turned and walked directly to the back of the room. And there was my cousin, still writing. He stopped to give me a pencil and to teach me how to make circles. I completed the entire booklet of about eight pages and a second one.

For my third book, I asked Denis, "Can I do something else?"

"I'll teach you the alphabet. Start with the letter A, like this." I wrote A's for a few pages. "Do you want to learn the next letter?" he asked.

As the day passed, I learned many letters. But, I didn't know what to do with them.

And so went the days.

Four days later, the shadow told me she called my parents to the school and for me to wait for them. That's when she told my mother and father, "Diane is smart. She can learn. She answers my questions—even the ones for the second grade. Maybe she needs eyeglasses."

My father explained, "The day Diane was baptized. Some of the water ran into her eyes and with the cold weather, she suffered severe infections in both eyes. The doctor told us Diane would be mostly blind and may never see well." My father wiped is eyes and continued, "We'll take Diane to the optometrist in the morning and have her eyes checked. Maybe he can help her."

The next day, my father left work, and with my mother and me, he drove from our small village to a big city fifty miles away. On the way, dad described what the doctor would do.

In the doctor's office, the man helped me sit in a large leather chair. I felt nervous, but not afraid. I promised myself I wouldn't cry.

The doctor placed a large cold metal object with two holes in front of my eyes. It felt heavy. When he inserted and changed many metal circles into the instrument, they made clicking sounds. At first, I saw a blur. When he finally finished the examination, I could see letters of different sizes on the wall. He handed me a paper. I recognized the letters Denis taught me.

"Can you read some of the words on this card?"

"No." Tears wet my cheeks because I didn't know how to read.

"It's okay. Can you see any letters?"

"I can see the letters ABCDEF...," I felt much better.

He said to my parents, "She should have been wearing glasses in her crib. I want Diane to have her glasses today. Could you return this afternoon?"

"We can take care of some errands," my mother said.

"We'll be back in a few hours," my father said.

When we returned to the doctor's office, the doctor said, "Diane, I have your eyeglasses. Let's try them on." He placed a plastic frame, with two clear lenses, on the bridge of my nose and adjusted the legs around my ears. What a miracle! I saw the face of a man wearing a knee length white coat. He also smiled a nice smile.

My mother asked, "Can you see us?"

I nodded yes. For the first time, I really could see what my parents looked like. My father was tall and handsome and my mother was shorter and beautiful.

At the age of six and one month, I could now see what others could see. On the way home, looking out of the car windows, I said, "Mom, Dad, I'm so happy. I can see so many things like trees and birds."

When we reached home, I asked my sister, "How did you get so tall? We weren't gone that long. And how did the knobs on the kitchen cabinets get there? They weren't there this morning, were they?" I asked my sister to show me a photograph. "I want to see what you can see."

The next day, I wore my glasses to school. I walked with my cousin without holding on to his hand. I felt happy and what a delight to enjoy a whole new world. I walked straight without the need to look at the ground under my feet.

Once we entered our classroom, I saw a large room with two rows of desks with double seats. I remembered how to find mine. Then I saw pictures on the wall and the alphabet written at the top edge of the chalkboard.

After I sat down, a woman entered the room dressed in a long black dress with a white pleated scarf around her neck and a silver cross. She wore an unusual headgear with a white bonnet and two long white panels down to her shoulders. She pinned the panels together behind her bonnet.

I asked Denis, "Why is she dressed like that? Who is she?"

"She's the teacher, Sister Ursula. She's a nun."

"Who are all those kids?"

"Those on this side, in front of us, are students in Grade One, and the ones on the other side of the room are in Grade Two."

"Wow! I was learning both grades at once."

I still answered all the questions until the teacher explained I was to answer only the questions addressed to me.

From that day until the day I graduated, my favorite subject was "Composition". I would write, and write, and I'm still writing.

Last year, I had cataract surgery. After years and years of wearing glasses, I can now read and write without glasses. My mother, who is still living, finds it difficult to understand how I can see. This time, I saw her eyes brimming with happy tears.

What a gift it is to be able to see, read, and write.

Diane M. Boilard

Diane M. Boilard is from Quebec, Canada. Diane and her husband, Richard, moved to Florida in 2001. The Florida Writer magazine published her short stories: Antarctica, A Friend Named Fred, and Heroes. An FWA member, Diane credits The Port Orange Scribes for their critiques.

The Replacements

In WWII, the Army Air Forces' recruitment posters, pamphlets, and movie trailers seduced "average American boys from average American families" to join the service. Two of those average American boys shared a wish to perform their patriotic duty from the air.

George Edwin (Ed) Farrar was the middle child of Carroll and Raleigh May Farrar's brood of nine from Atlanta, Georgia. Carroll Farrar owned a print shop until his health failed. Very ill, he could no longer support his family. Ed quit school after the tenth grade to replace report cards with paychecks. Aside from his job servicing vending machines, Ed brought home a steady stream of winnings from Golden Gloves boxing matches.

John Oliver (Jay) Buslee was the second child and only son of John and Olga Buslee of Park Ridge, Illinois. John Buslee was a partner in the Chicago firm Neumann, Buslee& Wolfe, Inc., self-described as "merchants, importers, and manufacturers of essential oils." On the road to a bright future, Jay studied for two years at the University of Wisconsin.

Though Ed's and Jay's lives had different starts and different expected futures, WWII brought them together. They both enlisted in the Army Air Forces. Ed began his military duty as an enlisted man and gunnery instructor. Jay followed the path of an aviation cadet and future officer and embarked upon pilot training.

***

The Eighth Air Force waged a fierce air battle over Europe fighting the Nazis, with numerous losses of aircraft and bomber crew after bomber crew. The American war machine constantly required new bombers and replacement crews to man the controls and guns of those bombers.

Ed's and Jay's paths crossed in Ardmore, Oklahoma, where they were selected to serve on a replacement crew and completed their final combat training. They would man a B-17 heavy bomber with Jay as the pilot and Ed as a waist gunner. In July 1944, Ed, Jay, and the rest of the "Buslee crew" were assigned to the 384th

Bombardment Group of the Eighth Air Force to fly bombing missions over Germany out of Grafton Underwood, England.

For the Buslee crew, the reality that their combat training had become actual combat came quickly. On their second mission on August 5th, their flying fortress, Tremblin' Gremlin, was pounded by heavy flak. They limped back to England with 106 holes in the fuselage; damage to the radio, brakes, and oxygen system; loss of two of the four engines; half the crew wounded; and a dying bombardier.

Their following missions throughout August and September were not as rough, but that changed on their sixteenth mission to Magdeburg, Germany on September 28, 1944. The Buslee crew manned the B-17 Lead Banana. After dropping their bombs and coming off the target, their group was startled to find themselves on a crossing course with another group coming in. Wallace Storey was piloting a B-17 behind and to the right of Lead Banana when "the lead ship made a sharp descending right turn" to avoid the oncoming group.

Storey saw the B-17 to his right, Lazy Daisy, slide toward him. He responded quickly and "pulled back on the control column to climb out of her path." Moments after the near miss, he saw Lazy Daisy continue her slide and collide with Lead Banana. Lead Banana cracked in two, just past the ball turret. Lazy Daisy's wings "folded up and both planes fell in a fireball," spinning into the clouds.

***

The boys' families held out hope, and waited for news of their sons. Three of the nine men aboard Lazy Daisy survived, but Ed Farrar was the only survivor of the Buslee crew's nine aboard Lead Banana. The Farrar family learned Ed was a prisoner of war on New Year's Eve. Near the end of January 1945, the Buslee family learned Jay died in the collision.

Ed sustained serious injuries in the collision. He was unable to walk when confined in the StalagLuft IV prison camp. Only able to shuffle his feet at first, Ed eventually regained his mobility.

On February 6, 1945, the prisoners were marched westward out of the camp. Known as the "Black March," it began during one of Germany's coldest winters on record, with blizzard conditions. With very little food, the prisoners marched by day and slept in barns or out in the open at night, never knowing their intended fate.

On May 2, 1945, after eighty-six days and five hundred miles, the British liberated the column of men in which Ed Farrar marched. The prisoners, described as walking skeletons, were returned to health before they were returned home.

***

Months later, Ed finally made it home. By then, Ed's own father was bedridden, but Jay's father was eager to visit Ed to learn everything he could about the mid-air collision that killed his son. John and Olga Buslee traveled to Atlanta to hear the news in person. Before they returned to Park Ridge, John offered Ed a job as a salesman for his business. Ed did not want to leave home so soon, but he accepted the offer and the opportunity to restart his life.

Ed moved into the Buslee home as Jay's parents would not hear of him living anywhere else. Ed helped fill the void left by their lost son, easing a small portion of the pain in their hearts. John Buslee taught Ed sales skills and life skills and helped him return to the normalcy of civilian life. Ed lived as the Buslee's son and thrived under John Buslee's tutelage. He walked a new path toward the man he would become, and toward a success in life he would not have attained without John's help.

***

Ed had two brothers who also fought in WWII, and he had not seen them since his return home from war. He learned they would both be home for Christmas, and they arranged a reunion in Atlanta. Ed was the last to arrive home, on December 16, and found that his father's condition had worsened. Carroll Farrar had delayed the business of dying until he could see his three boys together, home from war. A few days after Ed's arrival, his father was admitted to the hospital. Carroll Farrar died on December 20, just five days before Christmas.

In January 1946, once again reluctant to leave his family, Ed returned north to the Buslee home. As a man who had just lost his father, Ed was welcomed back by the man who a year earlier had lost his son. A beloved father and a precious son could not be replaced, but Ed Farrar and John Buslee stepped into those roles for each other to help ease their shared sorrow.

Ed and John needed each other in a way neither would have expected before WWII. They both traveled a new, unexpected path that would not have existed without the tragedy of war. The war had ceased to wage over Europe, but the aftermath of war continued to wage deep within both men. For Ed Farrar and John Buslee, WWII meant not only victory, but also loss, healing, learning to live with an altered version of the future, and starting over.

Cindy Farrar Bryan

Cindy Farrar Bryan is an author, researcher, and website analyst living in Ocala, Florida. Cindy won five of Emory Schley's 2013 Ongoing Tale competitions in the Ocala Star-Banner newspaper, and won the Star-Banner's 2014 The Shadows in the Alley story contest. Cindy sharpens her writing skills with her blog, http://thearrowheadclub.com.

Empty Girl

The man in the suit gazed over my body the way Daddy used to appraise a donkey. Daddy would open its mouth to check the teeth. He'd lift each leg to examine the hooves. He refused to pay more than the animal was worth.

As I stood still in a dress that stopped at my knees, the man circled me. He smelled my black hair which draped over one shoulder. When his breath hit my neck, a bad taste rose in my throat, like sour milk.

Outside, rain gently tapped the windowsill. It rained a lot more in Portland than back home in India.

When my sisters and I were younger, we often pretended to be animals. As the oldest, I chose first. I was a brown mare with a long, black tail and a shiny mane. Tani chose a cat. Yema, a rabbit. At a nearby soccer field, we'd wait for the boys to finish their games and leave. I'd gallop on all fours while Tani prowled and Yema hopped. Our saris got filthy. Mommy scolded us for not being proper girls.

Once, we played until sunset. We should've gone home, but we were having too much fun. Two men approached us. One shouted in a foreign language. The other spoke Hindi and said, "You are on private property. You must come with us. You're in a lot of trouble."

I was too young to understand it was a lie.

We approached the men with our heads down. He grabbed my youngest sister, but she bit his arm. He yelped, releasing her. Together, my sisters ran away, but the man commanded me not to move. Both men carried me off, so Tani and Yema must've made it home. When I thought about that, it made my circumstances a little easier to bear.

The man touched me. I flinched. I shouldn't have done that. His hand caressed my bare shoulder, startling me out of my daydreaming.

Mr. King glared at me. His pale eyes were hateful, his hands balling into fists.

If the man in the suit didn't take me, I'd be whipped for my mistake. Mr. King's girls were obedient and welcoming to all visitors, never allowed to recoil from any man's touch. Even this slight infraction meant that he'd strip me naked and whip the backs of my legs with his belt in front of all the other girls.

I was a horse. I was for sale. I must be examined.

The man in the suit stood in front of me, nodding. "She'll do quite nicely," he said in an English accent. I'd learned to distinguish English from American men. Most were American, but some came from other countries.

Girls stayed for a long time in Mr. King's cramped apartments unless a wealthy man wanted to buy one of us. I didn't know how much Mr. King asked for, but several men had examined me, shaken their heads, and said, "Not worth the price."

As a horse, I had worth and value. As a girl, I was empty inside.

"You belong to Mr. Carpenter now." The wicked smile on Mr. King's face made lines across his cheeks and forehead. If the devil walked around in skin, I believed he'd look like Mr. King. "Gather your things, Rita." He'd given me that name. Nami died, he'd said, and I should forget her. Rita always pleased the man before her, no matter what, even if he beat her.

Daddy used to say that a good owner never beat the donkey. The animal must be treated well. Otherwise, it wouldn't budge when he wanted a ride, or it would kick him when he walked behind it. And who could blame the donkey?

I quickly stuffed my few dresses and underwear into a bag. I wasn't allowed to cry. If I displeased Mr. Carpenter, he might beat me worse than Mr. King.

Beside the bed, I lowered onto my hands and knees. I imagined myself as a horse that must go with my new owner. I picked up my bag.

In the living room, Mr. King stuffed an envelope into his pocket.

Mr. Carpenter lifted an arm. "Rita, are you ready to go?"

"Yes, Mr. Carpenter." I took his arm and followed him out of the living room. I never noticed the musty aroma anymore except that Mr. Carpenter's cologne smelled lovely, like the spring rain.

We took the elevator to the ground floor. All the while I held his arm. He took my bag from me. "I'll carry that."

We exited the building. The rain had stopped. A ray of sunlight peeked through the clouds, warming my face. So far, Mr. Carpenter was kind. I shouldn't expect that to continue, but I prayed for it.

Another man in a suit and hat opened the door of a black limousine. I went in first, sitting on the fine leather seat. Mr. Carpenter slid in beside me, but left room in the middle.

As the driver pulled away from the curb, Mr. Carpenter turned to me. I waited for a command, expecting the worst.

His expression changed. His eyes, brown like my skin, saddened. "I'm sorry."

I didn't know why he said that, and I didn't know what to say in response, so I kept quiet.

"I wish there was more I could do." He leaned forward, hands on his knees. "What's your real name?"

"What would you like it to be?" I replied with a smile.

His chin dropped. He brushed his fingers through his wavy, blond hair. "I have a sister called Pam. She disappeared long ago. It's difficult not to give up hope, but I'll keep looking for her as long as I live."

Men shared strange and secret things with me. Mr. Carpenter's pain must become mine. "I'm sorry about Pam."

He lifted his gaze. To my surprise, tears rolled down his cheeks. He wiped them away. "I went to Mr. King's in search of her. In every place I fail to find her, I buy someone else and set her free."

It was a cruel joke, but I was a good horse who didn't show displeasure. "Mr. Carpenter—"

"My name is Richard Kensington. I bought you and I'm giving you your freedom. Will you allow me to help you get back to your family, wherever they are?"

Too stunned to reply, I crossed my arms and pinched my elbows, a bad habit. Was this a trick? Did he toy with his possessions?

"Please, tell your name."

I hesitated. That was my secret, a hidden treasure I didn't share with anyone. If this was a trick, I might get beaten later. But if not…would he really take me home? "Nami."

"That's pretty." His kindness reached his eyes when he smiled. "Nami, I will see you safely returned to your family before I continue my search for Pam. I promise."

Although it sounded too good to be true, Mr. Kensington kept his promise. That day, I was no longer a horse or an empty girl. I was Nami again, on my way home.

Bria Burton

Bria Burton's speculative fiction has been featured in anthologies such as Welcome to the Future and magazines such as The Colored Lens. She leads the FWA St. Pete Writers Group, a critique group, and serves as an FWA Board member. At St. Pete Running Company, she's employed as a blogger.

Miranda Monday

Outside the Perez Museum in Miami, arcs of heat rise off the pavement like sea waves. Inside, a few multicolored families mingle in the glassed atrium, dispersing into the galleries. I stand by the Cuban Art collection and watch for kids with sticky fingers. I see again the woman who visited the painting of "Miranda" for months, and marvel at her transformation from sickly to healthy. Today she is wearing heels, her face has color, and she just smiles at the painting – she's not crying. How curious.

I remember the first time I saw her, my first day on the job after getting kicked off the football squad at the University of Miami. She looked like an old woman, leaning forward as if falling against "Miranda," her hand outstretched, fingertips together in the Spanish gesture of sending a kiss. I stepped forward to stop her and saw that she was not old, but rather, seriously sick. Her eyes were red from crying, and there was a twisted smile on her face. Weird woman; she stepped away and I relaxed at my post. Then she came back many times, only on Mondays, and again, today.

I remain vigilant because this is an expensive painting, authenticated by experts, and valued at $1.2 million. Still, I am curious about this woman, why she comes just to see this painting, and her physical change over six months.

So I walk up and smile, nodding. She knows who I am and says "hello" with a radiant smile. I try not to get too close, lest my size and bulk intimidate her. "You really like this painting, huh?"

She looks around, then back at me. "She's my sister," she whispers nodding at the painting; then softer, "was."

I stand shocked for a moment, really? Then I see the family resemblance, now that the woman is healthier. "Really," I say out loud in agreement.

"It's a secret," she begins. "My sister; she has saved me again! She died in 1994," she adds with a wistful, sad tone. "I never saw her since the day this portrait was given to her."

"Really," I repeat like a dummy, "I mean, that's amazing." I find that she is drawing my interest. It is early in the morning and the gallery is mostly empty. I don't think I'll get in trouble for this conversation.

She smiles again and now there are tears in her eyes. For some reason, I find myself blinking to clear my eyes. I step closer, intrigued. "Tell me about it."

"Well, she was fifteen when the painting was finished, right before her quinceañera party in Habana." She speaks softly, looking sideways at the painting, as if afraid that Miranda might hear her words. "Papi had the painting done as a gift for her." She looks at me to gauge my reaction.

"Yes, we were well-off, but not spoiled," she says a little defensively now, "not like kids today... And Miranda was always mi ayuda, my protector. Always there for me, but ..." she shrugs. I think of my little brother Demarcus and a lump forms in the back of my throat. Demarcus, eleven years old and shot dead last month. Where was I, his protector?

The woman goes on slowly, "She was my idol. I was only ten, still a little girl, and she was beautiful and kind and popular. I envied her everything, but in a good way. After her quinceañera, I came to the US to a boarding school; she was supposed to come later. Then the Revolución came, and I never saw her again. She died of liver cancer at thirty-five."

"Sorry," I say. I know about death.

"I almost died of liver cancer myself, something genetic, the doctors say. That was last year, when I went to Cuba for a last visit to my family's grave and to Miranda's grave. With my son. Then the most amazing thing happened."

I nod; this is amazing so far.

"I went by the old house where we used to live, in Vedado. I went up to the gate, and a caretaker came out, a nice old man. I told him this used to be my house before... He asked us in."

"The living room was different, but the dining room still had our dining set from fifty years ago. I sat on a chair I last saw as a child and broke down crying. My son worried about me, but I was ok, as well as anyone with liver cancer can be."

"They let me look at my old bedroom, and there in a closet, unbelievable, I found 'Miranda.' They thought it wasn't worth much, or maybe they felt bad, but they gave her to me. My sister."

I nod, fascinated by this story but wondering, is this for real? I look at her face, and she seems normal, although very emotional.

"You were the owner of the painting?" I ask.

"Can't answer that," she replies smiling, "but 'Miranda' now belongs to all, she belongs to you."

I feel the truth in her story, and for the first time really look at "Miranda." I see the portrait of a beautiful Hispanic girl, so alive. I feel the warmth and innocence of her gaze, see the smile filled with hope and belief that all will be well, that all manner of things will be well ... captured in the loving strokes of the painter, Raul.

I can't speak for a moment, and I have to look away and clear my throat. "How did she save you?" I ask hoarsely.

The woman looks at me, hearing something in my voice.

"Well, with the money from the painting, I was able to get treatment for my cancer. I am in full remission. Miranda saved me again." She turns and speaks to the painting like it was a person, "Miranda, you made it, you came to America!"

I have to get away. I run to the bathroom and get inside a stall, my knees weak. I do something I haven't done for a long time. I take out a picture of Demarcus taken when he was ten - blazing smile, pure joy in his features. He had won a bear at the fair and I see in his eyes the same look as in Miranda's eyes.

I start to cry like I haven't since I was a kid. I hold the picture of Demarcus against my cheek "All right, little brother, I'm going to … I'm going to finish school like I promised you; I'm starting over."

Outside, I hear a woman's heels walk by, confident, loud. I blow my nose, wipe my eyes and hurry out, but barely get to see her walking away in the atrium. And what can I say to her that she doesn't know already? Miranda belongs to us all.

I go back to my post past the painting, but I dare not look up. I know that she is still there shining, blazing irresistibly from fifty years ago, still hopeful. Eyes brown, like my brother's.

I blow a kiss at her the Spanish way as I walk by. Thanks for saving me too, Miranda.

David Cantillo

David Cantillo's family moved to the US from Cuba in 1968. Since then, he's resided in the Midwest and Florida. He holds degrees from the University of Miami, Coral Gables, St. Thomas University, Miami, and from Wayne State University in Detroit, Michigan. He is married and the father of three.

A Perfect Companion

"Here's the grocery list. Chicken pot-pie would be nice for dinner. Walk the dog before you go."

"Yes, Edwina.Dog, grocery store, chicken pot-pie.Regular crust or puff pastry?"

"Puff. Use egg wash so it's shiny. I'll see you around 5:30. And, Troy, the garbage cans are getting stinky. Hose them out."

Troy smiled and kissed Edwina's cheek. "Have a nice day, Dear."

That afternoon, Edwina entered her elegant house, a place suitable for successful CEOs. Her company, Autom-O-Tech, provided components for the Perfect-Companion Corporation, builders of customized companion robots. The company lived up to its motto "more lifelike than real" so well that Edwina owned one—Troy. A good lover, her number one requirement, he was stellar in the sack. He kept house, was a reasonable cook, and had impeccable manners.

Most customers ordered their companions physically attractive, buff bodies, big boobs, model-like faces. Edwina didn't want anything obvious. When well groomed and tuxedoed, Troy was moderately handsome. Edwina and Troy Benedict appeared to be an average husband and wife, just the way she wanted it.

One spring Saturday as Edwina relaxed outside on the chaise, her peace was disturbed.

A woman's voice called, "Hello."

Edwina took a deep breath, rose from her lounger, and nodded to the speaker.

A middle-aged woman extended her hand over the arborvitae. "I'm Violet Burns."

Silently Edwina grumbled, "Oh, how I wish Violet would burn." They shook hands.

Violet spewed nosy questions. Where from? Occupation? Children? Then she went straight for the throat with deeper questions, ending with, "I noticed Troy shops at the same grocery store I do. I suggested we ride together. He's so funny. He said I'd have to ask you if we could share rides. What a sense of humor."

Edwina eyed Violet, but tried to keep her stare from revealing how she loathed idle conversations. "Are you asking my permission?"

A PERFECT COMPANION

Violet took a step back from the hedge. "He was just kidding, right?"

Edwina chose her words carefully. "Of course, but he wouldn't want to inconvenience you with errands, like bank deposits (a lie--all her money transferred electronically) or stops at the dry cleaners (they delivered) or getting items at the pet store (okay, legit.)

Violet's shoulders slumped. "Okay. But since we're neighbors, we should get together. How about Bridge?"

Edwina remembered she could play Bridge, but she didn't want to do it with Violet. Whoa, if the man weeding the pansy bed was Mr. Violet, she surely wasn't interested. All hairy, a double spare tire, and wearing a wife-beater T-shirt, his name had to be Rufus or Bluto, something rough and dirty.

Violet waited.

Edwina said, "We don't play Bridge. And don't want to learn, really."

"Okay. I guess I'll see you around."

Edwina gave Troy instructions to avoid Violet and Bruno-guy. Change the routine, whatever it took.

Troy managed to circumvent the neighbors, but Edwina wasn't so lucky. Violet appeared when Edwina came home, or worked outside on weekends. If Edwina didn't develop some kind of relationship, it might appear she had something to hide, so she let Violet "in" as little as possible.

Violet took up jogging and ran the same time as Edwina to chat. "Troy is such a nice guy. You're lucky."

No response.

"Either his mother or you did a really good job molding him into an excellent husband. He seems perfect."

No response.

"Odd though. Two days ago, I saw a van at your house. It looked like a 'Perfect-Companion' van, but I only saw it for a minute."

Edwina halted.

"Of course," Violet continued, "maybe it came by accident, you know, faulty directions or..." The words trailed off, an obvious opportunity for Edwina to respond.

Edwina, smiled outwardly as she had learned in her Yale MBA courses, but fumed internally. Perfect-Companion vans never came to the house uninvited. "Interesting," she commented.

Edwina thought the matter had dropped, but one afternoon as Violet walked her dog, she hurried to Edwina's car. "Saw that van again, today. Figured you'd like to know."

"You mean you'd like to know," Edwina thought.

"Come on, Girlfriend. Fess up. Troy's a Perfect-Companion, right?"

Caught off guard Edwina said, "Yes. But truthfully, he's not all that perfect." It was out now; she might as well tell Violet what the snoop wanted to know.

Violet absently dropped the dog leash. "Do tell."

With clenched teeth, Edwina let go. "Okay. Troy was perfect at first. A good cook, tidy, never argued, and dependable in social occasions.And the orgasms.Oy! The orgasms...even better than I specified."

67

Violet's jaw dropped. After a couple of attempts, she got words out. "Great orgasms? Like, uhm, did you order him…you know, extra large?"

"No, normal size. He was just super in the sack, knew exactly what I wanted."

"Oh," Violet said dreamily.

"But now," Edwina groaned. "The orgasms are pitiful—if at all. I'm not satisfied. He doesn't do it for me anymore. His cooking doesn't have the same verve. He's, well, become…boring."

Violet toyed with her hair. "Machines fail. Maybe he isn't working at full capacity. That could be why the van came out."

"Maybe. I'll check it out. Anyway, this is just between us, okay?"

Violet crossed her heart and zipped her lip. "Not a word."

By the time Edwina stepped over the threshold, she'd resolved to order a new companion. Troy had been with her for eight years, the usual run. She consulted the manual. It suggested trying something completely different on renewal. Great idea. Young, handsome, muscular.

Since she did her best thinking Monday through Friday, quietly staring out the double glass windows of her beautiful corner office, she waited until morning. At her desk, Edwina carefully considered Troy's replacement. Maybe she'd like to stay home, letting the companion work. Perfect-Companion offered an option for that purpose. Not only could you create a past for them, they could go somewhere and plug in to experience a virtual workday. Why, there was an unused closet not far from her office! It had a chair inside and a "private" sign on the door. She could give her new robot a job, maybe janitor?

She worked it out and placed her order. The van would be there next Saturday with the new companion.

At home, she could barely stand to look at Troy, and being near him made her nauseated. She couldn't wait.

Saturday morning at ten, the Perfect-Companion van pulled into the Benedict driveway. A uniformed man opened the rear of the van and guided an air gurney into the house.

Edwina let him in. Strange, she didn't remember Troy coming in covered like that. Troy dried his hands from washing dishes and joined them, expressionless.

The attendant aimed a device and pressed a button. A thump on the floor heralded the end of the old robot. "You are the only client who thoughtfully programs your unit to grow tired of the relationship. Sometimes the companions see the end coming and get depressed. But, like clockwork, every eight years you get a new one." He pulled the sheet away. "Here's your new guy." He activated the new companion's mechanism. The robot sat up.

Troy smiled. "Hello, Bruce."

Patricia Crumpler

Patricia Crumpler is a full-time retired person, happily writing, painting, and when possible, traveling. She lives in Parkland, Florida with her husband and three dogs.

The Plan

I parked as close to the curb as I could. Attracting attention with a sloppy parking job was the last thing I needed. I shut off the engine, closed my eyes, and mentally ran over the plan one more time. Cooling metal tick-ticked, dry leaves rattled across the hood.

When I opened my eyes, Caleb sat in the seat next to me, smiling with that gap-toothed grin I'd so loved. "You're visualizing, aren't you, Mom? Coach says we should do that before every at-bat. I always visualize me hitting a homer," he said in as serious a voice as an eight-year-old could muster.

I reached over to tug on the bill of his baseball cap, but my fingers met empty air. Caleb wasn't there. He'd never be there again. When that monster killed our only child, I accepted comfort from no one and sank further and further into despair. Robert almost gave up on me. He'd felt the same overwhelming sadness at our son's death, but he'd worked through it. Trying to pull me along the grief process with him had almost proven fatal to our marriage. I'd healed at a slower pace—thankfully Robert remained steadfast. I'd finally caught up to him at the anger stage.

The sound of a barking dog brought me back to the task at hand. Using the visor mirror, I adjusted my oversized sunglasses and hat. I plucked my phone from the console, tapped on my Memo App and read the information on the screen one more time: "Jordan Gaines, 523 Georgetown Avenue. Single mom (Carol) leaves 7:30 a.m., home at 5:15 p.m. Monday-Friday. Taylor Middle School, Bus leaves 7:15 – home 4:30, Soccer Tuesday and Thursday 7 p.m. Edgewood Park."

The time on the phone showed 4:27. In my rearview mirror, I watched a school bus lumber to the curb a block away, and spew out a ragged line of children. Only one walked in my direction: Jordan. He dragged the toes of his tennis shoes with every step, and slouched under the weight of his bulging red backpack.

Jordan let himself into the front door of the house three driveways down from my spot on the street. I waited five minutes, then pulled the keys out of the ignition, clicked out of my seatbelt and opened the car door. Sucking in a determined breath, I stepped onto the curb. I dropped the keys and phone into the pocket of my windbreaker and heard them rattle over the envelope nestled there.

THE PLAN

If a person looked like they belonged, no one paid them any attention, so I walked down the sidewalk with confidence and purpose. A gray-haired man clipped roses in his garden across the street. He looked up and waved at me. I smiled and waved back.

Pine needles covered the walkway leading up to Jordan's front door. Caleb would have loved raking them into a pile and practice-sliding through it. I shook my head to clear my thoughts. Caleb was then. This was now.

I pressed the doorbell button and listened to the ding-dong echo through the interior of the house. "It's certainly not Avon calling," I whispered while swiveling my eyes right then left to see if any neighbors might be watching; not a soul in sight. Even Mr. Rose-clipper had quit for the day. Overhead, tree limbs rubbed together with a moan in the wind, and jittery wrens scolded from a nearby shrub.

I stabbed the button a second time. I hoped he wouldn't answer, but then I heard the sound of metal sliding across wood, and watched the doorknob turn. A small gap opened, and a sliver of Jordan's face appeared. The smell of burned popcorn wafted out from behind him.

I pushed my toe against the bottom of the door to wedge it open. With a motherly smile, I cocked my head in the non-threatening way I'd practiced in the bathroom mirror at home. "Hi, Jordan. Is Carol here?"

The gap widened. Jordan stared at me. "Noooo?" he said as though asking if that were the right answer.

"Silly me," I said, "I forgot, she's still at work. Would you please give this to her for me?" I slid the envelope from my pocket and slipped it through the opening.

Jordan's skinny fingers pulled it inside.

"Thank you, Sweetie." Stepping away from the door, I said as though an afterthought, "By the way, Jordan, you should never answer the door when your mom's not home." Heading back down the sidewalk, I heard the door slam and the deadbolt grind back into place.

***

I sat at my computer and waited while the word processing program loaded. Our son's cat, Snowball, leaped onto the desk purring and rubbing his face on the corner of the picture frame that held Caleb's little league photo. I pulled the vibrating ball of white fur onto my lap, stroked his soft coat with one hand, and reached over him with the other to maneuver the computer mouse. Opening the document with the list of names and addresses, I moved the cursor to Jordan's name, double-clicked, and deleted him. Highlighting Andrea's name, I copied and pasted her information into the letter. It now read:

The decals on your car advertise to the world that you have a child named Andrea, the school she attends and what sports she plays. Because you are so compelled to brag about your child, I've been able to find out where you live, your daily schedule, and when your child is home alone. I've watched Andrea practice, and I've watched her at school. I've watched her let herself into your house after school where she is alone until you come home from work.

I am a concerned parent, but I could just as easily be a pedophile. Your carelessness and vanity make your child a target that could get her abducted and/or killed like my child. You are supposed to be her protector. Do your job!

Snowball jumped to the floor as I turned on the printer. While ink whooshed onto the generic copy paper, I picked up the photograph of Caleb, then noticed Robert standing in the doorway.

"Did you do it?" he asked.

I nodded, still staring at Caleb's sweet face.

"Do you want to go on with this?"

"Yes," I answered through clenched teeth. Tears threatened to erupt. I blinked them away. "I did the first one. You do the next," I said. "It will make you feel better."

I stood and slid my arms around my husband, and buried my cheek against the softness of his flannel shirt. The warmth of his body and the sound of his steady heartbeat grounded me. I let out a ragged sigh, clinging to our dead son's picture.

Terri Hoffman Curtis

Terri Hoffman Curtis is the author of two children's books; Sly Fly and the Gray Mare, and Sly Fly and Gray Mare at the Rodeo. She lives in Daytona Beach and Colorado, loves knitting and motorcycle riding.

Operation Fresh Start

I lounged back in the patient's chair as relaxed as if I were in my own living room. Dr. Kent McKinnon, my family doctor, had called me to his office to give me the results of my annual checkup. As he sat down on his stool, I expected he would tell me once again that I was in fine shape and to keep doing everything I was doing.

Medical problems were what other people had. Hospitals were places where I visited friends and members of my family who were not well. I hadn't been in a hospital as a patient since I was young. I felt fortunate; I felt healthy. This was six years ago.

Dr. McKinnon told me a blood test known as AST showed signs of irritability in my liver. He spoke in the calm voice of a friend. No stress. No sign of worry. My AST count was 51, just a bit above the normal range of 10 to 40.

Dr. McKinnon asked if I had any stomach pain.

"No," I said. "Absolutely none." Nevertheless, he thought I should have an ultrasound on my abdomen. This was just a precaution.

"Thank you," I said, and I headed back to my newspaper office, pleased to be able to think about the next day's paper and not about my health.

I went to a medical lab for the ultrasound. A few days later, the doctor's office called to say Dr. McKinnon wanted to talk to me again. I went back to see him. "Your gallbladder is a bit thick," he said, quickly adding that my gallbladder might always have been thick.

I listened, more focused on his words than I had been previously. Dr. McKinnon mentioned the word "cancer." That dreaded word startled me, but I relaxed as soon as he said he had never seen a patient who had cancer of the gallbladder in his entire career. Considering that I felt so healthy, I couldn't imagine that I would be his first patient with a cancerous gallbladder.

Dr. McKinnon arranged for me to have a CT scan, which showed a lump in my gallbladder. He thought I should see Dr. Craig McFadyen, a surgeon, and talk to him about it.

I went to see Dr. McFadyen even though, based on Dr. McKinnon's experience, I assumed my gallbladder probably wasn't cancerous. Not knowing much about my gallbladder, I did some research and learned that this small organ is attached to the liver and stores bile, which helps the digestive system.

Dr. McFadyen seemed to have gone to the same medical school as Dr. McKinnon. He, too, talked in an easy, friendly manner. Dr. McFadyen didn't even tell me what I should do; he wanted me to decide whether he should remove my gallbladder. He just pointed out that it doesn't perform any vital role. We can easily live without one.

With the modern surgical technique known as laparoscopy, Dr. McFadyen could remove my gallbladder through a small incision in my abdomen. A lab would then analyze it to see why it was thick. This simple day-surgery had only pros and no cons. "Let's do it," I said.

We set a date, and I went to a local hospital. After the operation, I returned home with only a small bandage over the incision. I felt well enough to climb our stairs two steps at a time. The operation had been only a minor intrusion in my life.

A few weeks later, Dr. McFadyen wanted to talk to me again. He had received the lab report on my gallbladder.

"Cancer," he said when I saw him.

"Oh." That was all I could say. I felt vulnerable. I was no longer in control of my life. I listened closely to every word Dr. McFadyen said. He told me the gallbladder has four layers, and the cancer was in the first two, but had not spread to the outer two. If it reaches three and four, it may be fatal.

As a precaution, when the gallbladder is cancerous, doctors open up the abdomen and remove parts of the liver that might have been infected by the cancer cells. Dr. McFadyen arranged an appointment for me with Dr. Mohamed Husien, a liver and cancer specialist, and we set a date for the operation.

This would be major surgery. After the operation, I would remain in hospital for a week and then spend several weeks recuperating at home. The more I thought about it, the less vulnerable I felt. I realized that the blood test, the ultra sound, the CT scan and the day surgery had given me the opportunity of having an operation that would re-start my life without cancerous cells quietly growing until no doctor could stop them. I had reason to hope. I felt blessed.

As I lay on the gurney waiting for Dr. Husien to start operating, everyone in the room seemed somber and quiet. I felt confident and relaxed so I decided to lighten the mood. "Don't let these guys drop me on the floor," I told the anesthesiologist, who was young, blond, female and quick-witted. "You'll never know if we drop you," she said, and the whole operating room erupted in laughter.

I wasn't laughing when I woke up several hours later. I couldn't sit up. Every time I moved, a knife seemed to slash my abdomen. The only way I could minimize the pain was to lie absolutely still. I felt helpless.

Later that day, two occupational therapists held my arms, eased me out of the bed, and helped me take a few steps to the other side of the bed. That was as far as I could walk.

Slowly, day by day, I regained my strength. I went home after a week, and I climbed our stairs very, very slowly, one step at a time.

The type of cancer I had may recur within five years, but if it doesn't, patients are usually clear. My five years have now passed.

I felt incredibly fortunate when during the fifth year I celebrated my 65th birthday, and I'll always feel incredibly fortunate. Now, I don't just say "thank you" to Dr. McKinnon and his staff. I say, "Thank you for saving my life." I also tell everyone — friends as well as casual acquaintances — to have a checkup every year. That checkup may give you a chance to start again, a chance you might not otherwise have.

Ian Darling

Ian Darling worked as a reporter, editor and editorial writer at newspapers in Canada. He wrote Amazing Airmen: Canadian Flyers in the Second World War, a book about aviators who survived ordeals during World War II. He is currently writing a book about American aviators.

No Prom Like An Old Prom

There were times in my life when I wished for—no prayed fervently for—another chance. A do-over. One of those times came sharply into focus when I saw my son in his rented tux preparing for that teen-age rite of passage, the Senior Prom. As I watched him walk to his car, a corsage in one hand and my credit card in the other, my mind flipped back to my own high school days and unerringly made the connection to my secret teenage crush, Norma Sue Moon.

Norma Sue met the qualifications for every teenage boy's fantasy: Shapely of body and long of limb, with blonde hair that bobbed gracefully as she bounced courtside in her skimpy cheerleader outfit. In English Lit, she sat so close behind me I thought I could hear her heart beating in her bountiful chest. A sweet scent of ripe apples hovered over us, perhaps from her shampoo. Or perhaps from the lunch bag that had been sitting beneath my desk for three days.

In my hormone-fueled state, I imagined Norma Sue's blue eyes gazing at the back of my head, marveling at the artistic nature of my well-greased ducktail. Of course there were other fantasies, but with the Senior Prom only weeks away I had only one thought on my mind—well, maybe more than one—and that was to ask Norma Sue to accompany me on that special night.

In my head I pictured how I would turn to her, the very epitome of cool in my tight Levi's and white tee shirt. She would return my knowing smile with an incandescent smile of her own, her eyes hiding intimate secrets, somehow both innocent and inviting. I could hear myself saying the words, "What time should I pick you up for the prom?"

She, of course, would say, "I'll be ready whenever you arrive."

As one agonizing day passed on to the next, I continued to fight excruciating mental battles, pushing myself to pop the question.

Go ahead and ask her, the positive voice encouraged. She might surprise you and say yes.

Hah! Another voice countered with a sneer, In your dreams.

I tried. Lord knows, I tried, but the words tumbled together inside my head and lodged in my throat, as if I'd swallowed great gobs of oatmeal. With only a week left before the prom, I gave up, telling myself it was crazy to expect anyone as beautiful as Norma Sue to be seen with me. I was sure she'd long ago been asked—and accepted—an invitation from the captain of the football team.

This left me with another dilemma since I still needed a date and I was sure most of the eligible girls had already been asked. Here is where my cousin Vinnie Scungilli came to my rescue. Like his mother Aunt Virgi, Vinnie wasn't much to look at. Family lore had it that when Vinnie was born, the startled doctor took one look at my cousin, and hauled off and slapped Aunt Virgi. But Vinnie had a heart as big as the heavens, and made friends everywhere he went.

I knew Vinnie also had a thing for Norma Sue. Who didn't? But he was wise enough to know she was out of his league. He had lined up a date with Amy, and informed me that Amy's friend Rosa Marie was still available. With her thick glasses and spindly figure, Rosa Marie would never be mistaken for Norma Sue, but she said she'd love to go with me, and seemed to mean it.

Rosa Marie Frangipani lived in an apartment above her father's store, Frangipani's Bakery & Fish Market. I can close my eyes and still smell the delicious fragrance of baking bread as I passed the bakery on my way to school. The fish market, which adjoined the bakery, added its own exotic aromas.

Mr. Frangipani was a tall, imposing man who seldom smiled. I remember walking into their second floor apartment the night of the prom. Rosa Marie's father greeted me in broken English, and told me to have a seat while I waited for Rosa to make her appearance. The day had been scorching hot, and heat seemed to radiate through the floor from the bakery below. As we waited, I became aware of sweat gathering under my collar, under my arms. Droplets formed on my nose and rolled down my face. Mr. Frangipani surveyed his daughter's date with what I took to be disdain, taking in my sweating face and the soggy tuxedo before traversing down to my neon red and green striped socks, which I had selected as a fitting accessory to my red cummerbund.

I squirmed uneasily as the room seemed to take on a reddish glow. By this time, the purple orchid I'd been clutching was almost ready for the compost pile, and I was struggling to think of something to say to break the awkward silence. Rosa Marie saved me when she swept into the room accompanied by her mother.

I leaped to my feet and thrust the corsage at Rosa Marie. "For you," I said, trying not to stab her as I pinned the purple flower to her brown dress.

We eventually made it out of the apartment, and joined Vinnie and Amy who had been waiting for us downstairs in Vinnie's Ford.

At the prom, we made our way onto the dance floor. I'd watched American Bandstand religiously, preparing for the big night, and I was soon shaking and jerking like my cummerbund was on fire. Despite my graceful moves, I collided with another dancer. Turning to apologize, I found myself face-to-face with Norma Sue Moon.

Eyes downcast, I mumbled, "Sorry."

I expected a look of scorn or a vacant stare since I wasn't sure Norma Sue even knew I existed. Instead she surprised me with one of her blinding smiles.

"Oh, hi," she said, "I knew you must have already had a date."

With that, her partner spun her away, leaving me in a state of shock. The rest of the evening was hazy, the after-prom party loud and boozy. I lost track of the times I kicked myself for not having the courage to invite Norma Sue. We might have ended up together at the prom after all, although I admit Rosa Marie and I had a good time.

But there are no mulligans in life. No time machine to whisk us back to relive an embarrassing or pivotal moment we wished had turned out differently. Everything, or so we're told, has a purpose, and I certainly wouldn't change the direction my life took after I left high school.

I seldom think about my school days, having left them behind long ago and moved more than a thousand miles away from my childhood home. I've tried to keep in touch with Cousin Vinnie, who recently retired as head surgeon at Johns Hopkins. We haven't seen each other in years, but we share the occasional phone call, and I always look forward to the annual holiday card we receive from Vinnie and his wife, Norma Sue.

Vic DiGenti

Writing as Parker Francis, Vic DiGenti pens the award-winning Quint Mitchell Mystery series and dispenses monstrous lies he calls stories. He's also been known to fabricate a few yarns about his schooldays, but never about his love for Norma Sue Moon. That's his story, and he's sticking to it.

What Happens in Vegas

He could be an illusion, another mirage among the many flung up by the rolling heat-shimmers on the desert road. But the closer she gets, the more clearly he takes shape, solidifying from a wavering shadow to a man, suitcase in hand, thumb out, pointed west, toward Vegas. Everything in her tells her to give the Vector more juice, make the mirage-man a dwindling flicker in her rear-view mirror, but what the heck. She knows what she knows, and what's the empty seat beside her but a waste of premium leather? So instead of passing, she coasts off the road and pops the locks.

He isn't the kind to run up beside her car and launch himself into her passenger seat with nervous, half-laughing apologies. No, he moseys like a man with all the time in the world, and stops and stands outside the bubble of glass and steel, tall, lean, his jeans as faded as his chambray shirt, his eyes as faded as the sky. Tired eyes, seeing…what, reflected in the dark-tinted windows? Himself? The thunderheads building behind him? Or does he see through the solar tint to the woman behind the wheel, plump, middle-aged, in a too-young dress all wrong for the desert and Joshua trees?

She fingers the window switch and opens the glass a crack. Heat and the odors of sand and hot tar seep in. "It's unlocked," she says. "Put your suitcase in the back seat."

"Sure, sister," says the faded man. The suitcase smells of dust and sun, and the desert heat rushes in as he lays it on the seat. "Mind if I carry this in my lap?" he asks as he ducks into the passenger side. It's an instrument case, not large, with a round flare at one end.

"No problem. Go ahead." She glances at the case. "You play in a band, or are you a solo act?"

A slight smile creases the edges of the hitchhiker's weathered face. "You could say I've been part of a band," he says softly. "But this one's a solo gig."

"I thought it might be," she says, and thinks, You looked so much younger in the paintings. Her eyes slide back to the case in his lap. "Saxophone?"

The faded man smiles again and doesn't answer.

"French horn?"

He laughs.

"Bugle, then."

"You're in the right family," he says, but nothing more. There is silence for many miles until the sun rides low, gilding the fronds of the palm trees that flick overhead.

"Where to?" she asks, as mountain-tall buildings close in around the road.

The hitchhiker leans his head back against the headrest, squinting against the rays of the sinking sun. "The Mirage," he says at last.

"Not the Stratosphere?"

"Nah. I'm close enough to God already."

Sundown gives way to twilight as the Vector coasts toward the Mirage, and like a night-blooming flower, Las Vegas bursts to life. One moment they're rolling through shadow, the next the Vector is a black hole in a sea of blazing color. Dapples of light slide over the car's hood and windshield like raindrops, vanish, are replaced by more.

"The Mirage," she says, looking up. She is one car among many streaming into the bright gape of the casino's entrance. The attendants frown when she parks under the portico, but they keep their distance from the diamond-bright gleam of the million-dollar car.

"I'm mighty obliged for the ride, sister," the man says. If he had a hat, the woman is sure he would tip it.

"My pleasure," she replies. Her passenger opens the door. The air smells of chlorine and car exhaust, and the wail of a police siren rips through the night. "And that's a trumpet in your case."

"You knew?"

"And I saw a new heaven and a new earth: for the first heaven and the first earth were passed away," she quotes softly. "What will you play? Taps?"

"I was thinking 'Nearer My God to Thee'."

She laughs and watches him gather the worn instrument case and the suitcase that smells like Time itself. As he turns to close the door, he stops and leans inside.

"I like the dress, by the way, Sister," he says. "It's a big improvement on the habit."

"Why, thank you, Gabe." She pauses. "You don't mind if I call you Gabe, do you?"

"Not at all. I won't say goodbye. We'll be meeting again soon."

"It wasn't a sin, was it?" she asks. "Renting this car, knowing I wouldn't have to pay for it?"

"Maybe just a little one. I sure enjoyed the ride, though."

She beams. "I did, too. Anything you'd recommend while I'm waiting for the concert?"

"Roulette. Roulette's always good," says Gabriel. "See you on the other side." He tips her a two-fingered salute and closes the door. By the time he reaches the casino doors he already has the trumpet in his hand, shimmering like a mirage in the neon lights.

Karen Dillon

Ocala native Karen Dillon is a long-time writer of fantasy, horror, and mystery fiction. She loves horses, hates spiders, and works in a library repairing all the books.

The Son in the Telescope

Mama hadn't said much in the car ride over. She'd been relatively mute the past twenty-four hours too. It could've been a tactic. Ignoring the issue. The silent treatment. The thought it could be premature mourning almost made me rethink my decision.

She stared out the window as we approached Canaveral. Though it was time to be cherished, the secondhand on my watch ticked with velocity, my heartbeat increasing in tandem. I swallowed hard. A deep breath as the road bent, straddled on either side by the sabal palm I'd come to know so well.

I turned to her, but her gaze was lost in the funeral running through her head. My funeral. My voluntary procession. I began to know something of the bouncing knees and disquieting stares of those who spend their last minutes with a dead man walking.

The car stopped. I thanked the driver and got out, circling around to help Mama. I opened the door and held out my hand. She scooted toward me, averting her eyes. Her wrinkled hand grasped mine, the diamond wedding ban representing thirty-two years of marriage before Papa's untimely death refracting the sunlight in a wheel of dancing colors.

We could have walked farther to say our last words, but the moment must've compelled her. Her arms flung high above her head over my shoulders, her face sobbing into my chest.

I could feel a tear drip down my cheek. It landed on her head, right in the center where her grey hair was parted. She had to feel it. It was like an anointment.

"Why?" That was the only word she could muster.

"We've been through it, Mama." I pulled her away to look into her eyes. She couldn't bear to see me. "Too few people can do this. I'm older. I've lived my life here. I've lived a good life."

"I won't have anybody left. My blood is gone."

"You have friends."

"I wish I could go back in time and take back that telescope. I wish I could erase that Christmas."

It wouldn't have helped. I developed my interest long before she even got me that telescope. Though I knew she'd crumble under any mention of the word again, I did take the liberty of purchasing one last night. It would arrive in five to seven business days. She'd appreciate it in the long run.

"This isn't goodbye." It likely was, but the hope of my return had been keeping her going. That, and the thought of bad weather to scrub the launch.

"They'll find a way to send people to come get you."

"Anything is possible."

The reality was far more hurtful. That was the deal I'd come to accept. I would hold the honor of being among the first crew to land on Mars, but it was to be a one-way trip. No resources to fuel a return.

I grasped Mama's hand and kissed her on the top of her head. The lilac of her shampoo reminded me of youthful summer breezes up north with the windows ajar. She pulled away and cupped my jaw between her warm hands.

"You are my boy." The words hung in the thick Florida air, choking me for a brief moment.

"You'll always know where I am." My voice cut gently. I released her hand and backed away. Her knees buckled, and the driver caught her to hold her up. I had to keep going. Stopping to help would make the pain worse. "Please be sure she gets to the viewing area safely."

I turned my back to her and sobbed as I hurried away. Her face would be a memory, one that would only smile back at me in pictures—relics of a life I used to know.

With each step toward the building, I could feel the ground changing. Morphing. Red dust appearing before my feet. An endless plain of rocks thrust up from extinct volcanoes. A new life. New dreams. New adventures. I wondered if they would thrill me the way I always hoped. I wondered if I'd miss breezes and humidity. I wondered if when I finally got to look back at Earth, my tears would fertilize the soil of a barren planet.

Allen Gorney

Allen Gorney is an actor, author, playwright, and screenwriter from Orlando. He is also a professor in the Film Production MFA program at Full Sail University.

A Time to Be Born

Lucretia bathed the baby as if he were still alive. She gently smoothed and stroked the tiny fingers and hands with warm water. She blotted the crown and face with a washcloth.

Buck stood behind her and placed his arms around her waist while Lucretia leaned back against him for support and continued her task. His beard brushed against her hair. He inhaled the lightness of her scent and felt the weight of her being.

The heavy sadness drained her and pulled on her weakened body. Birthing always took its toll on her, but this was different. Hours before, she felt life leave the newborn. His tiny lips were unable to hold her breast, his mouth too weak to take nourishment.

Buck and Lucretia were alone in the cabin on Wolf Creek. The midwife left more than a week ago. The children sent off to Buck's father's homestead in Holly Grove.

Gaps in the shutters allowed first light to creep in, gray and lifeless. The fire dwindled and the lone candle by the washbasin cast a feeble amber glow throughout the room. The empty loft for sleeping children was silent and cloaked in darkness above the ladder.

"Why?" she asked.

"Only God knows," he whispered. The words seemed hollow, even to him.

Eternal quiet filled the space as the light in the cabin intensified. No movement, no sound, except the breathing and non-breathing. The rain that washed the roof was now silent.

She leaned hard against him, lifted the still form from the earthen bowl onto the cloth, and dried him. She wrapped the lifeless newborn in a blanket.

Buck helped her toward the wood rocking chair, eased her in, and watched her move gently forward and back, eyes closed, the bundle held tight. He realized she was probably searching for God. He stirred the embers in the fireplace, added fatwood and split-oak to bring warmth. He kissed the top of Lucretia's head and lightly squeezed her shoulder.

A TIME TO BE BORN

After he pulled on his cavalry boots, he closed the cabin door behind him, and walked across the clearing toward the outbuildings. Buck unlatched the large door, pulled it toward him and entered the musty barn. He let his eyes adjust to the light, looked towards the end of the barn and saw two horses and a mule, still in their stalls, patiently waiting for food. He forked hay into their troughs.

With saw, hammer, and carpenter square in hand, he straddled the cobbler's bench. He knew the dimensions by heart. This would be the fifth one he built in five years. When the small box was finished, Buck took his knife and carved "William - January 14-23, 1873" into the top. Hot, salty tears formed stars on the rough pine lid. Buck watched them seep into the wood.

A passage from his Bible came to mind: "To everything there is a season, and a time for every purpose under the heaven. A time to be born and a time to die."

He spoke aloud, "Lord, William's seasons weren't long. Let him rest with You. Your ways are mysterious. Your will be done on earth. I ask You to give me strength for this day."

Stillness returned to the barn and he heard the soft splat of raindrops spilling from bare branches onto the wood shingle roof. He forgot about the rain during the night. It seemed like so long ago.

Alone with his thoughts about his life in Alabama, he recalled the work it took to clear the trees from the hill for this homestead. He remembered the hunt for wolves, deer, bear, and fishing for trout and bass. Most of all he thought of his family's large presence in the settlement of Walker County. Memories of the war came—brother Levi killed in Mississippi. Two other brothers captured by the Yankees at Big Shanty, Georgia, and released after the surrender at Appomattox in 1865. He recalled the aftermath of the war: the devastation of his native land, the poverty, the bitterness, and the violence of the hooded Night Riders.

Buck's heart lightened somewhat when he thought of the good in his life: three healthy boys from his wife Elizabeth before she died. His marriage to Lucretia produced three additional vigorous children. The rebuilding of his life was slow, but it was steady. He resumed farming, though not on the scale as before the war, but he provided for his family and kept his faith in God.

Buck led the mule outside the barn and hitched her to the wagon positioned under the lean-to. He watched white smoke climb from the rock chimney of the cabin, curl against the sky and vanish into the wind. He stopped the rig at the porch and carried the casket to the cabin, put it on the table, took out the bathwater and brought in the bucket of drinking water. The small, blanketed form rested in the cradle next to the fire.

Lucretia accepted the water ladle, and drank long and deep several times. He removed her long black dress and veil from the trunk and helped put it on over her nightgown. Her swollen feet finally went into the shoes and the dress squeezed her abdomen.

Buck picked her up and carried her in his arms to the wagon hitched behind the mule. She felt his strength when he lifted her to the seat. She watched his tall, lanky frame go back into the cabin and return with his coat and the box with William in it—the lid now secure.

He placed the chest on her lap. She pulled her shawl tight, placed both hands on the pine box and looked straight ahead at an unseen horizon. He climbed up, took the reins, put his right arm around her, and with his left, directed the mule to the burying ground at Holly Grove.

Patrick Guttery

Patrick Guttery, a native of Daytona Beach, returned to Central Florida, after a career in the architectural and durable product side of the hospital industry. He is a member of the Daytona Beach Writers Group, and has a deep appreciation for history.

My Bathroom Door

Gillian

I stop in front of the mirror and run my across over my stomach. Still flat at 47 years old. The hair's still jet black and shiny, though I got help with that. I turn and check my butt. Not too saggy. The lines in my face are the give-away, but they aren't bad. Any other time I'd smile at what I see.

Instead, a shiver passes up my spine because I'm in my bathroom and Michael's in the bedroom.

The first time I walked out of a bathroom naked to a man, Ted was a junior at college. I was a year behind. We were at his aunt's cabin near Whiteface Mountain that summer. I was drunk. I'd never done something like that before, and the alcohol helped me along.

Two years later, on our wedding night, Ted didn't complain at the huge task of unhooking the 44 buttons on the back of my dress. We weren't new to each other by then and the wedding-night sex wasn't the best. But we were married and I fell asleep with my head on his shoulder, looking forward to building our lives together.

Part of me still loves Ted. He ate at work the first two years we were married so we could see Seattle because I'd always wanted to go there. Then he agreed to move there because I loved it.

He sat wordless with me when I found out I couldn't have kids. He let me be angry and irrational and a bitch for longer than he should have. He held me six months later when I broke down crying for no reason while we made love.

He never left for the 30 hours between my mother's stroke and her death. He silently handled the arrangements because I couldn't.

Even now, I can still feel his hands, thick and powerful. I can feel his breath on my neck as he stands behind me, arms wrapping me like a shield. He was big and solid and immovable and he made me feel like nothing could hurt me.

He took me places I didn't know existed, simply by being mine. And he took me to hell when I found out what kind of man he really was.

Back in the present, there's noise on the other side of the door. A murmurring.

"What?" I ask.

A couple seconds go by.

"What?" Michael says.

"Did you say something?"

A short delay, then "No." Not an emphatic no, but I didn't realize that until later.

***

The sky was turbulent that March Thursday afternoon when everything fell apart, ragged clouds racing inland toward the mountains. The wind that pushed them found every gap in my clothes. A coffee-colored leather jacket, black slacks, and my favorite heels. I don't have those clothes any more. I don't have a lot of the things I had that day.

Three police cars sat in front of our house.

When I pulled up, the police were taking him out of our house in handcuffs. They took all of our computers, too. Even my work computer.

"Mrs. Hyatt?" The cop's eyes were hard on me, making me feel small and guilty.

"Wh-what's happening?"

When the cop told me, my eyes went to Ted's and found nothing. His silence told me everything and in that moment, the lie of our lives together became as plain as day.

Eight-hundred ninety-six counts, they said. One for each picture. I don't know how I found out, but there were eleven hundred sixteen kids in those pictures.

All those years, Ted was mine. He took me in his arms and made me feel secure. And all those years, he was a monster. He was my worst nightmare. And somehow I had no clue.

"I love you so much it hurts," I told Ted the night we moved into my dream house in Seattle. Twelve years and five months later, the day he was arrested, I found out what that really meant.

I lost the house—lawyers aren't free. I lost most of my friends. I lost my church and my workout partners and the good will of the people I worked with. They'd ask how I didn't know, why I didn't stop it. It wouldn't have hurt so much if I weren't asking myself the same questions.

Everything we built was a lie and I was stupid enough to believe it. Maybe I looked the other way because of the house and the marriage.

Kids are abused because guys like Ted want the pictures. And guys like Ted want them because women like me don't say anything. Maybe I wasn't a victim. Maybe I should have known. Maybe I was an accessory.

I don't like living in Florida. There aren't mountains and navy blue lakes. The grass doesn't kiss your bare feet when you walk across it. But down here, people don't know who and what I am. Down here, I don't feel the eyes on my back and the judgements on my heart.

I met Michael when he saw me reading a Robert B. Parker at Barnes and Noble.

"I miss him," he said. "Since he died."

As soon as I looked up, his eyes dropped, and then came back to me.

"I'm sorry. I didn't mean to disturb you."

Ted would never have apologized.

Michael's eyes were brown, not blue. And he was small and his hands were thin and calloused. I didn't intend to talk to him. I didn't intend to ask him to buy me coffee. I didn't intend to eat dinner with him that weekend.

Our first date was four years and sixteen days after I packed everything in my car and left Seattle. It took another three months before I decided to tell him about Ted. My heart stopped at his long silence. I almost got up to leave, but he took my hand.

"I don't know what happened. But I know you. And you couldn't do that to someone." When he smiled, I felt warm for the first time since the afternoon when they took Ted. That's when I decided to do this.

So I'm standing naked in my bathroom, my clothes heaped on the floor like the armor I never really had. And he's waiting for me. Out there. He knows what I am and he's still waiting. I ought to be happy, but it scares me. I'm shivering and staring at the door like it's a death sentence, running water in the sink to buy time. But I can't stay in here forever.

Michael's not redemption. He's a salve, a step toward a world where redemption might be possible. He's the first blade of grass you see when the snow starts to melt.

My hand goes to the doorknob and I take a breath.

Then I turn the knob and step into the rest of my life.

Chris Hamilton

Chris Hamilton has been an FWA member since 2005, but has been writing forever. His inspirations include Robert B. Parker, Jamie Morris, Julie Compton, and snarky, witty people he knows only on Facebook and from conferences.

Two

He had once been known as Juan, a teacher helping children. Now he could help no one except his only friend, a dog, as homeless as he.

Old and bearded, his ragged shirt hanging over torn pants tied round his waist with string, he smelled of urine and cast off clothing. The laces had fallen from the ripped holes on the top of his shoes, lost, perhaps in the gutter. Since the mudslide that wiped away all he once lived for, he had squatted everyday in city doorways where he could shelter from the rain, holding a can as bent and wrinkled as himself, hoping for a coin to buy the next meal. Most people hurried by without looking at him.

He shared his loneliness with a coarse-haired hound and his memories, shrunk to a few isolated scenes, like photographs pinned to a corkboard of his life, separated by blank areas of forgetfulness. The dog leaned against him, trailing a rope from its skinny neck.

One morning, a little girl tugged herself free of a woman's hand as they passed. She stopped to stare at the man as very young children will. He looked up at her with a smile, crooked and stained, with gaps where teeth had once been. She gazed back, her face solemn, head bent forward, peering shyly from under long lashes, as if sorry for something she might have done, and doubting her own innocence.

She held out her hand, a cookie in her fingers, the edges ragged from her teeth and damp with saliva. The direction of her gaze told him it was for his dog.

The woman dragged the child away. The girl glanced up at her, then at the man in the doorway with his dog, and threw the cookie to him. The woman hustled her to a waiting car where a driver in uniform, as crisp as the winter morning, took her umbrella. He held it aloft and opened the car door. The woman thanked him in English, then she and the quiet child climbed in.

The bearded man who smelled of urine had not eaten in two days, but he broke the cookie and gave most to his dog, who sniffed, then gently bit at the softened edges as if it knew they must share and eat slowly to make it last. The man chewed what was left.

TWO

He pulled a small photograph from his pocket, the wrinkles in the paper ageing the face that smiled back. His eyes moistened with memories. Fingers deeply stained and ending in nails chewed to the quick, smoothed the creases, and the face grew young again. A wet drop fell on it, though whether from the rain or from his eye he was not sure. It didn't matter. He wiped the photograph against his shirt.

Instead of the solemn little girl who had stopped beside him, the face in the photograph glowed with life barely begun. He had not given her a puppy because he had not understood her need. By the time he learned, she had been taken. He had been unable to rewrite the past.

He had seen the woman and her crisp driver before. She had passed his doorway many times, like so many others, as if he and his dog did not exist. The little girl he had never seen.

On the next day, and the next, the woman dragged the little girl past his squatting place toward the car. The little one looked at him from under her sad eyelids and no one said a word.

By the fourth day he felt the heaviness of the silence between them. This time she stopped again. She strained against the woman's hand toward the dog. The dog pulled against his own restraint, its tongue lolling, and the white tip to its black tail beating time to secret thoughts.

The little girl looked at the dog, but the woman would not let her touch it, and the man wondered why.

"He is safe," he said.

The little girl said nothing. The woman told him her granddaughter had not spoken since her parents had been lost. He knew what she meant, loss being a tragedy they shared.

On the next day, the man who had once been a teacher told the child his dog's name was Two. She didn't reply. "Because I am Juan," he said, and smiled at his own English joke. She reached out her hand. The dog licked it and morning sunshine spread over her face. She smiled at the dog, then at her grandmother, and the dog licked her fingers again.

On the fifth day she laughed as Two licked her fingers. Her grandmother gasped and hugged her, but she pulled away and leaned toward the dog.

"That is the first time she has laughed since…" the woman said.

The man, who had been known as Juan, held out the end of the dog's rope to them both. "She must have the dog," he said. "He has fleas. You can clean him."

"But he is yours," the woman said. "Why?"

"Because," he said, and shrugged. "Every child should have a dog."

When they had gone he looked at his crumpled photograph. He knew she would approve. He could not let the dog see him again in case it wanted to return. In the afternoon he found another doorway where the woman and the little girl and Two would not find him, but it was not so sheltered and he felt the chill.

Late in the winter, fever struck him. A city van picked up his body to carry it to the mortuary, but he still breathed so instead it took him to the Sisters of Mercy. They cleaned him, exorcized the smell of urine, trimmed his ragged beard, and laid him in a bed with a clean nightshirt, the crumpled photograph placed like an icon on the small locker beside his bed. The man lay thinking of a little girl, sometimes not knowing which one, aware he had begun his final contest with the quiet release spreading through his body. He knew he would never again sit in a doorway with his only friend, a dog who had brought laughter to a little girl.

That's where the woman and her granddaughter found him.

The little girl came close to the bed and stared at him in her solemn way.

"Two," she said.

"I have come to thank you," her grandmother said. "She has started to speak again, to her dog, and sometimes to us."

He smiled through the tiredness that would soon separate them forever.

"What can I call you?" his voice a whisper, like the breeze blowing through the window.

"Angela," she said.

He repeated it to himself, leaving off the final A.

Her grandmother thanked again the man who understood a child's loneliness, and he smiled.

When they left, he held the wrinkled photograph so he could see the young face. As he watched, the creases dissolved for the last time.

He lay, arms crossed, still smiling, holding the photograph, when a sister pulled up the sheet over his body.

Bob Hart

A retired veterinarian, Bob lives with his wife, Veronica (Ronnie), in Ormond Beach. His writing credits include the Florida Writer and previous FWA Collections. An RPLA award winner, INDIE finalist and 2012 International Chapbook Competition winner, with three published books available from Amazon, he is currently writing a political thriller.

Poisonberry Wine

February 1
Dear Ashleigh,
It's been six weeks since I sent you the first draft of Poisonberry Wine. I'm surprised you've made no comments. In the past you've been so quick to respond with great suggestions for improvements. I suppose you're busy with your new husband and house. I hope you're loving them both. In the meantime, if you haven't already, don't bother reading the book. I'm attaching the revision based on my editor's comments.

She says the poison wine details are too specific. I discovered the recipe in an 1800s medical book I found at a garage sale. The publisher is afraid she'll be sued if anyone tries to use it. She also thinks the husband ought to be far meaner; mean enough that the reader will cheer when he dies and will have more sympathy for the wife. So, I've changed the recipe, made the man meaner and hope you'll enjoy the revision I've attached.
    Hugs,
    Grandma

***

February 15
Dear Grandma,
I'm sorry I haven't written. I never received the first version of Poisonberry Wine. I like the revision very much. It's probably like your last book; you always do so well when you rewrite. I have no suggestions. Joe and I went up into the mountains to stay at a cabin for a week. Did you see the pictures online? We are both well. We're dieting–we gained so much weight since the wedding. I'm doing better than he is.
    Love,
    Ashleigh

***

February 18
Ashleigh,
How odd that the first draft never made it to you. I checked the email address and it's the same one I'm using here. I love the photos, but all I saw were a log cabin, a fireplace, and snow covered ground. Oh, and one photo of Joe watching a football game. I'm guessing you took all the pictures. Maybe next time you could have Joe take one of you. I can't imagine you needing to lose any weight, but I'd love to see the new slender you.

The book is at last in its final revision. There were still a couple of errors and one small plot problem. It should be out by May.

Grandma

***

March 12
Dear Grandma,
We decided to sell our house and move to that log cabin we stayed in. I know with your arthritis you won't ever be able to come stay. It's cold, damp, and really remote. I won't have internet access unless we go into town, which Joe will do every day because of his job.

Ashleigh

***

March 15
Dear Louise,
When is the last time you spoke with your daughter Ashleigh? Is she all right? I worry about my granddaughter. Her notes seem so remote, not at all like her old bubbly self. Is there a problem with the marriage? Sometimes it's really frustrating living so far away.

Love,
Mom

***

March 15
Hi Mom,
Actually between work and college applications for the twins, I haven't been in much contact with her. Probably about as much as you. She and Joe were fine at Christmas. Now that you mention it, she did seem more remote than usual. I attributed it to it being her first Christmas away from home, even though they visited for a little while on Christmas Day. Now that they've moved so much further north, I don't know when we'll ever get to see them. It's not the same, is it, once they leave

the nest? How is your new book coming? Will I get to read it soon? Finished revising?

See ya,
Louise

***

April 12
Dear Ashleigh,
My publisher is planning a big online launch party for Poisonberry Wine. Would you like to participate? I saw Joe's photo of the new "mancave" he made out of the garage at your cabin. Pretty neat. Do you have a space of your own?

Hugs,
Grandma

***

April 18
Hi Grandma,
Don't worry about me. I have my own space. And I love being with my hubby. Sorry I can't make your party. BTW Joe sends and delivers messages for me now that we're in the mountains.

Ashleigh

***

April 28
Hi Mom,
I attended a seminar up in Watertown last weekend so stopped by Ashleigh and Joe's. Lovely remote cabin. Last I heard she lost her job so I figured she'd be home, but no one was there. I left a note on the door and sent an email. Their yard looks beautiful. Lots of new shrubbery and a beautiful tulip border. They've done a nice job in the little time they've been there.

Twins are arguing about whether to go to the same college or not. Gotta run.
Louise

***

June 15
Dear Ashleigh,
I have to say I'm very disappointed in not hearing from you in such a long time. I keep worrying that something's wrong, but then, if something were wrong, I expect your mother would let me know. I hope you're happy. What do you do with yourself all day up in that cabin?

Love to you and Joe,
Grandma

P.S. Poisonberry Wine is doing well. Not quite flying off the shelves, but getting good reviews.

P.P.S. A reader claiming to be a forensic pathologist says my made up poison would not kill anyone, but might cause a person severe stomach cramps and loss of weight – they would most likely go to a doctor who would be suspicious. I'm glad I left out the original, deadly, poison in the revision and explained the fake poison in the end notes. I had no idea readers checked things out so carefully.

Your grandmother

***

June 16
Dear Grandma,
That's interesting about the poison. Joe lost a lot more weight than I did, but he is also a lot bigger than me. He loves his job at the computer store. I like the quiet at the cabin.
Love,
Ashleigh

***

August 15
Dear Mom,
I know the call was painful. You can't begin to imagine how sick and desolate we felt when we learned about Ashleigh. Eight months! Eight months she's been gone and he never said a word. Buried her at the cabin in the woods. A hiker's dog found the grave. It crawled in under their fence. Too gruesome and ugly to tell you about. It was in the local news. All her emails to you since the beginning of the year– he wrote them. The police and the district attorney say he'll probably get life in prison. I wish they still had the death penalty. Everybody's worried about his rights and a fair trial. What about my baby girl? If he was unhappy with her, why didn't he just divorce her? Did you hear that he poisoned her wine? Like something you might write. I read your latest book, Poisonberry Wine, and was relieved to see you created a fake poison. Imagine if Joe had used one you'd written about.

As we start our lives over without our beloved Ashleigh, the twins are set for their senior year in high school. We all miss Ashleigh as I know you do.
Love,
Louise

Veronica Helen Hart

Veronica (Ronnie) joined the FWA in 2002. Since then she has had seven books published thanks to the support of her spouse, Robert, and her writing groups. This story marks her 5th appearance in the Collection series. She is also a multiple RPLA and EPIC winner.

Career Revisions – Starting Over

My life career was all planned out. I was a hotshot on the trumpet, played in the high school marching band, and received medals at music festivals at the State level. The Assistant Band Director of the Michigan State University band, who heard me play at a competition, invited me to come and take lessons with him during the summer. I would go to State, get a degree in music, and be a professional musician or a band director.

***

Then an apparently insignificant event initiated a series of events that dramatically reshaped the rest of my life! It was July 1950, and at age 15, I was on a camping trip with a group of Scouts from Michigan at Philmont Scout Ranch in New Mexico. Near the ranch headquarters, I climbed a high wire fence to be safely away from a grazing buffalo, and, not wanting to drop my camera, I watched a mosquito bite my arm. A mosquito bite was a trivial thing that would be of no consequence and soon forgotten.

Back in school that September, I was First Chair trumpet in the high school marching band, played in the school dance band, and music became the center of my activities and my plans for my future.

Then one day at home, I lost my balance and fell! In a few days I was unable to walk. Something was drastically wrong! The doctors in the small towns nearby were unable to diagnose the problem, so my aunt took me to Chicago where I was seen by the neurologists at the University of Chicago Clinics. A spinal tap revealed the presence of encephalitis; a virus carried by mosquitoes that attacks the nervous system. I was almost completely paralyzed, and years later learned that encephalitis usually resulted in death or mental incapacitation.

My life was saved by the miracle of prayer. After four months in the hospital, I began a slow recovery, and was able to return to high school the following September walking with arm cuff crutches. I was unable to play my trumpet, and my new limitations forced me to focus on studies instead of physical activities. Missing a year of high school gave me time to mature, and with Mom's help, my grades improved significantly.

***

Always an optimist, I started Music School at the University of Michigan, still walking with crutches. Unable to play the piano, a requirement in Music, I transferred to Michigan State University, and completed a Bachelor of Science degree in a survey of business, graduating with honors. Looking back on those five collage years, I think the most important thing I learned was how to learn more effectively.

***

My career plan had been revised, and I was starting over again! With my specialized business degree in hand, I got a job in Florida that lasted a few months until the economy slipped into a recession. After a couple of other jobs didn't work out, I realized that the plan wasn't working, so I went home to Michigan to work at a Boy Scout camp for the summer of 1960 while I figured what to do next.

Realizing that my best asset was my voice, I returned to the University of Michigan for two years to earn a Master's degree in Speech, with a new goal to become a high school speech teacher.

It was August of 1962, school would start soon, and I had no job offers. I received a surprise phone call from the chairman of the Speech Department at Penn State University inviting me to join a new intern program as a 3/4 time Instructor and 1/4 time as a Phd candidate. The thought of more graduate work was not appealing, but it was a job, I would be a teacher, and at a University!

Three years at Penn State prepared me to be a teacher, and ended with a delightfully orchestrated answer to prayer that raised the curtain on twenty four years of adventure. After praying for months for God to end my desperate loneliness, I was "set up" by a colleague using a transparent ploy to meet a graduate student friend of hers by returning a college bulletin.

I returned the bulletin on Valentine's Day, and knew immediately that my prayer was answered!

Two and one half months later, I proposed on May Day. The very next day I received a surprise offer to teach speech communication at the University of Hawaii for one year, replacing an instructor on leave. What we thought would be an exciting one-year's honeymoon, became twenty four wonderful years in Hawaii teaching at the University! Apparently, God was facilitating my career path!

***

The residual effects of encephalitis began to creep up on me during the 1980's, and I was finally unable to keep up with the classroom obligations, so I retired early from the University at the age of fifty five in 1990. My wife and I moved to New

Port Richey, Florida. Hurrah! My rewarding teaching career was over! No more starting over; I was retired!

***

One day, I was watching my wife chase a green tree toad around the living room trying to capture it under a paper cup. A floodgate of memories opened of animals, birds and critters I enjoyed as a child growing up on my grandfather's farm, and I was inspired like never before to write many rhyming poems based on my experiences. The enthusiastic response of friends, who suggested publishing my stories, led me to wonder if God had another career plan in mind for me, and retirement meant another revision, and starting over again!

***

A collection of my rhyming stories was awarded "Best Submission for Children's Writing" at the 2005 Florida Christian Writer's Conference. The award affirmed my new direction, and a new dream began forming. I followed "coincidences" to establish my own publishing company to self-publish one of the stories. I was naive enough to think my beautiful hard cover children's book would fly off the shelves! Everybody who saw the book loved it and usually bought a copy.

Shoppers on Amazon and in Barnes and Noble stores didn't buy it.

It was a big surprise when my book won best in the children's category and Book of the Year in the Florida Writer's Association Royal Palm Literary Awards! I am starting over again! I now had a new "career" purpose in life. The rhymes help children learning to read, and maybe my life story of challenges and starting over will give the disabled and the discouraged hope that God has a plan for them too, and they can start over and achieve their dream. Challenges are gifts that God entrusts to us to make us stronger and better, and to prepare us for His purpose. Focus on the abilities we have, not what we don't have - then revise and start over.

When I'm working on rhymes; when I see the children's faces when I read my rhymes; when I hear their applause - there is music in my heart! My career path has circled back to the beginning - my heart for music!

Robert Z. Hicks

Bob has degrees from Michigan State and the Universities of Michigan and Hawaii. Bob taught speech communication three years at Penn State, and 24 years at the University of Hawaii. Bob has self-published two children's picture books. He and his wife Betty live in New Port Richey, Florida.

The Smile

Sunset tints the studio windows in a wash of translucent gold, tangerine and lavender. The day's last rays fall upon a cloth-draped, poplar panel leaning against the wall. Light dispels the shadows of procrastination and reveals the artist's most formidable foe, an unfinished work. As gloom disintegrates like rusty chains in an ancient dungeon, she is set free by the misty light of dusk.

He drew other sketches of her and reluctantly conceded them to his apprentices. He didn't know if they completed the paintings. But, he did know this particular portrait had haunted him for over a decade. It traveled with him, never finished, always near and always waiting.

The commission no longer mattered. Years past, and the patron abandoned it. The portrait evolved into much more than mere monetary reward. Over time, in his quest for perfection, he transformed her until she barely resembled the woman who once sat in his studio.

He had walked away from the work many times to pursue other ventures. His focus splintered into brilliant, curious fingers, exploring the myriad of innovations streaming into his brain. Wonders of nature, anatomy, and the universe; fantastic flying machines, devastating war machines and idealistic visions of futuristic cities. His notebooks teamed with meticulous drawings of his revelations. These thoughts consumed both his genius and his time.

Yet this evening, his genius finds its trysting place in her unfinished portrait. Desire, opportunity and artistry align in a fragile almost magical balance.

He seizes inspiration and vows to begin again. This time he will finish it.

Placing the panel upon his easel, he uncovers it. Dust trickles from the cloth. Minuscule particles, a stark reminder of his neglect, scatter and dance in the air before settling on the stone floor in a gray hush. He ignores the other unfinished works which litter his desk, his studio and his mind. To look at them is the same as to look into a mirror and see his own limitations glaring back.

He gathers his finest brushes of varying thicknesses crafted from sable, ermine and weasel hair. Finely ground minerals mixed with linseed oil create a muted pallet of earthy brown, green and blue pigments. The bristles gently caress paint across the gesso underlay, his expert strokes, imperceptible. Ethereal clouds of subtle tones, unfettered by boundaries, drift and evaporate into smoky whispers.

Behind her, he paints a landscape stretching across the horizon. The foliage of Florence, Milan, Venice and a dozen other places live here. Places where reality bridges imagination. Places where men may live, dream, and love freely among the perfect imperfections of nature.

The artist steps back and studies his work. His eyes glisten with tears as they meet hers. An unspoken promise passes between them.

The perfect light soon vanishes. A deep indigo blankets the sky, lit by the pale half-moon and a handful of glittering stars. He stops to light lanterns and candles so he may continue painting.

Others beckon to him from within the paint. He coaxes them to the surface. Their images, radiant in his mind's eye, funnel down through branches of bone, nerve and muscle into fingers wielding a slender, wooden stick tipped with a plume of animal hair. He channels only the purest essence of their beings and skillfully filters them through his hand, stroke by stroke.

Tiny revisions to the eyes suggest the hint of a mischievous soul. Oh, Salai, you little devil. He painstakingly applies luminous layers of flesh-colored paint. The skin warms beneath his hand like the memory of his mother's cheek pressing against his own. My dearest, Caterina. A few dabs of his brush perfect the nose. A long-held breath puffs through the nostrils with the faintest sound of a relieved sigh. I have not forgotten you, my loyal Melzi. Her soft hands relax on the chair's arm and remind him of a gentle touch from long ago. Sweet, young Albiera.

The brush touches her lips. They come to life in a marriage of moist light and expressive shadow. The corners of her mouth curve ever so slightly upward. La Gioconda, my joyous one. He recalled the musicians, the haughty, white Angora cat and the sleek, spirited Greyhound who entertained the woman while she sat in his studio. He knew it wasn't a melody or stroking the soft fur of the animals that provoked this smile. No, it is something more. The fleeting glimpse of her amusement is now captured forever in paint. Her lips are so lifelike, they threaten to part and speak their secrets. He forces himself to set down his pallet and brush on the table.

Is it finished?No, not yet. He adds one more stroke, here, then another, there. His joy and passion thrive in the creation, of transferring his knowledge of anatomy, light and shadow into something tangible. Yet the laborious, tedious painting tires him.

He doesn't adorn her neck with exquisite jewels or embellish her clothing with fine embroidery. Extraneous things would only hide the soul and the soul is what he strives to paint. Her features are plain, yet beautiful in her wistful realism. The gentle hollow of her throat appears to pulse.

Is it finished? He slowly exhales and backs away.A bittersweet wave of accomplishment washes over him, and then sadness ebbs in its place and lingers. His brush will never touch her face again. The single thought expands until it becomes a dark, bottomless chasm. To sign his name would declare the work finished. He could not commit to completion. He would not commit.

Her eyes follow him as he moves about the room, gazing at her. She will always be his favorite for countless reasons; the techniques he used, the innovative composition, the secrets he cleverly hid within the paint and of course, the smile.

The master's lips mirror her enigmatic smile. Secrets sealed beneath a cloak of transparent glaze, tricks of light and veils of smoke, obscure the truth in plain sight. He has created a collage of himself, his loves and his lovers, all hidden within one glorious face.

We are together now my loves, bound forever in one eternal mask.

Dawn's gray glow shrouds the studio. Exhausted, Leonardo lays on his bed and closes his eyes.

I wonder if others will ponder the secret of your smile?

Christine Holmes

Christine is a graphic designer pursuing her second dream of becoming a fiction writer. A member of the FWA's Daytona Beach Writers Group, she is currently working on her second horror novel. Originally from New Jersey, she has lived in Florida for thirty years, is married and has one son.

The Drive

I feared this drive. Shivering, the cold Sunday morning after Christmas made my teeth chatter. The minivan's wheels crunched over salted streets. I passed houses weighed down in slushy white.

My wife and kids were still asleep, warm in their beds. I breathed and raked a hand through my thinning, graying hair. Marriage.Kids.Mortgage.Bills. How'd I get this old?

I turned onto the onramp. The highway lines blurred and my mind cleared, leaving nothing else to think about but him.

Granddad.

The stench of his stale cigars and smiling yellowed teeth were carved into my memory. It had been seven years. No, nine. After my third kid was born, making the trip was impossible. That's what I told myself. Our weekly calls turned into monthly calls, then every once in a while calls, and then never. The less we talked, the less we had to talk about. I actually blamed him for wasting my precious time. When we did talk, I knew he heard irritation in my voice. Even as a child, he had a knack of sensing my silent barometer, slipping me candies when Mom forced veggies on me and a wordless hand on the shoulder when tears welled up.

But now... he was gone.

Dad's phone call while I was in the middle of cycling the kids through their nightly routine left me breathless. I hung up and stared at my wife like someone had just murdered my childhood. I've been in a daze ever since, packing, rescheduling, staring.

An hour passed and the dark morning lightened, but the freezing remained and made me want to pee. I pulled the car to the side of the road, jumped out, and ran to nearby bushes. Finished, I moseyed out and was half way back when I realized the minivan was gone. In its place was a blue and white car.

I stared. The highway was desolate in both directions. I spun from the bushes to the car.

A cold wind blew and I stuck my hands into my jacket pockets.

Clink.

THE DRIVE

My keys, but they felt different. I pulled them out. They looked strange yet familiar. I ran my finger over a Dodge insignia. I looked at the blue and white car and gasped.

"It's my..."

I stepped up to the car. It stood empty and quiet as if waiting for someone. I swept a hand over its slick roof. A pair of white racing stripes ran along the top. The sexy curved profile looked great even now. I hadn't thought about my Dodge Viper for years.

I opened the door, slipped inside, and breathed in the aroma of leather. From the rearview mirror hung a college graduation tassel, class of '92. I touched the dangling strands.

I gripped the key, stuck it in the ignition, and turned. The engine roared.

Overwhelmed, I laughed.

I ran a hand through my hair. "What the...?" I looked in the mirror. My head was covered with dark, wavy hair. My eyes looked bright and alert. I pulled at my face.

Car still rumbling, I looked down the highway. I had no idea what had happened, or what was happening. Still, I needed to get to Granddad's funeral.

I closed the door and shifted into gear. The engine's throttle was just like I remembered. The vibrations, the press against the seat, the immeasurable chills.

My parents thought I was crazy buying a brand new Viper right out of college. I had no job, student loans over my head, and no way of paying for anything. But Granddad believed. He gave me a pirate smile and punch to the shoulder from the passenger seat. The glint in his eyes negated the entire sensibility speech Dad had hammered me with. I didn't even mind Granddad lighting up a cigar in my new car. He believed in me. That was all I wanted.

So lost in my euphoric memories, I almost ran over a transient sleeping in my lane. I jerked the wheel. The car spun. I struggled.

The car jolted to a stop.

I breathed. A giant semi blared its horn at me. I was cockeyed in his lane. I hit the gas and wrenched the wheel until I was fully in the median.

The truck flew past. A gust of wind rocked the car.

I unbuckled and stepped outside. The bum still lay sleeping in the lane. I crossed the icy road and ran to him.

I knelt. "Hey, buddy." I touched. The pile of clothes shifted revealing a trash bag, no man.

Disgruntled, I jogged back up the road.

I stopped. Dodge Viper was gone. Instead, there stood a cream-orange AMC Gremlin hatchback, my first car. I crossed the highway and circled it. Empty and idling, its keys hung in the ignition. I opened the creaking door and sat. Even in the cold, I smelled the B.O. The engine clunked, struggling to maintain idle. I grabbed the wheel remembering how much I loved this piece of junk.

I shifted into gear and drove off. A car honked and swerved around me. The wheel shook nervously.

I moved my leg and knocked the rabbit foot keychain dangling from the ignition. I grabbed it.

105

Granddad handed me the keys on my fifteenth birthday, rabbit foot and all.

Dad snatched them away from me.

"Oh, come on." Granddad's stubbled face bent into a smile. "Who's going to be my designated driver?"

Dad's eyes burned at him. "Wouldn't be a problem if you'd lay off the booze."

That night, Granddad snuck to my room, threw a jacket over me, and whispered, "C'mon, boy."

We snuck out and I drove this crappy Gremlin through darkened city streets, Granddad laughing next to me, beer in one hand, cigar in the other.

Now, heading down the highway, I felt the weight of no longer having such a powerful man in my life. He was a horrible influence and I loved him for it. Unlike my peers, he'd get away with everything, filling me with a whirlwind of childlike adventure.

I looked at my body. It was thin, scrawny. I was a teenager.

I turned off an exit, maneuvering through familiar streets I hadn't seen in years. Same trees, same houses, same unpaved roads.

My heart leapt. The sadness of losing Granddad had somehow evaporated. I felt excited, happy.

I whipped around a tight curve, closed my eyes, and shouted, "Yahoo!"

I felt cold wind over my face.

Opening my eyes, I was no longer driving. I rode my blue bicycle. Granddad had painted my name on its side. Legs pumped the pedals. I was a kid.

I laughed, sped down Granddad's steep driveway, and slammed on the brakes.

His small, red house stood in front of me, the wooden porch he built himself looked fresh.

The front door opened.

I ran and jumped up the steps.

Granddad stepped out. "Hello, boy."

I hugged him, then looked up. "Tell me a story."

He gave me his pirate smile, cigar dangling, teeth yellow. "Ever tell you about the boy who time traveled?"

We walked in. I shivered inside, hungry for his story.

I knew it was going to be good.

John Hope

John Hope, award-winning short story, children's book, and middle grade fiction writer appears in multiple anthologies and collections of the best of the Florida Writers Association. Mr. Hope, a native Floridian, loves to travel with his devoted wife, Jaime, and two rambunctious kids and enjoys running.

Read more at www.johnhopewriting.com.

Coming to America

The early morning sun peeked through flowered curtains and flowed across the room to gently caress the sleeping form with light. Hye Young stirred beneath the coverlet. It was 9:00 p.m. in Korea. But she wasn't in Korea anymore. This was America. And it was the beginning of a new day.

Hye Young opened her eyes. Twin beds separated by a small nightstand dominated the center of the room. A large dresser and bureau clung to the sides. She looked at the wooden door of the closet. Already it held more clothes than Eldest Sister ever had. She sighed and sank back into the pillow.

The first time Hye Young heard the word "adoption" she was at her grandparents' house. She and her little sister, GiEun, had run through a rainstorm to Grandma and Grandpa Birum for the special treat of a spaghetti dinner. The Birums weren't her real grandparents. Grandma Catherine and Grandpa Lee were missionaries from America who had unofficially adopted the five orphaned Kim sisters. Many times when they were ill and oldest sisters had to work, Grandma would care for them. When there wasn't enough to eat, she would bring over food. Grandpa built a little house in the Birum's back yard so they could be close. Hye Young loved it. It was a tiny brick building nestled under pine trees at the top of a mountain. She would sneak out late at night and watch the lights from the town below wink out one after another.

That night, Grandpa took their picture, wet and dripping from the rain. It wasn't until later that Hye Young discovered why. Soon Eldest Sister sat down and talked about adoption and the prospect of moving to America.

"Will we go together?" Hye Young asked.

Eldest sister sadly shook her head. "No. This is only for you and GiEun."

Of course, GiEun wanted to leave right away. What could you expect from a kid. She was only seven and didn't realize that it meant losing all they had in Korea. Hye Young was eleven and knew better.

"I don't want to go and live with strange people. Why can't we stay here?"

Eldest sister grew quiet and her eyes shimmered. "It would be better for you. I can't support us all anymore." She dragged in a ragged breath. "This way you would have parents to care for you. You would always have enough to eat and would go to American schools."

Hye Young crossed her arms and glared. "I don't want to."

Eldest sister turned away and quietly pulled out the bedding for their sleeping mats. Tears flowed down her cheeks and splashed onto the blankets making small dark spots.

Hye Young turned away, still defiant. She tried to ignore the tears.

But I don't want to go! She told it to her grandparents. She repeated it to GiEun. Hye Young was born in Korea and she was determined to stay there.

Then one day, a letter arrived. It was from the woman who plotted to steal Hye Young away from her family. Grandmother brought the letter with the strange stamps and writing over to the small brick house and offered to read it. At first Hye Young wanted to run away. Her mind screamed, "Don't listen!" But she never said it aloud and GiEun wanted to know what the foreign letter held. So Grandmother opened the envelope, carefully unfolded the paper, and read.

Dear Hye Young and GiEun,

I want you both to know how much my husband and I love you and pray for you. I know that leaving your home and all you know is hard. I wish I could make it easier. I promise that you will never lose touch with your sisters. We will write and call and one day, you will return to visit. I promise we will try to be the best parents for you. Please know that whatever decision you make, we will always love and pray for you. That will never change.

Yours in Christ,
Mother and Father

Hye Young could feel her heart melt. A part of her always wanted a mother and father. Could she actually find a new family in a far country?

"I want to go," shouted GiEun.

Grandmother sat very still, her eyes fixed on Hye Young's face.

"Then we'll go," sighed Hye Young. "We'll go."

Grandmother smiled. "I know it will be hard, but I think it best."

And so the months flew by. There were endless forms to fill out and during the entire time, Mother kept writing and sending little gifts. Mother and Father had a toddler son and baby daughter. Hye Young secretly was glad for the prospect of having a new little brother and sister. She liked babies.

The day finally arrived when they held their passports, their visas and their plane tickets. It was a tremendously long trip. The end of it tired even GiEun. Hye Young held tightly to Grandmother's hand as they threaded their way off the airplane and up the ramp to the airport.

There stood a man and woman she recognized from pictures. Mother and Father! Little brother and baby sister laughed and ran to them, as if they always knew Hye Young and GiEun were their sisters.

There was another long trip in a big van back to the place Mother and Father called Florida. Hye Young didn't know how a country could be so enormous. But they finally arrived at their new home and discovered that they had their own room and actual beds. Exhausted, Hye Young dropped into the one by the window and fell into a deep sleep.

The sun woke her. She rubbed her eyes and looked over at the second bed. GiEun was missing. A sudden panic filled her. It had always been her job to look after her little sister.

Hye Young threw back the covers and leaped across the room. She tore open the door and raced down the hallway. The sound of laughter stopped her. She peeked around the corner. There was GiEun, sitting at the table with their little brother and baby sister, eating breakfast. Mother was in the kitchen. When she noticed Hye Young standing in the hallway, she came over with a smile and wrapped arms around her. Hye Young couldn't understand the words, but she recognized the tone. It was love. She had a mother. It dawned on her that she no longer had to be the one to look after GiEun. Mother would look after them both.

With an answering smile Hye Young allowed herself to be led to the table and into a new life.

Sharon E. Johnson

Sharon Johnson moved to Florida over thirty years ago and raised a family, taught school, and tried to stay sane – unsuccessfully. After the death of her parents, she now writes paints and attempts to climb trees (also unsuccessfully).

Author

I looked at my husband. At seventy-five, still the handsome man who once set off a frenzy in 7-11 when mistaken for Sean Connery. He slumped in his usual spot on the couch. Lying flat had become uncomfortable. He even slept there at night. The concentrator panted like a dragon, pumping oxygen to his only lung.

"Hey, look at this." The morning paper rustled as he flattened the page. "They're having a Florida Writers Conference in Lake Mary week after next. You have to go," Jerry said.

"Never heard of them." I placed my steaming cup of coffee on the table. "How long does it last?"

"Ummmm, about three days."

"I don't know. This is kind of last minute."

"But your writers group is falling apart. You need to get serious about being a writer. No—author. I'm not gonna call you a writer. You're an author."

What does an author look like? A seventy-one year old grandmother with graying hair and thickening waist? Could I imagine my picture on the back cover of a book? If Jerry could, I could.

"With a cheerleader like you, how could I go wrong?" I smiled and shook my head. "But let me learn more about this group, see if they're legit. If they pan out I'll go next year. Okay?"

Though supportive, Jerry also had good instincts when he critiqued my work. Oh, he tread lightly, apologetically even, when offering criticism, but I insisted he be honest because he was invariably right.

Even so, I didn't take his suggestion about the conference. I couldn't. Not right then. I felt suspended in time, rooted to the one spot he and I were always together. If we just stayed very still in place maybe time wouldn't move. Jerry had not been able to make it past nine holes of golf when he played a few weeks before. Prior to that, he had paused only twice for each of his surgeries. It had been nine years since doctors discovered the lung cancer. Statistics predicted fourteen months of life expectancy at the time. Almost eight bonus years. Good years. Celebrating our 50th, then 51st anniversary. Boating with children and grandchildren. Celebrating holidays. I felt it would last forever.

A week into the last of three consecutive hospital stays, I talked with him about his release. The Christmas tree still stood as it did when I rushed him to the hospital the day after Christmas. We would tackle that when he was stronger.

"We'll have a belated New Year's Eve celebration when you get home too."

His long, graceful fingers gripped the sheet at his waist. His eyes focused into the distance. "I'm not coming home this time."

"Of course you are. You always come home."

But he didn't.

When beeping from the bedside monitor slowed, then slipped into a piercing, steady wail, its stillness crept into my body. I didn't move. I soaked in Jerry's every feature one more time, from the strong brow bone to his magnificent nose. Somewhere in the space behind me, I was aware of our children rushing from the room. A light touch on my shoulder. My oldest son. I laid my hand on his and, like a drunk, repeated over and over, "I'm half a person." My eyes filled, but didn't overflow.

In the months that followed, I experienced living alone for the first time in my life, but rarely felt alone. More than once at bedtime, the sickening sweet smell of a gift bar of soap I'd forbidden Jerry to use filled the room—weeks after I'd thrown it away. He loved to tease me once in a while by lathering with it. Jerry had hated green. The color suddenly looked bilious to me. I pitched all my green clothing. Finally I could buy my favorite chunky peanut butter, but it grew stale, half eaten. I replaced it with his smooth. Maybe I was more than half a person. When new situations came up, I knew exactly how he'd respond. There was no question about the next Florida Writers Association Conference. I would go.

The following October I walked into a cavernous hall filled with strangers at the Marriott, Lake Mary. Florida. The smell of steaming coffee, eggs and bacon felt welcoming. A low rumble of voices eventually quieted as workers sectioned off smaller spaces with rolling walls. After the first workshop concluded, a familiar feeling washed over me. It brought me back to a day many years before. At the lunch break of a one-day mini-conference in Maitland I had stepped outside and called Jerry.

"How's it going?" he asked.

My voice shook with excitement. "There's a whole room full of people in there just like me!" I felt the same as I did back then, and hoped he knew.

Banquet night a smiling woman sat at a back table, with an empty seat nearby. She invited me to join her. It seemed everyone was from another area, and I expected her to be, but Joan lived in Sanford. I invited her to visit my old writing group. She accepted, but though she enjoyed the other writers, our methods weren't a fit for her. Nor for me any longer, I realized.

Two years later we met again at the conference, where she, Bruce, another writer, and I decided it was time to act. Surely there were enough local writers to start a critique group. We held first meeting at the Lake Mary Library March 14 the following year. Later Bruce's work forced him to drop out of a leadership role, but he remained a member.

Joan and I pinch ourselves often to be sure all that has happened is real. In a little over four years Seminole County Writers Group has attracted talented, serious writers dedicated to improving themselves and others in the group. Each year as many as ten of our members' stories are printed in FWA Collections. Several members have won multiple Royal Palms Literary Awards, and have published short stories, and novels. We've also become close friends. Who knows you better than one who reads your work?

Yes, I had to start a new, unfamiliar life, but Jerry led me to the start-over point—as an author among authors.

Beda Kantarjian

Beda has published short stories online and in print. Her stories have appeared in five Collections, including a Top Ten in 2013. Along with several creative non-fiction finalists, she placed first in 2012 and second in 2014. She is a co-founder of Seminole County Writers group.

Catching My Breath

Going home was like a tonic for me, one of those caffeine-and-vitamin packed zingers that zap the life back into the worn out husk of your soul. We had been living in Florida for more than two years, on the far side of the globe from South Africa and all that was familiar to me for the first 30 years of my life. It had been more than two years since I had taken a vacation, more than two years since my parents had seen their only grandchild. I had reached that stage of burn out where just waking up annoyed me. The cat irritated me with her big green eyes demanding breakfast. My three-year-old child was almost more than I could bear. I wanted to be gentle and patient but all I could see was the list of chores I would never get finished and a family making more and more demands on me when I felt I had nothing left to give.

It was time for a break. I booked the flights for my daughter and myself to fly home.

We were living in Florida on work permits with applications in for our Green Cards. It sounds simple. In actuality the stress was excruciating. We were giving everything we had to make a business and our lives work here with the ever present danger it could all be taken away at any time. If we were turned away, we would lose everything. I feared for the safety of my daughter, if we were forced to return to live in South Africa, a country with the highest rape and HIV statistics in the world and where child rape is commonplace.

As our departure dates grew closer the stress seemed to grow even greater. I was often in tears and tired all the time. Knowing we were going home soon seemed to be the only thing to hold onto.

The journey would take three airplanes and four airports. I planned for every eventuality from hunger to headaches, extreme boredom to diarrhea. I even took my heavy scrapbooks to share with my parents. They had missed more than two years with their only grandchild, time gone forever. How could I begrudge a few hefty scrapbooks in my luggage? I pack them wrapped in blouses and shorts, stuff antibacterial wipes and headache tablets in my purse, check our passports and tickets and it was time to go.

I'm have always been nervous before an international flight and this was no exception. I imagine the worst case scenario and by the time we were ready to check in, I was ready to throw up. I clenched my teeth, rubbed my sweaty palms on my pants and tried to look nonchalant beneath the scrutiny of airport security. Next up was a seventeen hour flight with a three-year-old!

I was born in a steamy African city, an eclectic mix of poverty and posh, third world and first, wrapped in tropical dark green trees and scented by the Indian Ocean, a thousand curry spices and the lives of a million people. This city is surrounded by hills of sugarcane and the fog of industry, sprinkled with post-colonial architecture and sprawling squatter camps.

We arrived exhausted, searching out the familiar outlines of my mother, father and brother, stopping in the middle of the airport tarmac to wave in their direction. Thankfully all our bags arrived, including my precious scrapbooks, and then that dreamed-about moment finally arrived. We were hugging our family, smiling through tears of joy and exhaustion.

The next morning bright sunlight flooded my parent's small, garden cottage. Fresh flowers everywhere were like jewels in pools of sunshine. Familiar pieces of furniture stirred memories as I touched worn surfaces with my fingertips.

The next few weeks were utterly glorious. We drove north through the sugarcane encrusted hills to my favorite wildlife reserve. There is a smell that is a mix of dirt and wild grasses, dung and the acid smell of animal. For me it is the smell of paradise and our thatch cottage with its wide verandah and panoramic views of the African bus, was a little taste of heaven. Each day we would pack fruit and icy juices and drive for miles to watch elephants, giraffe, zebra rhino and other wildlife and birds. We visited the Drakensberg, or Dragon's Back Mountains, dry silhouettes of craggy peaks towering over us in impossibly beautiful sunsets and sunrises. We snuggled in beds piled high with soft blankets and duvets and basked in the golden warmth of log fires. With each passing moment in the beauty of our surroundings and the love of my family I felt the tension slip further away. I felt my old energy and enthusiasm creep back. The days were icy, clear and dry, sharp winds stinging my eyes and freezing my nose red. We watched noisy troops of baboon and flocks of Guinea Fowl. As soon as the sun ducked behind the mountain the iciness flooded back and we lit the log fire in the lounge. It crackled and spats, warming my hands, my back and my soul. I was beginning to unfurl, regenerate.

Our last week we spent time at the beach; crashing waves pounding rocks, wide sandy places, tangy salty air and the smell of wild coastal vegetation. I cannot visit those familiar beaches without the flood of a thousand seaside holiday memories haunting me at every turn. Wild, sun-bleached hair and salt on my lips, diving into the cool ocean to be pounded and rolled around by strong waves and currents, lying on towels on the sand in the sun, eyes shaded by whatever book I was reading at the time. Vividly I recalled the sting of a cool shower on fresh sunburn and the delicious aromas of meat roasting over a fire in the evening. Each beach day brought back memories, of schools of dolphin surfing and leaping in the shining water and whales blowing just beyond the breakers. Grampa bought ice-creams that melted quickly in the mild winter sun. It was cool in the shade but the skies were bright blue and the sun was warm. Our apartment had unobstructed views of the beach so even after we brushed the sand off our feet to go home, we could continue to enjoy it. I would lie in bed and hear the waves crashing on the rocks, pounding as they have for thousands of years before I ever heard them. I felt refreshed and whole again, ready to get back and get on with life again. I felt sated, satisfied, filled with images, sights, sounds and smells that nourished my soul. I savored them and held them close.

Flying back to Florida I was far more relaxed. Once again I was going home, this time to my new home and my new life. I was thankful for the peace in my soul. Replenished and refreshed I was ready to say my bittersweet goodbyes and start again.

Colleen Kastner

Colleen Kastner is a writer and artist who happily survived immigration to the United States from South Africa. She lives with her husband in Florida and is a new member of the Florida Writers Association.

Always Apart of You

For now, I am warm and almost comfortable, the best I've felt since my world shattered. You're close, so close that your body heat is the warmth that surrounds me. Your familiar scent is the only smell that fills my nostrils.

At moments like these, I could almost be content with my new world, even though I'm losing you.

I know I've already lost you. The life-bond that united us is broken. I don't have you all to myself any longer. Others surround you. Your voice brims with laughter and affection as you call to them, "My Zorito, my Maxito."

They respond with happy, lilting tones. "Mommy!"

Who are they? How can I become who they are to you—treasured and loved?

The sensations and sounds that rupture from my bowels shatter the idyllic peace. I panic as you push away from me. No, no, no. My whimpers become wails as your heat gives way to cold, and your scent gives way to a barrage of unfamiliar odors. Don't leave me.

I scream for you to come back.

And there you are. Your hand is gentle against my stomach. "It's okay, sweetheart. It's just a dirty diaper. No need to get all worked up about it."

I thought you were leaving me.

My sobs don't let up even though you are back. Every time you walk away, even if just for a moment, reminds me that I'm not you any more.

Moments later, once again clean and dry, I desperately nuzzle any part of you I can reach. I have to keep you close. I want that feeling of security, of identity.

You sigh. You sound tired, exasperated. "No freaking way. You can't possibly be hungry again. I just fed you."

I'm not hungry. I'm not thirsty. I just don't know how else to be you once again. Suckling from you is the closest I can come to recapturing the feeling of being immersed in you, when you were the only thing I could hear, see, taste, smell, touch, love.

You tense when my mouth closes around your breast. Somehow, the contact hurts you, but you don't pull away. Your deep breaths anchor me as I draw from you. Moments later, you relax too. Your arm closes around me, drawing me even nearer.

During these precious moments, the shattered pieces of my old world reshape into a fragmented view of this new place where I find myself.

It is almost as wonderful as the world I lost. All it needs is one piece to complete it.

I find that missing piece when you speak, your voice brimming with awe. "My Kencito."

Yours. I settle into the embrace I know will always be there. I am already treasured and loved.

I think I understand now. I am not you, but I will always be a part of you.

And this new world will be beautiful since, like Zorito and Maxito, I get to call you Mommy.

Jade Kerrion

Jade Kerrion writes science fiction, fantasy, and romance at 3 a.m. when her husband and three sons are asleep. She is the author of Life Shocks Romances and the award-winning Double Helix series, and aspires to make her readers as sleep-deprived as she is.

Melted Ice

I nervously bounced on toes and practiced my opening comments.

"Did anyone bring ice?"

Jennifer's question caught me off guard and hollowed my stomach. I felt my face redden.

Despite severe reservations I had volunteered, and paid $2,500, to be the sole sponsor of Meet Your Elected Officials Day. I had been told the county's top business leaders would be there. The very same people I needed as customers if my company was going to survive its first year.

Jennifer stood across the County Building's small lobby with a confused look. A pair of bright orange coolers, filled to the brim with bottled water and soda, sat on either side of her. Our eyes met. She smiled and tilted her head like my mother would just before she asked me to do something.

"Dammit, Jennifer, this cost me $2,500 and there's no ice? You can't be serious."

"I forgot."

Her shrug annoyed me more than the words, but to keep my company from being embarrassed I volunteered, once again. "I'll go out and get ice."

"Oh, Henry, you're wonderful."

Wonderful my ass. Instead of meeting potential customers and getting face-time, I had to be an ice-gofer. Lost face-time meant lost opportunity and lost return on my investment.

In the two miles to the grocery store I flipped off a bicyclist, a bus driver, and a lady in a white Cadillac. They earned my extended middle finger because they cost me time, and potentially money.

There were only two cars in the grocery's parking lot. Good. The sooner I got back, the sooner I'd be able to start making money. After all, I had a business to run, not a charity.

I hurried in and looked around. A stark white ice chest stood against the far wall next to a beer display. As I marched by the green-haired, gum chewing cashier, I called out, "Just getting ice, don't go anywhere."

Of course the bags were frozen together, but half a dozen bruising fist slams loosened four of them. I almost dropped my cargo when a lady dressed in dull gray scrubs pushed her cart into the checkout lane ahead of me. A Spiderman-pajama dressed toddler stood amongst her items and clung to the cart's red plastic lattice.

Dammit, I can't catch a break.

The cashier methodically scanned the lady's store brand items. One…by one…by one. Each accompanying BEEP felt like money disappearing into the Bucket of Lost Opportunity.

I held my tongue and looked down to see drops had created gray measles on my newly polished shoes. Then I noticed the lady's once white sneakers. Pink sock showed through cracks near the little toes.

Her name tag proudly proclaimed City Assisted Living Center. A small, glued-on, green strip with white letters said, Ester.

The toddler, about three years old, pointed across the conveyor. "Mamma, M's."

"No Joshua. I only gots a little money 'til payday."

"Mamma, peez," his face wrinkled up, ready to cry.

"Hush. You'll get some of this cereal when we gets home."

"That'll be $9.42," the clerk announced.

I'm not sure, but thought I heard a whimper.

Ester laid down eight crumpled bills and examined a palm full of coins. Her fingers and mouth moved in unison as she counted. "I got $8.98." Her voice cracked.

Green-hair rolled her eyes. "That's not enough."

"How much am I short?"

"I don't know." Her shrug irritated me.

"44 cents," I offered in an effort to hurry things along.

Ester looked up. "Thank you, sir. I'm not good with numbers." Her lips smiled, but her eyes held tears. That face told a thousand stories of stress, exhaustion, and lost hope.

Ester picked up the hot dogs. "These are on sale, did they ring up at 89 cents?"

The cashier scanned the paper slip. "Yep, 89. Want to put them back?" The condescending grin further aggravated me.

"No, that's tonight's dinner." Ester looked beyond me but I don't think she saw anything tangible. I admired that she still had pride and refused to let tears flow. Using the back of her hand she wiped each eye. "What can I put back for 44 cents?"

The cashier popped her gum and glanced at the slip again. "The chicken noodle soup's 48, that'll do it."

Ester hesitated. "Okay, I got crackers to eat…need to lose a few pounds anyway." Ester straightened, and lifted her head.

My stomach felt empty, but I was sure not like this woman's.

That can of soup resurrected a deeply buried memory from when I was eleven. While delivering newspapers one cold winter night, I passed Mr. Jurisic. He carried a white cardboard pizza box. That pepperoni pizza smelled so good. When I got home two hours later I had the only thing we could afford for dinner, a can of chicken noodle soup. My heart sank and eyes moistened. Emotion took over. "I'll pay it." It came out like a gum ball rolling down the chute. Once it started, there was no stopping it.

Both women looked at me. Their faces said, 'Are you sure?', but not in the same way.

"Thank you for the offer, sir, but I can do without lunch one day." A tear trickled. She wiped it and bit her lip.

"Maybe you can, but it would please me if I could pay it for you."

"No, sir. I'll take the soup off."

I looked at the clerk for help.

Her hands went up surrender fashion. "I get paid by the hour, you two work it out."

"Please, Ester. Nothing's gone right today. I've felt obligated to volunteer for all kinds of crap the past month, but this, I want to do."

Ester wiped another tear. "Okay, but write down your address and I'll send the 44 cent Friday when my husband gets paid."

"No need, just take care of your son, and help someone in the future. Okay?"

"Yes, sir. I surely will. Thank-you."

I held out a twenty. "Add a bag of M&Ms and four bags of ice to the bill."

Ester gasped.

The cashier muttered, "Really?"

"Yes," and I nodded.

Ester eyed me up and down. "Why you want to do that?

It took a couple of seconds, but the answer pushed its way through the darkness like a seedling emerging from the cold ground into the sunlight. This was the first time in years I had volunteered to do something without expecting something in return. It felt good, like the new beginnings that Spring brings. I pointed at the can. "Chicken noodle soup's one of my favorites."

Ester's smile brought warmth to me for the first time that morning.

Outside it felt much warmer than when I walked in despite the forty pounds of ice I carried.

About to drive away, I looked at the string of wet spots that marked my path from store to car. They made me wonder. Did those drops come from the melting bags of ice I carried? Or, the ice melting around my heart?

Bruce H. Kubec

Born and raised in Pittsburgh, Pennsylvania, Bruce has enjoyed careers in banking, entrepreneurship, and telecommunications. His passion, writing, produced multiple Collections stories and several published books (one an RPLA 1st place winner). He married Nancy 40 years ago, they have 3 children and one grand-child. He lives in Longwood, Florida.

Help Wanted

Maggie stared at her reflection in the glass door. The hairdresser had assured her the new cut would take ten years off her age. It did make her feel younger, so maybe it was true. For a second, she remembered the snow-white mane that had flowed over her shoulders, and the forty pounds she'd left at Mac's gym. Then she smiled.

A bell jingled as she opened the door to the art-supply shop. Toward the rear of the store, a young man leaned against the wall behind the checkout counter, his red t-shirt not quite covering the sliver of white belly protruding above his belt. He seemed engrossed in a magazine and did not look up as she approached. After a minute of being ignored, she cleared her throat. "Excuse me. My name is Mar... I mean Maggie Tillman. I'm inquiring about the job opening." She had shortened Margaret to Maggie, but sometimes, under stress, Margaret still slipped out.

The man's eyes remained focused on the page. "What opening?"

"There's a Help Wanted sign in the window."

"Oh, that." He glanced her way for a second with a quick, mocking smile. "We should take that down. I'm pretty sure I'll be staying after all. Sorry." A lock of unkempt hair fell over his left eye. He tossed his head to put it back in place then refocused on the open page.

Maggie shrugged and started for the door, but stopped midway down the aisle. She needed this job. What, exactly, did "pretty sure" mean? She turned back to the man. "I'd like to speak to the owner anyway, if you don't mind. I'm very well qualified, and if you're not sure. . ."

He plopped the magazine down on the counter, and leaned heavily on both outstretched arms. This time he didn't smile. "Can you operate a cash register?"

Sweat trickled down her back. "I've never operated one of the modern ones, but I could learn. I have years of art experience."

"Yeah, I'll bet you do."

What a jerk. She hated the flush of red crawling up her face.

"If you can't operate a cash register, I think we're done."

Okay. That's it. Job or no job, this guy needed to be put in his place. "So, who is the owner, your Mommy or your Daddy?" Ah, the question seemed to surprise him.

"My mom. How did you know?"

"A wild guess." She heard snickering coming from the opposite wall. Embarrassed by their exchange being overheard, she decided to end it there by waving a hand in the air as she headed out the door.

She sat in her Volkswagen Bug with her head back and eyes closed, squeezing the steering wheel. A moment later, a rap on the side window startled her, and two women motioned for her to roll the window down. When she did, the taller one spoke. "We overheard that conversation with Nathan in there. You should come back tomorrow when Kathryn's here. She needs help in the store—no matter what you heard."

Surprised and grateful for the woman's forthrightness, Maggie nodded. "Thanks, I will."

The next morning, Maggie watched from her car as a slim and trim, neatly-dressed Kathryn unlocked the door and went inside. When the lights were on and the CLOSED sign had been flipped to OPEN, Maggie followed. As she approached the counter, Kathryn greeted her with a smile, "Good morning, Maggie."

Maggie stopped in her tracks. "Good morning. I'm surprised you know my name. I honestly didn't think your son would tell you I was here."

"He didn't. My friends did. I had to go out of town yesterday, so I asked them to come and make sure he opened the store." She hesitated for a few seconds then added, "My son isn't very reliable."

"Well then, may I talk to you about the job opening?"

"Yes, of course, but please allow me to apologize for my son's behavior. Customers have complained, too. He wasn't taught to behave that way."

Maggie believed that, and Kathryn seemed nice enough. "Your friends said I should come back today. So, what is the job, exactly?"

"He used to be such a nice, responsible boy. I don't know what caused the big change in him."

"Yes, well, young people out on their own are often influenced by their peers. It happens. Would you like me to fill out an application or something?"

"He isn't out on his own, he lives with me." Kathryn rubbed her forehead. "His father died eight years ago. Nathan came home from college to help me settle things—and never left."

"I'm sorry," Maggie said, and meant it in every way. "Maybe I could tell you my qualifications?" She wanted to get on with her interview.

"I wish he'd go back to school or get a real job. I'm really sick of him hanging around."

Kathryn's topic of conversation would not be derailed, so Maggie gave in. "I don't mean to interfere, Kathryn, but why should he?"

"What do you mean? He's twenty-eight years old, for one thing."

"What responsibilities does he have?"

Kathryn proceeded to pour out the truth. Nathan did nothing. She not only managed the store, but also did all the household chores, and even hired out the lawn cutting. As she spoke of this, her voice grew louder and little droplets of moisture appeared on her upper lip.

Maggie studied her own manicured nails, deciding if she should go on. "And consequences? What about those?"

Kathryn pulled up a nearby stool, sat down, and sighed. "I take care of those, too. But, what can I do? He's beyond retraining at this point."

"I'm not so sure it's him that needs to be retrained. Perhaps if you stop doing for him, he would take care of himself."

"I can't simply stop. Just like that."

"Look at me, Kathryn. A year ago, I was a frumpy, overweight woman about to turn sixty years old. I spent my entire adult life enabling an alcoholic husband—taking care of his consequences. One day, I decided I didn't want to do it anymore, so I stopped. Just like that. I took my life back. Once I decided, it was easy."

Kathryn stared toward the front window, tapping the counter with her fingers, and said nothing.

Maggie knew she had gone too far, said too much. After a moment, she turned down the aisle.

As she opened the door, Kathryn called to her, "Wait, Maggie. What about the job? When can you start?"

"I think I already did. See you tomorrow."

Peggy Lambert

Peggy is the current leader of the Port Orange Scribes, and has been a member of the FWA since 2012. Her stories have appeared in the Florida Writer Magazine and the 2013 Crime collection. She gladly gave up Ohio winters over forty years ago and now lives in Daytona Beach.

Ira's Bride

Ira walked out of the doctor's office slower and a lot older than when he had gone in. He looked at the steps leading down into the subway.

Not today. That day he did not have it in him to go down into the tube.

It's nice out; I'll just walk. A mile isn't that far. He wasn't ready to go home just yet. He needed to think about what he had been told.

After four blocks, with sweat pouring off his brow, Ira knew this had been a bad idea. For over forty-five years he had thought nothing of the half-mile walk from his brownstone to his tailor shop. But that was a long time ago, and he had been much younger back then. He sat on a bench and struggled to catch his breath. For the first time in years Ira hailed a cab.

Ruth knew as soon as Ira walked through the door that the doctor's news had not been good. His shoulders sagged a bit more, and the crooked smile and gleam in his eyes were missing. Ira never complained, but after sixty-two years together Ruth knew her husband. She could see his pain reflected in his eyes.

"Well?" she asked impatiently.

"He said I have the heart of a seventy-year-old."

"How about the rest of you?"

Ira thought back to the doctor's words.

"Mr. Levinson, the cancer has spread throughout your body. I am sorry. There is nothing we can do for you."

"How long do I have?"

"I'm afraid, no more than a month at best. I will prescribe a strong pain medication, but you will want to get in contact with Hospice soon."

"The doctor gave me some pills that he said will take care of whatever ails me." He could not meet Ruth's eyes.

"OyGevalt! If he has a pill that will cure what ails an eighty-six-year-old man, I just might take a few of them myself," she said, forcing out a laugh. For the first time, since they had gotten married, Ira didn't laugh at one of her jokes.

"Come. Come into the kitchen. I have lunch on the table—and I don't want to hear you're not hungry. You are too skinny and your clothes are starting to hang on you."

They ate in silence. Ruth knew her husband was keeping something from her, but Ira was a proud man and would tell her when he was ready, so she did not push.

Ira spent that afternoon at his desk. He first looked at their investments and then took out all the paperwork Ruth would need when the time came, including the key to their safety deposit box. They owned their home and the only bills they had were the monthly utilities. Financially, Ruth would be fine.

"I was thinking, my love. Why don't we invite the children over to dinner on Sunday? We have not seen them in a while and I miss our grandchildren."

"I will call and see if they're available and instead of cooking, though, why don't I order in from the deli? This way we won't have a big mess to clean up and we will probably have enough leftovers for a few days."

On Saturday Ira went to the Synagogue for the first time in years. He said that he wanted to see a few friends he had lost track of over the years. He came back looking a little tired, but smiling.

The sparkle in Ira's eye returned Sunday. Everyone laughed, ate, and tried to keep the children from destroying their grandparents' house. There were plenty of hugs and kisses to go around. Ruth watched her husband. It looked like he was trying to hold onto every last moment with them. By Monday the gleam in his eye was gone again.

As the days went by, Ira became more lethargic and depended more and more on his magic pills. When he started to sleep past his normal wake-up time, Ruth knew in her heart what Ira had been keeping from her.

One night as they lay next to each other in the dark, she asked the question she really did not want the answer to but needed to hear.

"My husband, how much time do we have left with each other?"

He was quiet for a moment. "Not much, my bride."

Ira had called her his bride since the day they had exchanged their vows. Even though Ruth had told him she was too old to be anyone's bride, he would say, "You will be my bride, until my last breath."

With tears in his eyes, Ira told his wife. "I love you so much but I'm afraid, I've never been without you."

"My husband, do not be afraid. I will always be right here with you. Now go to sleep. You need your rest."

As Ira slept, Ruth relived their last sixty-two years. They were not always easy, but she had never once doubted Ira's love for her. What would she do without him? She never thought she would have to worry about that. Until now.

Ruth no longer woke Ira when he slept. When he was asleep, he was without pain. He no longer had an appetite, so Ruth ate only when he slept.

The angel from Hospice came. The morphine she administered dulled any remaining pain Ira had. His last days were spent saying goodbye to his family and the few friends he had not out-lived. Ruth never left his side.

One night Ruth awoke when she felt Ira's feeble hand grasp hers.

"Ruth, I loved you even before I knew what love was. Remember when I first told you that you were going to be my wife?"

"Ira, I was twelve. What did a twelve-year-old girl know of love?"

"But my father talked to your father and an agreement was struck."

"Without my knowledge!"

"Are you sorry?"

"No, not in the least. You have given me a life filled with love. What more could I have asked for?"

"When I die I don't want you to be alone. If you wish to remarry you have my blessing."

Surprised, she looked at him and then saw the crooked smile and long lost gleam in his eye.

"Your bride will never be another's bride. Now go to sleep, you old fool."

Ira never woke up. He died in the comfort of his home with the one person that had meant everything to him.

Ruth grieved his loss but cherished the joy he'd given her.

***

Ruth didn't start over in the true sense of the word. She more so carried on as a volunteer Angel of Hospice. She helped others in their time of need giving them the courage to move on like they had given to her. She told her children it was her new calling in life.

When her time came, she was not afraid. She would be reunited with the love of her life. Ira would have his bride back in his arms again.

Stephen Leitschuh

Stephen Leitschuh wrote strictly for enjoyment for five years before deciding to get serious about his work. In 2012 he joined the FWA and Author's Round Table in Mount Dora. He published his first novel, A Little Bit of Death in 2013, and his second, Esther and Me in 2015.

The Sweet Scent of Spring

When Mama called us her little angels we would all laugh, glancing at each other in delight, knowing we had a bit of the devil in us. Becky was the youngest, the 'peanut' as we would call her. Next, was Sophie, whom Becky called 'Soapy.' I was the oldest, named Elizabeth after my aunt who died when Mama was still a little girl.

We lived on the upper floor of a South Boston tenement building near Dorchester Street and West Broadway in a two-room apartment. Our bedroom was shared with Mama and Papa; a large drape separated our beds, which was not sufficient to block the snores from one side and the giggles from the other.

Papa left suddenly one day. Mama said he went off to fight in the war, but I doubted her story because it happened so suddenly; one day he was gone; no goodbyes. I was twelve and knew more in my heart than my sisters. After the war we all knew he was not coming back. Mama began working by cleaning other people's houses and we sold newspapers.

Our morning ritual would begin by going to the bottom floor of the building to use the toilet, having to share it with several others in the building. After, we would gather in our kitchen, which was barely large enough to contain a table and chairs. The stove, an icebox that sometimes had ice in it and side table consumed the remainder of the space. The rest of the room was filled with our laughter and the glow of our mother who doted on us. More often our breakfasts were lean, but we didn't seem to mind because we were truly happy just being together.

After breakfast we would rush downstairs, off to our jobs selling newspapers on street corners. We all sold them, even Becky. After getting our batch of papers we would position ourselves at the busiest intersections. We defended three of the corners as our own; Sophie and I could handle ourselves, but we both kept a watchful eye on Becky, making sure she was not pushed around by some of the older paperboys. If we saw any sign of trouble we would come to her defense and those boys knew not to bother her again.

One day, after getting our morning quota of papers, we were traveling down an alley when we came upon a photographer. We were with of some of the other paperboys when the photographer asked us to stop and pose for a picture. We never had a picture taken of ourselves and we were only too happy to oblige his request.

For that moment we felt special; we were having our picture taken just like the rich people pictured in the papers we sold.

It happened in late October of 1918, the year of the great flu epidemic. By early November Becky became weak with the flu and Mama kept her in bed. Mama kept saying she just needed rest and soup.

We continued to sell our papers, going out each day while Mama would do the best she could taking care of Becky. Many people were becoming sick and the streets were almost empty because of the flu; selling newspapers became more difficult. After the third day of her illness we returned from our daily routine to find Mama, red eyes swollen with tears, sobbing next to the bed bearing the discolored and motionless body of our Becky.

When spring arrived the Great Flu was over. Many families lost loved ones, people we did not know. But the passing of Becky, left emptiness in our hearts, and had a name.

In springtime Sophie and I went out to sell our papers, and the sweet scent of spring embraced us as we stepped outside. I could not help thinking about Becky and her love of this season. It brought back memories of the three of us traveling together as a family. On that day she was with us in spirit, myself, wishing only to have that photograph of us when we were as one.

Christopher Malinger

Christopher Malinger is a published writer. His most recent work, The Object of Desire, appeared in Journeys VII; An Anthology of Award-Winning Short Stories published in 2014. Other works include a collection of short stories, Tales to Keep You Awake.

Colonial Midwife

Mary Neff placed wood on the crackling fire to keep the room warm. Despite the morning's crisp air, it was better than the bitter cold and deep snow the villagers experienced that winter. On the fringe of colonial expansion, Haverhill, Massachusetts was a tiny Puritan settlement.

Few people have a life-altering event define their legacy. Mary's experience was set in motion on the chilly morning of March 16, 1697. At that time, the fifty-one-year-old widow sat quietly next to the hearth at the home of Hannah Dustin after delivering the woman's ninth child.

The experienced midwife wrapped newborn Martha in a blanket, placed a recently knitted bonnet snug on her head, and laid her on her stomach in the family's well-used hand-hewn cradle. In response to the infant stirring, she gently rocked her back and forth. "Shhh, little one," she whispered. "You've been fed and changed into dry clothes. Let yer mum sleep." She tenderly caressed the baby's back and cooed, "You're the sweetest thing. You look like yer eight brothers and sisters. If you'd been twins, our community would now be one hundred souls." She chuckled, "Now I'll have to wait to deliver another wee one to reach that milestone."

Martha let out a few half-hearted whimpers.

"I'm awake," said Hannah as she eased herself onto her elbows. "Is she all right?"

Mary smiled. "She's fine, a bit restless is all. She ain't used to bein' outside the warmth of yer body. It's a big change from the last nine months."

Hannah glanced around her home. "It's quiet."

"Yes, it seems strange. Thomas took the children with him. I think they like bein' outside now the weather ain't so harsh. The soil started to thaw. He wants to ready yer far field for plantin' by removin' rocks."

Hannah heard the door latch lift. "Ah, it seems they—."

Mary shrieked.

A dozen fierce Abenaki Indian warriors burst through the door wielding clubs, hatchets, and knives. Mary grabbed Martha from the cradle and retreated toward the fireplace. Hannah leaped from bed and joined them.

The Abenaki charged the women and yelled unintelligible commands.

Mary held tight to the infant, seized the fireplace poker, and screamed, "Get away from us, you heathens, or I'll smash in yer heads."

An Indian ripped the makeshift weapon from her hands, tossed it aside, and cuffed her across the face. The terrified women watched helplessly as the invaders ransacked the house, broke furniture, and took pots, utensils, and anything else of value. Some Abenaki left to join others and continue the attack on Haverhill. Several, however, set fire to the house, hustled the two women and baby outside into the forest, and forced them north at a punishing pace.

As night fell, the retreating Indian band gathered their exhausted prisoners together and allowed them to rest. The fifteen terrified people huddled together while their abductors kept guard. Finally able to talk with one another, Mary learned the Abenaki slaughtered at least twenty neighbors and friends during the attack. Of these, half were children, including two of her nieces. There was no word of Hannah's family.

Hannah pleaded to Mary, "What are we goin' to do? I tried to feed Martha, but we moved so fast I couldn't get her to nurse. We ain'twearin' shoes and have only flimsy dresses." She hugged Martha. "My poor babe has only her light blanket, bonnet, and a shirt. We can't survive outside this time of year."

"We have to keep goin' until help comes," Mary said. The two curled their bodies around Martha to keep her from fussing.

After a restless night in near-freezing temperatures, the Indians herded the villagers farther from their beloved families. Compelled to walk over rocky trails and wade through icy streams, they clung together for warmth and security. Despite bleeding feet and numbing cold, they willed themselves to continue with the hope of rescue always on their minds.

The captors stopped about midday. After an animated meeting with vigorous pointing toward the English, an Indian ripped Martha out of Hannah's arms, grabbed the infant by her legs, and brutally killed her when he smashed her head against a tree. Inconsolable, Hannah collapsed into Mary's embrace.

The Abenaki then pulled aside three terrified hostages who had slowed their flight, bludgeoned them, and then scalped them in front of their horrified friends and relatives. Without remorse or concern, the Abenaki forced the remaining hostages to their feet and shoved them onward. Grief-stricken and fearing for their lives, the English could do nothing but comply.

That night Hannah vowed through tears, "I swear on Martha's body, I'll have my revenge. Those bastards murdered my innocent babe."

"Nothin' we do will be harsh enough," declared Mary as they cried and clung to each other on the cold ground. "They have the upper hand now, but we'll pay 'em back."

Three days later, the Abenaki left Mary and Hannah with a group of thirteen Indians on an island in the Merrimack River. Along with a fourteen-year-old boy, Samuel, captured two years before, their daylight hours consisted of grueling work and meager meals. With limited sleep at night while tied together, their futures appeared bleak.

After three weeks of intense deprivation, they gave up hope of rescue. "No one knows where we are," Hannah whispered to Mary while they cleaned fish. "The militia must not be able to find us."

"You're right," Mary said equally quiet. "We won't survive much longer like this. We have to escape on our own. But we can't let 'em catch us. If that happened, they'd club or knife us to death."

Hannah nodded. "Samuel's willin' to help. He's heard they're takin' us to the French. Those bastards offer bounties for English scalps and prisoners. They'll do anythin' to end New England settlements and expand their territory."

"We must act soon," Mary said. "I've hidden a hatchet." She lowered her voice more and explained her plan.

That night they stayed awake until the Indians were asleep, cut themselves loose, and enacted their revenge. With stoic determination, they split open the skulls and scalped eleven Abenaki. Only a woman and child escaped. They destroyed all the canoes except one for their use, gathered available food, and set off downriver. After they traveled three arduous nights and hid during the day, they reached their hometown and rejoined their joyous families.

Less than a week later, Mary once again sat at the bedside of a woman in labor. "I'm grateful to be home," she said to the young mother-to-be. "In our small community we need to help each other."

Three centuries later, hundreds of descendants, including the author, are in awe over Mary Neff's legacy of perseverance and fortitude. She survived a horrendous experience and returned to assist women bringing life to the hazardous frontier and unpredictable world of a growing country.

John Mallon

John Mallon is a retired economist. He is active in the Florida Writers Association and the Historical Novel Society. He has done extensive research on English history.

Coming To America

March 31, 2015

Sixty years ago today I set foot on American soil. What an anxious, yet happy, 18-year old immigrant girl I was as the ship docked in New York's harbor. I was especially glad to be back on solid ground because the voyage from Germany to the U.S. was a nightmare. The MS Italia, the vessel that transported me, other immigrants, and tourists, felt as if I were riding a roller coaster through the turbulent ocean which made me violently ill.

We left Bremerhaven in the middle of March, certainly not the best month weather-wise to cross the Atlantic. From Germany we cruised to Southampton, England, then to Le Havre, France, and finally headed towards the North American continent. Upon arriving in Halifax-Nova Scotia, some travelers disembarked. The rest of us continued the journey until we came to New York City.

Of the 11 days it took to reach our final destination, I was seasick for 10 and 3/4 days. I had hoped to explore the ship, meet other young people, and dance each night away, but it did not happen. Instead I spent most of my time on board in bed. The only activity I performed was to drag myself to the dining room every day and nibble some food because our cabin steward told me it would ease my nausea. But after each bite my stomach protested so I tried to get back to the solitude of my cabin without embarrassing myself, but only made it to the hallway outside the dining room. There I emptied my stomach's contents into a large, sand-filled container (huge ashtray). Retching became a daily ritual for the duration of the trip.

The Italia, though a pretty ship at the time, was nothing like today's luxurious cruise liners that are more than 1,000 feet in length. They now have stabilizers that allow them to smoothly glide through rolling waves without swaying unless attacked by a major storm.

As I lie in my narrow bed in the tiny, windowless cabin that I shared with a stranger, I feared that I might die. But while confined to the bed, I had plenty of time to reminisce about what had brought me to this moment in time and location.

When I was eight years old, my brother, two years older, and my mother, 32, received word that my 34-year old dad, a soldier in World War II, had been killed in

Croatia in October, 1944. Three months later, in January, 1945, another life-changing event occurred. Officials ordered that women with children were to be evacuated from Breslau, our hometown, because the Russian front was coming closer to the city. Although they told us that soon we'd be allowed to return, they lied. We never saw Breslau again.

We wound up in a Bavarian village with about 100 residents. Life as a refugee in our own country was difficult. We were poor, having lost everything after leaving our home except for the clothes we carried. Some villagers weren't friendly and treated us as if we were foreigners. A couple of years later, we moved to a small, nearby city because my mother just couldn't adjust to country life. When I turned 16, an idea crept into my head---I wanted to escape from this city because job opportunities were few and my future looked bleak. I longed to immigrate to America and start a new life in a new environment.

Until today I am wondering what I was thinking when, at that age, I wrote to the New YorkTimes and placed an advertisement in their paper, looking for any job in America. Was I too daring, or just too young and naive? Some of my mother's friends called me gutsy and courageous, others thought I was out of my mind trying to move to a foreign country on my own, having no relatives and no friends in the U.S., and speaking only the limited English that I learned in an evening class.

Surprisingly, I received 37 letters in answer to my ad---32 job offers and five marriage proposals. I chose one family in New Jersey with a teenage daughter who needed a live-in housemaid and began writing to them. I also wrote to one of the gentlemen who offered marriage but he turned out to be 25 years older than I was. I thanked him for his offer but declined.

After mailing my application for immigration to the American consulate in Munich, the long wait began. Two years later I was summoned to Munich for an interview with an embassy official. After answering routine questions, I was warned about the danger a young girl alone in the States could encounter, but I was confident that my job offer was genuine and didn't worry. Eventually, I received my visa to enter America as a legal immigrant. I was thrilled and couldn't wait to get there. My mom, naturally, was distressed and kept repeating that I should come home if I was unhappy or scared, but I assured her that I would cope with whatever I faced.

On my last night aboard the Italia, I, who felt adventurous and had no qualms about being alone in the "New World," suddenly worried what I would do if my sponsors weren't at the pier, but because they had paid for my passage, I hoped that they'd be there.

After disembarking, I went through customs with my two small suitcases filled with only a few clothes and one hundred dollars in my purse. Scanning the assembled crowd in the terminal, I said a silent prayer of thanks when I spotted a couple who held a sign with my name. As I had hoped, my sponsors were indeed waiting for me.

When they drove me through New York towards the Lincoln Tunnel and New Jersey, I was mesmerized by the sights and sounds of this world-famous city. I felt immediately at home and knew then that I definitely was going to stay in America. I promised myself that in the future, when I was fluent in English, I would come to

New York on my days off and visit all the famous landmarks I had heard and dreamed about. And I did.

In January 1958 I met a handsome, young Armenian engineer and we married in June, 1959.

We were blessed with two sons, and many years later with their lovely wives, and three awesome grandchildren.

In 1970, I fulfilled another dream of mine and went to college, part-time, and graduated six years later. After teaching for seven years, I decided to continue my education. In 1986, at age 50, I earned a Master's degree, specializing in English-as-a-second-language (ESL), because I wanted to give something back to the country that had been good to me---I would help new immigrants to learn English. What satisfying work it was!

Sixty years have passed since I arrived in America and I'm still in love with this country and appreciate all it gave me and allowed me to accomplish.

In retrospect, my wanting to immigrate to America at the age of 16 was the best idea I ever had.

Doris Manukian

Doris Manukian lives in Ponte Vedra Beach, Florida, with her husband of 56 years. They and their two sons also resided in Thailand, the Philippines, and Libya due to her husband's work. Doris primarily writes her family memoirs and has published numerous articles about her experiences.

The Party

Halfway down the lane to the mansion, the car shuddered and glided to a stop. The headlights illuminated a small sign that dangled, lopsided, from the lowest limb of an enormous oak tree. My eyes focused on the oversized red letters, Hoppengale. The headlights went dark.

"Damn the luck!" Roger squinted at the dashboard barely visible in the moonlight. "I can't understand it. We have plenty of gas, the oil gauge says it's fine, and the amp gauge indicates there is no problem with the battery. It's a vintage 1924 Chrysler Six and Mr. Stewart assured me it's been fully restored."

"I feel absolutely ridiculous in this get-up."

"Look, Ellie, Mr. Stewart was kind enough to invite us to his party. We're already in his driveway. I think we should go ahead and walk the rest of the way."

I stared at my fiancé. "I'm dressed in this too short 1920s black dress, jammed my feet into a pair of spike heels, had my hair done like a flapper and I'm even wearing a peacock feather headband. I agreed to attend this back to the 20's party because you said we'd arrive in style and have a really good time."

"Come on Ellie, we can still have a ball. The Mr. Stewart is eccentric and filthy rich. He and my boss said Stewart would sell me the car if we came to the party in it. I got a great deal. He even bought you the dress."

"You agreed to have me tag along so Mr. Stewart would sell you this heap?"

"Of course not, honey." He smiled at me.

"There is no way I'm going to walk more than a mile in these heels in the dark."

"I don't think it's that far."

I exhaled loudly. "I looked it up on the net. Hoppengale built this estate in 1921 for his new bride. The driveway is nearly two miles long. We couldn't have made it more than half way."

"You looked it up?"

I shrugged. "It's kind of tragic, really. Hoppengale's wife died three months after they moved in. He disappeared, and the estate was sold at auction because he didn't have any relatives. And it's a little creepy the guy who's throwing this party has the same first name as the guy who built the place? After all, Valentino isn't exactly popular."

"It's only a coincidence." Roger put a hand on the lever of his door, pulled up, and opened it a crack. "What if I walk ahead and you wait here? I'll have someone come back for you."

Lights and a car horn cut off my comeback. A man wearing a tweed coat, vintage racing goggles, and a tartan scarf pulled his yellow Stutz Bear-Cat beside our car. "Can I be of assistance, Mr. Wilson?"

"Oh, Mr. Stewart. We're having car trouble."

"I prefer to be called Val." He chuckled. "I'm afraid I only have room for one passenger. But, since I sold you the car, I feel responsible." He reached over and unlatched the passenger door. "I can take the young lady. I'll send my limo back to pick you up."

"You go," Roger whispered. "He's driving a car that's worth a fortune, he's my boss's best friend, and he knows we're engaged." He kissed me on the cheek. "You'll be safe."

I shoved my door open and climbed out. I snatched my fox stole from the back seat and stalked over to the Stutz. I dropped into the passenger seat, and without looking at him, I said, "Thanks for the help, Mr. Stewart."

"Please, call me Val. And no problem." He waved at Roger. "See you at the party."

Val shoved the car in gear and roared off. We were barely out of sight of Roger's car when a fog enveloped us. I shivered. A terribly uncomfortable silence hung in the thick air as he drove on. When we stopped in front of his mansion, I gave him a quick, "Thanks. I'll wait for my fiancé inside."

The mansion looked every bit the part of a place lost in the 20s. Servants in costume served guests decked out in clothes as reminiscent of the period as mine. I snatched a glass of champagne and parked myself on a loveseat near the fireplace.

When I looked above the mantle, my first sip caught in my throat. A painting of a woman who could have been my identical twin stared down at me. She wore a dress exactly like mine.

I was staring at the image when Mr. Stewart took a seat next to me. "You look lovely."

A shiver crawled up my neck. I took a long drink of champagne. "Who's that woman in the painting?"

Before he could answer, a man approached us. "Mr. Hoppengale, Sir." He bowed slightly. "Mrs." He nodded to me. "Should we announce the meal maam?"

My mouth dropped open.

"Certainly, Fredrick." Mr. Stewart waved the man off.

The air became stale—hard to breathe. I wanted to run outside, but his hand on my shoulder stopped me.

"I'm not here to go along with this sick charade. I don't know how you arranged to have that painting of me made or why you want me to pretend to be Hoppengale's wife. I'm an engaged woman. Roger's probably—"

"There has been no mistake, Roslan."

My pulse raced. "My name's Ellie, and my fiancé will be here any minute."

"I'm afraid he won't. I really am Valentino Hoppengale," he looked into my eyes, "and you are my wife, Roslan."

"You're crazy." I ran my fingers through my short blond hair. "You can't be him. You'd be over a hundred years old." My vision blurred, and my mind swam with strange thoughts.

He caressed my hand. "You didn't die. You were stolen away by a fellow named John Mathgen. In our youth we discovered the secret to bending time."

I tried to close my mind to what he was saying, but something in his voice drew me in.

"Please, let me go."

His hand tensed. I felt warmth slide up my arm as he continued. "Shortly after you and I met, John fell in love with you. Here." He handed me a photograph.

I stared at a picture of what could have been me standing between the man holding my hand and a much taller man with a thin mustache. It can't be me!

"When you rebuffed his advances, John cast a charm on you and took you into the future. I traveled the world, and through time, to find you. And now that I have, I've brought you back to the place and time where you belong."

I fought to clear my mind. My lips trembled. "You're insane."

"I'll prove what I say is true." He took my hand and replaced my engagement ring with a larger one and a matching wedding band. "You have a wine colored birthmark two inches below your navel. It reddens when you bathe."

I gasped as I looked into his dark eyes—the eyes of the man I'd married the year we bought the gleaming yellow Stutz.

Robert E. Marvin

Robert grew up in Van Wert, Ohio. He taught biology at Riverview High School in Sarasota for thirty-three years. He's written for the ACT and curriculum for the State of Florida. He's received two wards from Writers-Editors Network and was published by Writer Advice.

Reset

On the underside of the young woman's wrist the bit of red plastic and shiny stainless steel violated the sanctity of her flesh with obscene efficiency. Round, two inches in diameter and brilliant red, the button sank into her skin as if it had always belonged there. The tech was that good. The surgery that much better. The surface of the button had a single word printed in white. RESET.

"Give her a push," Sergeant Marks, crouched beside the corpse, held the dead girl's wrist toward his partner. "See if it works."

Lieutenant Franki Colletti, five years on the job and a rising star in DEA, grimaced. She hadn't yet developed the veteran's veneer of crude favored by her partner. "Jesus, Marks. A little respect? A young girl's dead." The young agent settled back on her heels. "Whoever's doing this is still out there. And we're four bodies down with no clues."

"I will if you won't, college girl." The senior agent turned his head and squinted. With his free hand he made a grand show of pushing the button embedded in the dead girl's arm.

"Cut the clowning, Marks. I told you, show a little—"

"Gaaa—holy Christ. Did you see that?" Sergeant Marks leapt to his feet. "She frickin' moved."

Indeed she had. Their corpse, before so tidily composed in the plush leather lobby chair of the new downtown Ritz—"We thought she'd dozed off. We didn't know."—slid into a tangle of arms and legs at the chair's foot.

Marks stalked back and forth. "She seized like. Jerked and shit. You saw it. Right?" He rubbed his balding head. "Oh man, oh man. Flung 'er out of the damn chair."

"That's enough, Sergeant." Franki stood and directed the rest of the crew. "Process this scene ASAP. I want Miss Doe on the table in the morgue within the hour. And someone give Dr. Joan her morning wakeup. Tell her she's got another customer." Franki snapped her tablet shut and headed for the car. Marks could catch a ride with someone else.

Behind the wheel, she ticked off the morning's events in her head. They find a fourth corpse, in a fashionable part of town. Well-dressed. Sporting a brilliant red RESET button surgically implanted in her arm. Only this time, Marks' button pushing act—he hadn't refined it since corpse number one—gets a response. Ritz girl jumps out of her chair and scares the bejesus out of everyone.

Well, now that's a clue.

***

Water gurgled in the background. Frigid morgue air carried disinfectant and formaldehyde stink that cleared space in the back of Franki's nose. She pulled on the lab coat the M.E. offered and gratefully buttoned it. "Something about this one, Joanie.Different from the others."

Dr. Joan, youngest M.E. in city history, dangled short legs off a stool and sipped a Starbucks. "You are correct agent. Would you like to know what that something is?"

"If you're not too busy?"

Busting chops was S.O.P. with them. Both brilliant overachievers. Both youngest in their departments. Both sisters.

"Her button," Dr. Joan pointed.

"What?"

The M.E. slid off her stool and picked an evidence bag off the table next to Jane Doe. Franki saw red plastic, assorted wires. "It failed. Look at her arm." Dr. Joan gently rolled the woman's arm over and peeled apart a dissection that traveled to the dead woman's neck.

"Okay—?"

"I know what this is. Remember you thought our first RESET button was some stupid escalation in the piercing wars? What outrageous thing can I stick in my body next?"

"It's not?"

"It's functional."

"Bullshit."

Joan wagged the evidence bag, "RESET's the perfect drug. Wired to the brain to trigger endorphins, serotonin, dopamine, God knows what else. Need a soul cleansing, toe-curling rush? Push the button. No drug to run out of. Perfectly legal and absolute genius."

"Gives drug pusher a whole new meaning."

"Hilarious. Keep your day job agent."

"But...this one failed?"

"Wires didn't die."

"Excuse me?"

"Whoever designed this did so with the idea that if the unit ever shuts down the wires die, get absorbed. Probably to protect RESET's true meaning from snoops like me." The M.E. examined the button closely and murmured, "So close. Almost perfect."

"How can wires die?"

"Bio-material, silicon-matrix...don't ask. But her wires didn't die and I followed them."

Franki took the evidence bag from her sister. "The ultimate drug. Feeling shitty—reset. In pain—reset. Life sucks—reset. Except it didn't work for her."

"Or, three others we know about. But how many are still out there, resetting as we speak?" The M.E. paled. "Sis?" She grabbed Franki's coat. "Listen to me—"

"What?"

"Tech like this? Genius like this? Expensive. My guess? Ungodly expensive."

"Thanks, Joanie."

Dr. Joan hopped back on her stool and sipped her coffee. "Just trying to help. Now go catch this asshole."

"I'll do my best." Franki shrugged off the morgue jacket.

"Do better."

Back at the department Franki sat with her tech guru following Dr. Joan's lead. Big as a bear he took up most of the desk. She sat on the edge of it. "Hadley, let's take a look at the bank accounts for each victim," she said. "Flag all the identical withdrawals."

"Like how much?" Hadley's fat fingers slapped his keyboard—he went through one a month—but no one waded through the ones and zeroes like he could. "I got possibles from $20 to $25,000."

"Check the big ones."

"Cash withdrawals. All four victims took out $25,000."

"Compare dates of withdrawal with dates of death."

"Damn, Lieutenant. You're good."

"Tell me."

"Each died within nine days of the withdrawals."

"Now what do I do with that?" Franki slipped off the desk and paced behind Hadley.

"Input more key profile markers. Look for patterns inside the kill zone. See what areas the victims overlap. Follow the money."

"Hadley, I could kiss you."

"Lieutenant," the big bear beamed. "My reputation."

"It could only help. Work your magic...."

***

Dr. Joan stood against the wall in shadow. "Thought that money comment would get you on track."

"Why'd you help me?" The morgue air made Franki shiver. No coat this time. The only light the one above the still-occupied autopsy table.

"You were so earnest. I couldn't stop myself. Besides—" Dr. Joan stepped into the light and rested her elbows on the table. "One of us has got to succeed in this shitty life."

"Look at you. Youngest M.E. in—"

"Blah blah.And blah. Now, if my freakin' button had worked? Major success." She lifted the sheet. "I was so close Franki. Perfect drug. Almost harmless." She dropped the sheet and smiled. "Almost genius."

"We can fix this Joanie."

"Already have." Dr. Joan peeled back a lab coat sleeve to reveal a newly implanted red RESET button. "Who knew Nature would only allow so many resets?"

"Joanie, wait." Franki rushed forward. "Don't do something stupid."

"Too late for that, Franki darling." Joanie blew her sister a kiss. "Maybe God'll give me a do-over in the next life. Please don't hate me." She pushed RESET and collapsed in her sister's arms.

Mark McWaters

Mark McWaters, married 32 years to Meredith, has an MFA in Creative Writing from the University of North Carolina and is an award-winning 25+ years advertising veteran. Creative Director/copywriter stints at several national advertising agencies kept his writing wheels greased. Multiple RPLA Collections, Short Fiction and YA Novel winner.

Taking the Bait

It was as if his "bachelorness" had been caught in the cool breeze from Lake Tsala Apopka, spreading out over the land, for they sensed it and came from great distances around the small cabin he had bought in west-central Florida. It started out with a few, but soon developed into a veritable plague of food-bearing locusts. He didn't know what to do.

Conroy Phelps wanted a quiet place to retire, a new start, away from the pressures of teaching. He enjoyed the students, whom he considered his children. He never married, not having found a need. What he didn't like about being part of the small college in South Dakota had been the almost oppressive academic turmoil of the administrative, often political, component.

The first days in Florida had been relaxing, sitting on the dock in the early morning sun, his usual black coffee and warm buttered blueberry Poptart on the railing. However, Frank Gomez, his next door neighbor, had warned him.

Frank was a short and wide man who had moved from the Caribbean and made a good living with a Latin restaurant in Tampa. He and Josefina welcomed Conroy to their community when he arrived.

"Conroy, I may be poking my nose into your business. Let me know. There is no lady in your life, right?"

"Where you are going with this?"

"You have a house. You have money, obviously. So, they will be coming."

"Soon? Who? What? Oh, must have something to do with property appraisers and increasing county taxes. Should have expected this."

"You don't understand. You're a single man."

"They tax on the basis of being a single man?"

"No, no. I'm talking about casserole ladies. They know who you are by now. They will be coming for you."

"Casserole ladies?"

"You don't know about them?"

"Never heard of such ladies."

"Listen, Conroy. I'm serious. The next few days, weeks, will be a nightmare. The first one has not shown up; I've been watching. Soon there'll be women at your door; standing with casseroles in their hands and big lipstick covered smiles."

"Casseroles? Nice. Free food! Is this some sort of service, a welcoming program?"

Frank, exasperated, "No, these are widows, old maids, single women for one reason or another. Some have little money, looking for a man to support them. They use casseroles as bait to catch a guy."

"What! I don't want to be caught. I've been a bachelor since I was born, and plan on staying that way. I'm here to restart my life, to live it simply."

"Fine. Don't get excited. Just wanted to let you know what will happen. I'm surprised they haven't shown up."

***

Frank was right. A trickle at first, then the dam broke. All sorts of women; all types of casseroles. The ladies would drive up in cars and pickups, others on motorcycles or bicycles, one on a horse. All with steaming, savory enticements.

"Thanks so much. Really appreciate this. So kind of you." What else could he say, not wanting to be rude? They left addresses and phone numbers. At first he dropped empty containers at their houses, but after a few outrageous incidents he called them to let them know they could pick up the crocks and pots. That didn't work; some persuaded him to let them in, with more unwanted advances.

"Call them when not likely to get them. Leave a message or hang up. Tell them the food was excellent; you left the dish on your porch. Don't answer the door. Hide out," said Frank.

He put empty casseroles on the stoop, never answering the door. Slowly the surge of casseroles stopped. Peace and quiet came to Conroy's world, until they started to come by water. Well, that's what he thought when he saw the long flaming red hair coming around the bend in the shoreline. But no, she had no casserole, only a bait-casting rod and reel.

She paid no attention; ignoring him as she cast purple-gold rubber worms at the reeds along the deep edge of the lake. Intense, she moved her jonboat into the cove, switching to a crankbait on a second rod. Then, she moved out and back into the main lake. No casserole.

Almost every Saturday and Sunday morning she worked the shore with focused effort, periodically catching a largemouth bass or feisty chain pickerel. Never looking at Conroy, she moved on past his dock, not casting toward him.

Conroy told Frank about her. "Yes, she fishes the lake a lot, particularly our shore and along that bend. It's a good area for bass. I don't know much about her."

***

It became part of Conroy's routine to get up Saturday and Sunday mornings to sit on the dock in a weather-worn Adirondack wooden chair to have his coffee, a shot of cream and a spoonful of sugar, crispy toasted blueberry Poptart. He watched. She fished.

Late May; the bass were active during this month according to Frank. She had come around the bend, casting the crankbait right and left, slowly reeling in line with slight fish-attracting twitches. Far out from the dock, she stopped the trolling motor.

"Mind if I fish your dock? Not having luck today. The big momma bass seem to be hiding. I don't fish people's docks unless it's ok."

Conroy blinked, "No, go right ahead. Not my fish."

He watched, curious. With careful casts she bounced a black rubber worm with silver flecks off dock pilings, letting it fall to the bottom. Then, slowly cranking her reel, gave the rod slight jerks. She tensed a couple of times, and then repeated her casting. Suddenly, she lurched back, the boat rocked and the rod bent in a sharp arc. An enormous fish leapt out of the water.

Conroy's coffee cup fell onto the dock, the Poptart into the water. He froze, bug-eyed.

The battle between woman and fish lasted a long time. Finally, she reeled it in, reached down and "lipped" it out of the water. Opening her tackle box, she pulled out a scale. Attaching the hook to the bass' mouth she weighed it. Smiling, she said, "10 pounds 8 ounces." Then, she bent over, lowered the fish into the water, moved it back and forth, and gave it a swat as it took off to the safety of deeper waters. "Go back to your babies Momma!"

Conroy was on his feet. She stood on the platform of her boat, looking at him. "Thanks. That was a good one. I always put the big ones back where I caught them."

"Yes, quite a show. I'm exhausted watching you."

"I'm shook up also. Always happens when I hook a big one."

"Uh, I was having a coffee, but knocked it onto the deck. Perhaps you might like a cup; I have a pot on the stove, fresh."

"That would be nice, seeing as we sort of caught that fish together. Cream and one sugar, please."

"Excellent. I'll go get some. Oh, would you like a Poptart? Mine fell into the water."

"Sure, blueberry if you have one."

"Blueberry? I always have blueberry. Back in a bit," a smile on his face.

John Charles Miller

John Charles Miller, Tampa, Florida, is a groundwater geologist and speculative fiction writer. Self-published works include Citrus White Gold (alternate history), You Can't Pick up Raindrops (short stories) and Dead Not Dead (parallel universes). Las Ruedas was the #2 short story in the FWA 2012 annual collection, My Wheels.

Blossoming Popularity

At first, Jen tried to hide her developing breasts. The summer before sixth grade, she and her best friend Rosemary frolicked on Manhasset Bay's beaches. Jen always covered up with a baggy T-shirt over her bikini—even in the water. But when she got wet, the teenage lifeguards took notice. They leered at the curves revealed by clinging fabric.

On the first day of middle school, Jen wore the new Maidenform bra her mother bought her, instead of the flattening sports bras she had used since buds emerged when she was 11. That morning's bus ride was a revelation. Every boy, from sixth- to eighth-graders, gaped at the distinctive mounds. Hugging a loose-leaf binder to her chest, Jen walked down the aisle with her cheeks burning under the stares. She spotted smiling Rosemary, who patted the seat beside her as an invitation to continue the customary pairing they had enjoyed throughout their elementary school years. Just as she reached her friend, a group of the eighth-grade boys called out to her from their haven in the rear of the bus.

"Hey, Blondie," they chorused.

Jen looked around, thinking they could not be addressing her. Not seeing any other blondes nearby, she gazed at the back-row boys, pointed to herself, and said, "Me?"

"Yup, you, Blondie. Come on back here. We want to ask you somethin'," said Don Lyons, the unquestioned leader of the pack, neighborhood charmer, and unrivaled hunk of Manhasset Middle School.

"Don't listen to those creeps, Jen. Just sit here with me. I want to show you my new pen." Rosemary patted the seat again.

Eyes glued to the popular boys, who had never spoken to her before, Jen muttered, "Be right back." She headed to the rear of the bus—drawn to them as if caught in a tractor beam. Despite knowing the dangers she had witnessed many times before, she could not resist the lure of popularity. Her common sense screamed, They're going to make fun of you. They're going to make you cry. Yet her legs continued moving toward the purveyors of ridicule.

As she approached, Don shoved one of his compatriots out of the seat. He smiled at Jen and patted the cushion next to him, exactly as Rosemary had done. It seemed like a harmless request, and Jen planned to sit for just a moment. She wanted to know what it felt like for the whole bus to see her, Jennifer Karwoski, with Don Lyons. So the formerly invisible Jen slid into the seat beside Don and stared straight ahead— afraid to look directly into the blue eyes she had long admired from a distance.

He leaned close, so close she could feel his warm breath on her neck, and said, "So what's your name, new girl?"

New girl! He thinks I just moved here. Jen's speech failed her. She turned toward Don and stared at him.

"Aw, you're shy. Why don't you put down your notebook? Here, I'll take it." He tried to pull it from the nesting place against her chest. "Come on, I won't steal it." Don placed the relinquished loose-leaf binder on the floor. "There, isn't that more comfortable?"

The fiery spirit hidden deep inside burst out with indignation. "I am Jennifer Karwoski, and I have lived three blocks from you my entire life. My father is your CCD teacher. And stop staring at my chest."

The back-row boys howled and poked their leader. To his credit, Don laughed too.

He stood up and bowed deeply. "My sincerest and deepest apology, miss." He plopped back down and grinned.

Out went the fire, quenched by a charming mea culpa accompanied by sparkling sapphire eyes that met hers. Jen returned the smile.

"So, Jennifer, I hope you're in my homeroom. No, wait...I remember. You're younger. See, I know you."

"Yes, I'm in Miss Castelero's—sixth grade. Who do you have?"

"Me and my boys got Mrs. Salerno. It's gonna be tough. She likes handing out detentions."

"Oh, I'm sure you'll be able to talk your way out of any detention, Don."

"Well, thank you, Jennifer. I guess you know me, too." With that he put his arm around her shoulders and leaned back with a sigh. "But I sure want us to get to know each other better."

Jen felt warmth rise up within her—not an embarrassing flush or an angry burn, but rather an enjoyable glow. She had garnered Don's admiration, starting her on the path to popularity. Jen tossed her long curls and straightened her posture—proudly displaying her attributes. Her mind whirled with prospects and nowhere among them did her best friend Rosemary appear.

Diane Mutolo

Between writing and editing legal treatises, Diane's imagination takes her on fanciful journeys that sometimes end up as prose. Her fiction appears in the 2010 and 2012 FWA Collections. Diane's short story "The Twin" won first prize in the 2011 Royal Palm Literary Awards.

Jumping the Fence

When Mom shrieked, my brother and I straightened up, wide-eyed. We'd done nothing yell-worthy. Before I could reassure Billy, Mom stepped between us, brandishing her flowered bed sheet. Brown spots stained one yellow bouquet. "Missy, which one of you is bleeding?"

"Not me," I said, racing through my chores. Mom brought us home early because Sunday school cancelled, and I wanted the time to read.

She checked me anyway. "You were jumping on my bed."

"Yeah," I queried my brother with one eyebrow, "in our socks." In the silent language of siblings, Billy affirmed his muddy cowboy boots hadn't touched the bed.

Glossy brown tendrils curled around Mom's face. I loved her hair, but Dad said those long, soft waves belonged in the bedroom, so she corralled them in scarves.

She grabbed Billy and scanned his perennially scabby arms and legs. "Thank heaven you're okay." Frowning, she dragged the sheet back to her door. "I simply can't imagine," she said, and stopped.

"Maybe Dad's hurt." We'd barely seen him. He left to do Grandma's chores when we arrived.

"Oh, it can't be." Her face puckered like she'd eaten something sour. "Not again." She sagged against the doorframe. "He promised."

We rushed to her, but hugs didn't ease her sadness or soothe her trembling shoulders.

"Mom, what's wrong?"

"I need to lie down. You two go on outside." Her smile wobbled. "You'll take the laundry downstairs first?"

"Sure." We crossed our hearts and hurried to please her.

Worried, I emptied my hamper onto my sheets, towed everything to the basement, and returned to help Billy. From his closet, he touched a pale finger to blanched lips. I squatted beside him and listened.

Mom's anguished cries carried through the wall. She never cried. Ever.

Billy pulled his blanket around us. We huddled together, a young Tonto and Lone Ranger, fogbound and shivering on the edge of a canyon we couldn't see.

Her sobs gradually slowed and the rocky landscape I'd envisioned materialized into random heaps of unwashed clothing. Like cowboys riding for shelter under blackening skies, we gathered his dirties and galloped along the hall. I trailed him, herding strays.

Funnel clouds created this same heavy, electric feeling right before they touched ground. Our school taught tornado drills, but I knew no way to protect ourselves from a storm inside the house.

Billy and I silently sorted clothes into piles. Above us, the floorboards responded to Mom's restless pacing with near-human creaks and moans. Unnerved, we could no longer rein in our jitters. Like panicked animals, we bolted for the haven of our swing set.

We laughed and chattered in the sunshine, giddy with relief. Billy swung in big arcs, but my clumsy feet dragged from legs grown too long. A neighbor kid wanted help building his cavalry fort and Billy went, but I'd outgrown that, too.

I scrambled under the sprawling lilac bush alongside the house and hugged my knees to soothe my thumping heart. The window above me hitched open and I heard Mom talking to Faye next door, her best friend.

Mom liked to perch on the sill while she chatted on the phone. I ignored the small talk until I heard the too-casual tone she used to disguise the importance of a question.

She asked Faye about her monthly visitor. Girls in gym class called it a "visit from Susie." I knew vaguely what it meant. Next year, in sixth grade, we'd get pictures and handouts.

"Stop lying, Faye. The sheets stink of your perfume." Her words exploded around me like hailstones. "Sorry isn't enough."

I curled tighter, battered by her bitterness.

"No. Stay away. Never speak to me again." She banged the receiver down twice and groaned.

I wanted to help, but I didn't know how. I wanted to run, but I didn't know where. I wanted to cry, but I didn't dare.

The phone rang and she leaned against the screen. "Hello, Russ. What's going on? I'll tell you." She walked off, fury crackling like lightning, and I missed her conversation.

Faye's husband told us jokes. I crossed my fingers, hoping he could cheer Mom. The window slammed shut and I dashed for the swings.

Mom called from the kitchen door, "I need some things from the store." Her voice shook. She took a breath. "Russ offered to drive. Stay in the yard until we get back."

Flushed from the run, I ducked my head. "We'll be fine. Don't worry."

Russ started his car, Mom scooted in, and they rumbled away. The pounding in my chest slowed and I busied myself with the S-hooks holding my swing, proud that I could make this one thing right.

By the time I had the chains fixed at the proper height, they'd returned, and Mom crossed the lawn clutching a drugstore bag.

She paused on the porch. "No problems?"

"Everything's all right," I lied. My satisfaction shriveled. Yesterday she would have complimented my mechanical skills. Or resourcefulness. Not today.

Fierce as a pioneer woman under siege, she nodded and went in.

I wandered across to the boys' stockade, praised their work, and shared their lemonade and cookies. Cramped inside, my shoulder caught the frame and one rickety section collapsed. While I reset the flimsy rails, they fired cap guns at imaginary dangers.

"Silly greenhorns," I laughed. "Fences work to keep things in."

Unsettled, I slipped into the house to find my latest library book, desperate for the familiar comfort of fantasy. I peeked in the kitchen, but Mom wasn't there. Only our telephone, a marked-up newspaper, and a notepad, filled with her beautiful script.

A tempest pounded in the bathroom shower. I tiptoed to my room, snatched my book, and hustled outside.

Later, my brother and I settled in to watch TV. The storm had passed, leaving the kitchen tidy, the bathroom empty, and Mom behind her bedroom door.

Dad came home, whistling like usual.

Billy reached over and linked pinkies with me.

The screen door closed. Dad took two steps into the room, and Mom appeared wearing her best suit. She held out her hand.

The three of us stared, speechless. Sunny brown curls no longer cascaded past her shoulders. Cropped at her chin and dyed dark red, they waved around her face like flowers in the wind.

"The keys," she said, staring straight at my dad.

No one moved.

Surrounded by light flooding through the door, she glowed. Beyond her, I glimpsed the flickering images of a new frontier.

Excitement flooded through me, completely releasing the day's tension. I felt weightless.

"Give me the keys." Mom took a step forward and Dad recoiled. "Crown Realty is hiring. They'll see me today."

Dad stuttered, clearly as unbalanced by the apparition as we were, and fumbled the keys from his pocket.

She plucked them from his hand and marched through the door. "Make your own dinner. I left your wife in the bedroom." Billy and I crowded in as Dad opened their door. On the neatly made bed, the folded coverlet perfectly framed those dark spots. Mom's curls, tied with pink ribbon, decorated Dad's pillow.

Tires screeched. Our car sped past the window like a prized Thoroughbred running free.

Bettie Nebergall

This is Bettie's fourth consecutive appearance in FWA Collections. A two-time RPLA winner, she placed 8th in the Writer's Digest 2014 Competition. Her book, "The First Seven, Stories of Deception," is available on Amazon. For more details, visit her website: www.bettienebergall.com. Follow her on Goodreads, Facebook, LinkedIn and Pinterest.

Marigolds

At half past midnight, the old man edged out the door onto the back porch of his son's farmhouse, quietly latched the door shut, and turned to face an onslaught of frigid wind. An Alberta Clipper, according to the perpetually perky TV weather-girl, not that he needed her to tell him what his aching bones already knew. After ninety-odd years on this earth, he'd confronted more kinds of weather than that blonde bubblehead knew existed.

He paused. Nothing stirred, no lights, no commotion ensued.

Ha! I got away with it, he thought. Nobody heard me sneak outside.

His family considered him a bit feeble and worried he might wander off, despite evidence to the contrary. In fact, he looked no older than his seventy-year-old son. Yesterday, standing side by side in Wal-Mart, an out-of-towner mistook them for brothers.

The old man had been charmed; his son not so much.

Better get on with it.

Icy blasts of crystallized snow pelted his face, and he turned aside to tug his stocking cap lower on his brow. He readjusted his scarf into a sheltering loop to protect his mouth and nose, leaving but a small slice of space above to peer out. He seated his fur-trimmed parka hood atop hat and scarf and tightened the drawstrings. He had a long ways to walk, and a frostbitten nose and ears were not on his agenda—not that it would matter in the end.

Perfect night for it.

Beside the porch door, lined up under the kitchen window, sat a line of clay flowerpots devoid of life and color, brown and twiggy with death. All but one; one small pot thrived with florescent orange marigolds, gleaming in the rays cast by a solitary floodlight attached to a battered wooden shed. Yesterday, somebody left that plant on the front seat of his son's unlocked truck, but while his son joked about "white trucks all looking alike," the old man saw it as a sign letting him know his time was up. However, just to be dead certain, he'd left the plant outside on purpose, hoping it would keel over. Didn't happen.

I better take it with me.

He snuggled the pot into the crook of his arm.

Looks like the one cousin Enoch showed me after my heart attack.

Enoch, a distant cousin the old man had never even known existed, had shown up at the hospital twenty years earlier following the old man's brush with death. He'd brought along a potted marigold eerily akin to this one. Enoch then congratulated him for "not going the way of all flesh" and explained how they were related. But now, for the life of him, he couldn't remember what happened to that marigold. Did Enoch take it with him? The old man had always half-suspected Enoch was merely a medication-spun hallucination; although, seeing this matching plant from the truck begged him to rethink things—like Enoch's blabbering on about things living forever.

Gripping the wooden banister with a mittened hand, he eased himself off the porch, gingerly stepping down the short flight of steps, taking care to find solid purchase in the yard. It would not do to slip and fall.

Easy does it. Easy does it.

He had his future to contend with, and he smiled to himself, imagining how he would never hear the end of it if he foolishly broke his hip.

He set off across the yard and cut through the vegetable garden, plowed under for winter, bereft of life. He had almost bit the dust here back twenty years ago on a glorious spring morning, which until that moment had upheld the rebirth of life.

He remembered how the agonizing pain squeezed his chest like an over-cinched belt. Face down in the dirt and home alone, he willed his face sideways and struggled to breathe, but his lungs would not draw. He immediately recognized the darkness settling along the edges of his vision; it mirrored the time he'd fallen off the garage roof, knocked unconscious.

Staring sideways at a row of spring's first succulent shoots of Bibb lettuce, he fully understood how this time when the light eventually shrank to a pinprick and winked out—he'd wink out too. Dead. Awaiting the inevitable, and as his focus tightened, he wondered if he'd see the oft-mentioned "light at the end of the tunnel."

Nope.

Instead, his field of vision narrowed and settled on an anthill. An anthill close to his face; so close he could feel ants crawling on him—on his chin, on his neck, along his jawline, across his cheek, and into his nose.

Oh, the horror!

Adrenaline jolted his body.

He sneezed.

And his heart hammered—once, twice, then thumped in rhythm.

He had lived to see another day, and another and another, piling up to now, today, resulting in a ninety-year-old man who for some reason or other still looked seventy. He had not aged a speck since his heart attack.

He blinked, coming out of his thoughts as the wind delivered a light lashing of snow, coming heavier on each swift gust as he trudged past the barn toward the tractor ruts leading into the back forty acres. His feet knew the way by heart, and he could have followed it with eyes closed. But not on a dangerous night such as this ripe with fallen branches and wind-tossed urban tumbleweeds of plastic bags ready to trip him.

They waited just inside the tree line near the river. Family. So many of them. Far more than he anticipated. All there to facilitate, soothe, and guide him. Men, women, boys, girls, several babies, old and young alike smiled, their voices a hubbub of welcome. They gathered around, drew close, clapping him on the back or patting him reassuringly.

Enoch stepped forward. "We've all gone through this—leaving our loved ones behind."

"My family will think I'm dead," the old man said and handed over the marigold.

Enoch put an arm around the old man's shoulders. "They'll believe you wandered away in the blizzard and the river carried you off. You know it's for the best."

"Yes." The old man sighed. "Now what happens?"

"It's time to leave," a young girl said and took his hand. "Come. The RV's are parked just through the woods."

He recognized her. A cousin.

Rebecca had been small for her age when she drowned in a quarry accident at about age fifteen or so, though her body had never been found. The truth of course differed. She had cheated death by surviving meningitis five years earlier and could no longer hide being eternally ten years old.

Just as he could no longer hide looking seventy for . . . what? Eternity? He didn't know how the family fluke worked, why most died or why a select few didn't. Some said it was marigold tea from the plant that flourished even in the savage ferocity of a blizzard, but it could be moonbeams for all he knew. Or genetics. Everybody was big on genetics these days.

Jean Axtell Nelson

Jean Axtell Nelson is former banking industry technical writer. In 2014, she won the RPLA Humor award and also had a story in the FWA's Collection #6. She lives in Belleview, Florida.

Come to Papa

I've waited outside his house every day for the past week. I usually park on the corner and watch to see if he'll come out, but he never does. One time I hung out under the hardware store awning and watched from across the street. That was a mistake. I must have looked too nervous and twitchy in my baggy T-shirt and Chuck Taylors because a cop pulled up and hassled me like I was a drug dealer.

When I told Rourke what I'd been doing all week he said it was a half-assed stakeout and I didn't really want to find him. "Dude, if you were serious, you'd just go knock on his door," he'd said, lighting a Marlboro. "Do you want to meet him or not?"

Rourke has no clue what it's like. He met his dad the day he was born, like most people. But I give him props because he tracked down my birth mother, Ms. Belacek, in Arizona.

She didn't want to talk on the phone but she gave me my dad's address. My hand shook as I wrote it down, feeling sweaty and sick as she began to pull away before she hung up. "Please don't contact me again," she said.

It's not like she or my dad would be impressed with how I turned out. On paper, I'm a shiftless loser, dropped out of college, fired from three jobs in one year. But I think if I could just learn where I came from I might figure out who I am. I might understand why I threw away a whole engineering scholarship because I was afraid to fail.

I'm staying at Meggie's apartment over the pet store. We met in school and we have a platonic thing going. She lets me sleep on the couch because she's a kind, decent person and she knows I have nowhere to go since my adoptive parents kicked me out last month. "Tyler, you've got to meet your dad," she said this morning, running her finger around the rim of her PETA coffee cup. "It could mean everything."

So now I'm going to actually walk up to the house and ask this guy if he'd like to meet his son after twenty-two years. The thing that blows my mind is Ms. Belacek told me on the phone that the whole time, my dad has been living a mile from where

I grew up. When I think about that I get this wrenching pain across my chest and it makes me want to go slam a six-pack.

I pull into the hardware store parking lot and walk across the street to 457 Weisert Road. The house looks a lot different up close than it did when I was hunched down in my Toyota half a block away. From there it looked sorta cool, like a gingerbread house. But when I sneak up along the side of the hedge I see the paint is peeling and the windows have some brown caked shit on them. So for a second I'm thinking maybe my dad is going to turn out to be some sloppy, crazed gangster waving a pistol. But then I remember what Meggie said when she left this morning: "Just man up and knock on the door. This wussiness is a turnoff." She'd raised an eyebrow weirdly at that point, almost like she was flirting with me.

The porch steps creak under my feet and I leap to the door because I want him to hear me knock confidently rather than creep up the stairs. I yank open the screen door and rap on the window pane. The screen door falls against me and I keep trying to push it away, annoyed, but it has a strong spring and it keeps flopping back on my shoulder. My heart starts pounding as I'm thinking this could turn out really bad.

I'm surprised how fast he comes to the door. He nods at me with his jaw clenched and leans his hand on the doorjamb. "I wondered when you were going to finally make it over here."

I'm unsure if he's being ironic or just pissed off. "Ms. Belacek told you I'd be coming?" I'm embarrassed at how high-pitched my voice sounds.

His face softens. "Ina calls me a few times a year. Come inside." It's then I notice his eyes. They look like mine. Washed-out blue, hesitant, on guard.

He steps back and waves me in and I follow him as he stomps through the house to the kitchen. He pulls out a chair. "Have a seat."

I sit and look around the room. Curled photos of dogs and motorcycles are mounted on the fridge with Miller Lite magnets. A toolbox and some electrical project take up all the counter space.

I can't think what to say. I've been planning this the whole week and I can't come up with anything. "So . . . " A clock ticks loudly on the wall and I want to get up and leave. Then I remember Meggie and her eyebrow. "So, Ms. Belacek says you've lived here the whole time, a mile away from me?"

"Yes." He folds his arms and leans back.

I'm afraid to ask the next question but I do it anyway. "Did you ever wonder about me? I mean, did you ever think—"

He jumps to his feet and walks to the fridge with his head turned to me. "Tyler, is it?" It freaks me out to hear him say my name and I nod like a jackhammer. He pulls a couple cans of Budweiser from the fridge. "You have to understand something." He clangs the beers on the table and plops back down in his seat.

"Look, I know, I have no right—"

"No, dammit, that's not what I mean." He opens the beer and the snap sounds loud in the kitchen.

I feel stupid for being such a wuss. "Okay, sorry."

"Ina moved to Arizona just after you were born, after she signed the papers. She didn't want anything more to do with me. I'd been back from the Gulf for two years—"

"The Gulf?"

"Desert Storm," he says, tapping his beer on the table. "I thought I could go over there and kill for my country, but . . . " Then he shakes his head in a frenetic, desperate way. "God! She couldn't understand what it was like seeing . . . in the desert. The bodies. Being scared all the time, even after I came back. She said I wasn't who she thought I was. He crunches the can in his fist, and some of the beer seeps out onto the table. I feel like an intruder, watching a fight between two people I've just met.

And the blue eyes that look like mine aren't even looking at me anymore; they're gazing out the dingy window over the sink. "I want to tell you about your mother, about us, and why everything happened. I don't know if you'll understand." He wipes a tear quickly, like he hopes I don't notice.

I sit back. "Actually, Dad, I think I might."

Kate Newton

A former criminal defense attorney from New York City, Kate Newton moved to Florida to write books and surf. Her novel Those Dark Places won Second Place in the 2014 RPLA and her short story What Lies at Our Feet appeared in the literary webzine Running out of Ink.

Fresh Step

Each time Ryan enters Walmart, he's surprised at how the shoppers have The Look. "How judgmental," he tells himself. "But true. And they push their carts like bumper cars and collide into each other, then offer a gruff, 'Sorry.' "Just cat food and litter," he mutters. "Best prices in town."

He selects the poultry and beef box of Meow Mix and adds several single serving containers of REAL beef in gravy, REAL salmon and crab meat in sauce and REAL chicken and beef in sauce, his cat's favorites. He carefully maneuvers around a cart in the middle of the aisle and eyes the boxes of Tidy Cats kitty litter, forty-pound box, thirty-five pound pail, thirty-pound bag, twenty-pound jug, scented, unscented, multiple cats, lightweight. A slim woman dressed in soft earth tones—long jersey skirt and loose T-shirt—tosses her silver-streaked gray hair out of her face and grabs the handle of a Tidy Cats thirty-five pound pail. In a wide arc, she swings it into her cart, the one blocking the aisle.

She glances at him. He stares at her, self-consciously brushing his too-long white hair from his eyes. What a lovely, wisdom-filled face, he thinks. She smiles as if he's spoken the words out loud. He's been doing that lately, filling empty silence by talking to himself, sometimes even to his cat, who sometimes answers. Maybe he should call his kids. Emma was the glue that held the family together, but she's been gone over six months now. He didn't think he'd make it through.

"Have you tried their lightweight litter?" he asks. "It doesn't work. It doesn't clump. So it's smelly. A waste of money."

"No I haven't," she says. Her voice is low, direct, earthy. "But a friend has and she says the same thing."

"Nice that it's not heavy, but it doesn't clump," he says again, then searches the four shelves of Tidy Cats for his usual unscented, thirty pound not lightweight bag, but can't find any. "Those are pretty heavy, aren't they?" he says as the woman hefts another thirty-five pound pail into her cart—clunk—sending it careening against the other side of the aisle.

"Yes, but I'm used to slinging bales of hay, so. . . ."

"Bales of hay?"

"Yeah, for the horses."

Ryan can't look away. He wants to tell her how pretty she is. She looks up at him and smiles again. Did he say that out loud? He looks in her cart. "Lots of kitty litter."

"Yeah. Six cats."

"Wow."

"A friend recently died and left a woman $40,000 to take care of her six cats. The woman took the money but left the cats. So guess who has 'em?"

"You."

"Yeah. Had to. Couldn't leave them to fend for themselves, could I? But so many cats."

"But what good karma you've made for yourself. And your friend on the other side knows. And she's grateful."

She laughs. Her rosy cheeks glow. Her teeth sparkle white, one in the front slightly chipped. How did that happen, he wonders. She tucks her hair behind an ear, soft curls cascade down her back. A strand sticks to her eyelashes. He raises his hand to free it, then stops. Silence echoes like heartbeats through a stethoscope.

A bumper car races around the aisle and crashes into Ryan's cart, scraping metal on metal. He hears a gruff, "Sorry," then repositions his cart out of the way and quickly scans other shelves for unscented, clumping, regular weight litter. When he turns back, he watches the woman's silver curls bounce behind her until she turns the corner, out of sight.

He feels abandoned, covered in gray haze like at Emma's funeral. He sighs and places two Fresh Step brand, twenty-five pound, unscented boxes into his cart. "Try something new," he tells himself, out loud.

At the check-out line, he reaches over and grabs a pre-roasted chicken from under the heating lights. "Smells sooo good," he tells the young man in front of him. A cart behind him bumps his softly.

"Karma," she says. "I haven't heard that word in years. I used to live on an ashram. Know what that is? Not many people do anymore."

"Yes. I lived on one in the seventies."

"Where?" Her eyes twinkle.

"Green Gulch, near San Francisco. Where was yours?"

"Green Gulch in the eighties!" She glances in his cart. "Those chickens smell sooo good." She looks at him, hesitates.

He stares into her hazel eyes as if hypnotized.

She raises her eyebrows, tilts her head. "Want help eating that one?"

His smile stretches so wide, words can't get through.

Joan North

Joan North lived on an ashram and Zen center for eighteen years. She currently lives in St. Augustine, Florida. Her short stories were published in The Florida Writer and FWA's 2013 collection as one of the top ten entries. Two stories were selected as finalists in 2012 RPLA competition.

A Rose by Any Other Name

Rose stopped coloring her hair. At first, tiny bits of grey peeked from her scalp. Soon, no trace of auburn remained. The soft, grey curls, framing her freckled face, made her skin look pale, but her eyes still glowed a vibrant turquoise blue. Her wardrobe colors migrated from burnt orange, rust and olive to silver, lavender and aqua, a further compliment to her new look. Outwardly, she had changed substantially, but inside she was still the happy, silly, Rose everyone at work loved.

One afternoon, Rose poked her head into my office. Worry filled her eyes. "I feel terrible. I'm going to the emergency room."

I jumped from my chair and grabbed my purse. "Can I drive you there?" I offered.

"No, it's only three blocks away. Joe is meeting me."

"Are you sure?"

"Yes," she said with a tone of finality.

I dropped my purse and sat down. I could not force her to accept my assistance. "Give us a call, OK?"

"Sure," she murmured as she limped slowly toward the front door.

Hours later, my phone rang. Apprehension welled inside me as I lifted the handset.

"They're doing more tests, but I may have pancreatic cancer," Rose stated bluntly.

I stared at the wall opposite my desk, thinking how can this be? "I'm so sorry," I croaked my inadequate response.

"Call you later," she said and broke the connection.

A CAT scan identified cancer on her pancreas and spleen. Surgery, radiation and chemo followed with good results. She enrolled in an experimental program of injections made from mice antibodies and hoped for success. Eventually, she came back to work a few hours each day. She laughed at the cheese party celebrating her return and proudly wore our gift of mouse ears to her injection sessions. We had to find things about which to laugh, otherwise we would all cry. Tears and sad faces would not help Rose.

For a few months everything was great... until cancer reared its ugly head again.

***

Unadorned wooden pews lined the stark chapel. Whispers echoed off paneled walls. Light fixtures hummed. Half a dozen baskets of flowers flanked a lace-covered pedestal table supporting a framed portrait of Rose, a jade urn, and a single red rose in a sterling silver vase. Above the table, a flat panel television flashed photo images selected and arranged in a chronological progression.

The room was full when the funeral director closed the doors. Rose's husband, Joe, thanked everyone for attending the celebration of her life and invited those assembled to share stories. Her son remembered a loving mother; younger siblings related humorous events; her mother spoke in proper British English of a loyal daughter; and friends shared touching memories. Joe finished the ceremony with an invitation to supper. He'd smoked fifty pounds of pulled pork. Neighbors brought side dishes and desserts. There was plenty for everyone.

The weather was warm and dry, so guests congregated inside and on the outdoor deck. At first, no one spoke, but soon the sound of people gathered in friendship filled the evening air.

I wandered into Rose's sewing room. My fingers picked at the remnants of fabric and thread scattered on the cutting table. Her scent still permeated the room. I breathed in heavily to make a final memory. As I turned to leave, I saw Joe standing at the doorway.

"Will you take something as a remembrance?"

"Oh, I can't."

"She would love for you to have something."

I removed two rhinestone headed pins from the pincushion. "These are unique, just like Rose."

"I thought you were going to speak at the ceremony."

"Couldn't do it. Not without crying."

"Can you tell me?"

"Last Halloween we wore costumes to work. Rose dressed as a witch. I imagine you remember the day-glow green hair. Took a month for her to wash it all out."

"She had no idea how easily grey hair absorbed green dye," he said with a chuckle.

"In this sewing room, she made a skirt with green pleats. But the most outstanding feature of the costume was that pair of lime green and fluorescent purple striped stockings. Those crazy hose with their horizontal stripes were unique, just like Rose," I said as I fingered the pins in my hand. "I'll never forget her."

I think of Rose often, but always on Halloween. The memory of her outrageous stockings always brings a smile to my face.

***

Years later, I sailed on a vacation cruise from Venice's Grand Canal through the Mediterranean. At my dinner table, I was delighted to meet passengers from several

European countries. One seat remained empty as the waiter began taking beverage orders. I heard the maître d' fill the chair across from me, but the face of the guest was obscured from view by the huge, placemat-sized menu. I made my dinner selection, closed the menu and placed it on the table.

My eyes widened in surprise as I looked at the newest guest. Rose's turquoise eyes smiled across the table! Realizing I was holding my breath, I exhaled slowly, smiled, and recovered my composure. The woman introduced herself in heavily accented English. She was Annemeike from Amsterdam, a widowed bank executive. I felt foolish for my initial reaction and made no mention that she reminded me of a deceased friend.

Annemeike and I discovered many common interests. We laughed, shared stories and soon became fast friends. The days passed too quickly.

The gala Halloween party promised to be an outstanding departure event. Passengers were encouraged to accent evening attire with handmade hats or masks using art supplies provided by the cruise line. Elaborate décor transformed hallways and dining rooms into spooky graveyards filled with zombies and bats or haunted houses with shrieking ghosts and skeletons. Flickering candles filled the ship with an eerie glow.

At our table men sported sailor and pirate hats. Women dressed as gypsies and wenches. Black paper cat ears and a fluffy, tissue paper tail accented my evening dress. The ship's photographer hovered, but since Annemeike had not yet arrived, he waited to snap a group photo.

Within moments the maître d' escorted Annemeike to our table. An elaborate, handcrafted hat and cape accented her cocktail dress. With a flourish of her skirt, she bowed a deep curtsey. I felt the blood drain from my face and goose bumps rose on my arms. Below Annemeike's short, black skirt were lime green and fluorescent purple striped stockings.

I forced a smile to my lips, but my hands trembled and hot tears welled in my eyes. We sat silently, our eyes locked together, for what seemed like an eternity. I would never know why Rose created her new life. What devils plagued her? I could not imagine.

When I could finally speak, I gazed at the menu and asked, "What looks good tonight?"

I saw the tension ease from Annemeike's shoulders. She glanced at me for a moment longer and smiled an unmistakable "Rose smile" before picking up her menu. She knew she would not have to start over… again.

Sheila Marie Palmer

Sheila Marie Palmer is one of those rare Sarasota, Florida natives. A decade of work in the court system provided background for the first two books of her Life and Death series. A member of FWA and MWA, she now lives with her husband in Pensacola.

Happy Dazed

I created this party, so why was I alone? Couples hung onto each other as they slow danced like koalas hugging trees. Remember the "twelve-inch apart" rule in high school? That didn't apply here. The couples were smooching on the dance floor. Mr. and Mrs. Robinson always hired me to provide the band and decorations for their annual anniversary matinee party, but I usually had a date. It was nice to have a man to hold onto, but since Pete and I broke up, this time felt different. This year, if I stood next to a begging man at the end of the Interstate off ramp and held a sign that read "I need a date for Saturday night," people would continue to throw money into his hat, and I'd still be standing there alone and dateless. It was time for me to revise my thinking, change my patterns, and jump-start my love life. Instead of driving right home and sulking after the party, my strategy was to stop at a sports bar, where men hung out.

I jumped into my Fiat, and drove with determination to Danny's Pub, a local sports venue and restaurant where silence was forbidden. The noise and energy felt like a Rolling Stones concert. I sat at the bar, then glanced around to see forty big-screen TVs showing a variety of programs from auto racing to ziplining and many sports in between. The friendly bartender asked what I wanted. I wanted to meet a man and start dating again, I thought.

"Just orange juice," I said. "Any single men here?" She just rolled her eyes. I pivoted my barstool to take a look at the selection.

The man at a table nearby, attired in a suit and tie, did not make eye contact to my dismay. This was the first time I stepped out since the breakup, so a flirtation from that man would make me feel special. Instead, a man at the table diagonally across from me approached. He wore light blue denim jeans ripped at the knee, a golf shirt, and long, messy, light brown hair.

That figures. The well-dressed individual who I want to talk to is ignoring me, and the slob is staring, I thought.

"Hello." Mr. Denim made his move. "I'm Hap, short for Happy."

"I'm Cecily." It fell out of my mouth before I could censor it. I should have said another name, but I liked his face and physique.

"What do you do for work? I'm an inventor."

"How nice. I'm an event planner. I'm here because I was in the neighborhood doing a party. I love your voice, Hap," I gushed.

"Oh, thank you. Merci."

"Oh, French. Are you from France?"

"No, from Canada."

"Oh, I was in Edmonton and Banff once."

"You were in Western Canada. I grew up back east in Montreal. Monreal." He pronounced it in French. "I'm from the country that has hockey as its national winter sport. But I live here now. Want to shoot pool?"

"No, I'm dressed for a party. I can't."

"Yes, you can. I'll be easy on you. Il est facile de faire." He led me to the lounge area. I wobbled on my high heels as I grabbed the cue stick.

"Hello, Hap." A man walked by and waved to my new friend.

A woman sashayed by and said, "Hi, Hap."

"You have many friends here," I said.

"I come here a lot," Hap offered.

Hap racked then broke the balls. Customers gathered around the pool table and watched Hap shoot the cue stick into the white ball into a solid red one. He sank it.

An onlooker shouted, "He shoots; he scores!"

"This is just practice, OK?" Hap shared a smile. "Your turn."

How hard can it be to shoot a ball at an angle with a wooden stick and get it into the hole? By now the crowd had grown, and my hands shook a little. "I haven't had geometry since high school, Hap," I said. I grabbed the cue stick and set up the shot. I pushed with great force. The cue ball exited the table and flew toward one of the onlookers. He ducked and avoided getting hit. "Sorry," I apologized.

"You moved your elbow." Hap stood behind me, repositioned my arm, and showed me how to hold the stick straighter. "I'll help you," he whispered in my ear.

He was so close, I smelled his cologne. His touch made me shakier; I didn't want him to know. "Wow, you're good at this. I really hate sports."

"You do?" Hap asked with his adorable French accent, "Pour quoi? In Canada we love our sports."

"Well, take baseball, for example. I could knit a blanket in between hits. And football, yikes, all I see is pain. And in hockey, the players are brutes, and they fight on skates on ice. They slide backwards. How stupid is that? They lose teeth. Nice teeth are important to me."

"Now we play seriously," he said.

***

Hap won the game with ease. "OK, young lady. I have to go to get to my job now."

"I thought you were an inventor."

"I am. I have to get to my scheduled work. Cecily, please give me your phone number."

I gave him my business card. "I had fun, Hap. Thank you."

"I enjoyed myself, too. Moi Aussi. Au Revoir." He kissed my hand that had just let go of the pool stick, winked, and sauntered away.

As I walked back toward the bar, I sighed and thought, Not bad for my first time in a long time looking for a new beau. Hap's kind of cute. I hope he calls me.

I continued down the hallway, and I noticed a dozen 8 by 10 glossy photographs framed and displayed on the wall. At my eye level was an autographed photo of a man smiling, a front tooth missing, stick in hand. The printed words below it read: Hap Montagne, Hockey Star.

Elaine Person

Elaine Person's parody "King Arthur" is in Random House's A Century of College Humor. Her stories appear in FWA's collections and The Florida Writer. Her poems are in Poets of Central Florida, volumes II and III and Florida State Poets Association's collections. Elaine co-edited anthology Looking Life in the Eye.

When I Grow Up . . .

August 1956

I awoke to a rooster crowing outside my window. I'd arrived at Uncle Mack's farm in Columbia, South Carolina yesterday, my parents letting me ride the shiny blue and silver Greyhound bus from New York all by myself. It was their present to me for having turned ten two months ago and getting all good grades on my report card.

My cousin, Teresa, ripped the quilt off me, yelling, "It's six o'clock, Tootsie! Rise and shine!"

That was the time I'd gotten up for school. But summer vacation wasn't over yet, and I wanted to sleep in. "Too early," I muttered, pulling the quilt back over my head.

Teresa snorted and yanked it off again. "No, just in time to help me feed the animals."

Animals, right. I'd always loved coming to Uncle Mack's to see all his animals. His farm was huge, just like in the picture books I'd read back in kindergarten.

We washed up, got dressed, and Aunt Beverly cooked us eggs and grits for breakfast.

We went to the barn, where Uncle Mack was mucking the four horses' stalls. I laid a small amount of alfalfa hay in each of the horses' hay racks while Teresa gave them fresh water. My favorite pony, Lucille, whom I used to ride when I was little, was still as pretty as ever with the white diamond-shaped mark on her forehead.

"I wanna be a veterinarian when I grow up," Teresa said, smoothing out Lucille's brown coat with a brush.

"That sounds like fun," I said.

"Yeah, but Mr. Clemson—the farm vet around here—said it's really hard and I should consider being a secretary instead. But I like taking care of animals. I already know how to splint a chicken's leg after watching Mr. Clemson do it so many times."

"Well, when I grow up, I'm gonna be a detective like Dick Tracy," I said, thumbing myself in the chest.

Teresa grinned. "You think Dick's ever solved mysteries on a farm?"

"Are you kidding? He solves mysteries everywhere!"

When the horses were happy, Teresa went to feed the pigs while I hurried to the chickens. I'd always loved feeding them the most. Sometimes I made a trail of feed and watched all the chickens happily follow me like the Pied Piper. Or I'd dance around and hum the song from Cinderella, pretending I was a princess while I tossed seeds and dried corn everywhere.

The chickens well fed, I returned to the barn to look for Teresa but was lured away by the meowing of cats nearby. I followed the sounds to an empty stall, where a grey cat and five little kittens were snuggled in a nest of hay.

The mama cat looked at me and meowed. The babies rolled around, wrestled, and pawed at her tail. One of the babies, an all-black one, had crawled atop several bales of hay sitting against the stall's wall. He stood on his hind legs, his paws pressed against the wall as he peered at Lucille in the next stall. He pushed off the wall, one of his hind legs overextended its step, and he fell.

I gasped and rushed over to catch him. I was seconds too late, but he landed on his feet and looked okay.

"You sure were lucky there," I said, picking him up by the scruff of the neck and returning him to his mama. Lucky. What a perfect name.

"Mimi had her babies two months ago," Teresa's voice said from behind me. "You want one?"

"I'd love one, but we're not allowed to have pets in our apartment."

"Aw, too bad." She left the stall, and I followed.

Teresa retrieved a roll of white bandages and a handful of Popsicle sticks from a shelf and stuck them in the pockets of her overalls. "I'll show you how to splint a chicken's leg."

We returned to the chickens, and Teresa ended up finding a wandering chicken who was limping around. She held it carefully in her arms so it couldn't fly away.

"Poor little thing," I said, frowning.

"It happens a lot," Teresa explained. "They'll wander near the cows and goats, and some of them get accidentally stepped on."

We went to the picnic table behind the house, and Teresa explained her splinting lesson. I got to hold the chicken steady while she worked on it, putting a Popsicle stick on both sides of its leg and wrapping it securely with the bandage. Afterward, we took the chicken to the coop.

I returned to the kittens while Teresa went off to check for more injured chickens. Mimi lay comfortably in her nest of hay, while the kittens—four of them—slept. Where was Lucky?

Oh no! I searched around the barn for him. I heard small cries, and my expert detective skills led me to Lucille's stall. Peering inside, I spotted Lucky lying beside one of Lucille's front hooves, mewing painfully. He tried to stand, but his back leg was oddly disfigured; it wasn't moving.

I gasped and swept Lucky up in my arms. I ran out of the barn, calling for Teresa, but she wasn't around. Uncle Mack was far out in the field on his big green tractor.

My heart raced. What would Dick Tracy do at a time like this?

I took Lucky to the picnic table, where the splinting items still lay. I don't think I've ever seen Dick splint animals' legs before. I tried to remember Teresa's lesson, carefully wrapping the sticks and bandage around Lucky's leg. Afterward, I carried him into the house and wrapped him in an old quilt to keep him comfy.

I rushed to the kitchen, found Mr. Clemson's emergency number sitting next to the telephone, and gave him a ring.

A car pulled up in front of the house a short while after, and I went outside. A man wearing a hat and thick glasses and carrying a leather bag got out of his car.

Teresa came out of the chicken coop, all smiles when she saw him. "Hi, Mr. Clemson!"

Mr. Clemson tipped his hat at us and smiled. "Good morning, girls. Someone call about a kitten with a broken leg?"

"I did, sir," I said, showing him Lucky.

Teresa's eyes widened. "What! How did he break his leg?"

"I think Lucille stepped on him. I found him in her stall."

Mr. Clemson examined Lucky. "Hmm... this splint is pretty well done. Did you do this, Teresa?"

Teresa opened her mouth, then closed it and shook her head. "No, sir. Must've been my cousin, Tootsie, here. It was her first time, too. Pretty good, isn't it? Course, she had a good teacher." She grinned. "Maybe one day I'll be a veterinary teacher at the university. What do you think, Mr. Clemson?"

"I suppose not much surprises me anymore." Mr. Clemson smiled at me. "This is some good handiwork, young lady. I'm impressed."

I beamed. Maybe it's about time I hang up my detective hat and get me a spiffy new doctor's bag.

R. M. Prioleau

R.M. Prioleau is a game designer by day and a dangerous writer by night. Since childhood, she's expanded her skills and creativity by delving into the realm of literary abandon.

Together

The sad-eyed beagle in the grainy newspaper photograph caught her attention even though she wasn't much of an animal lover. She'd only meant to volunteer, answering the phone or putting records in order, a job to fill a few hours. When the stocky, tattooed woman who took her contact information asked her to consider adopting, Julia laughed.

"Oh, I'm too old. I'm seventy-five."

A grim weariness seemed to settle over the woman, whose name, Julia later learned, was Estelle. "Don't you think one of our animals would be grateful to live even a few weeks or a month longer?"

A sobering pause ensued while Julia considered the question. "How many do you kill?"

Estelle's gaze never wavered as she replied, "About half."

They walked down an antiseptic-smelling hallway, where the metal bars lining both sides of a polished floor reminded Julia of scenes from The Green Mile. Surrounded by an array of jumping, yapping dogs, she noticed one silent bundle of black and tan fur standing stock-still on bowed legs. Its bat-like ears straightened as she approached and the tail began to wag.

"He's some sort of Chihuahua mix," Estelle said, "probably three or four years old, not likely to find a home."

***

"Damn dog," Julia griped as she shoved Bitty out the front door. "Couldn't even wait two minutes, could you?"

At that moment, she couldn't have cared less about getting a condo association fine for having an unleashed dog outside. She grabbed paper towels and a spray-cleaner from the kitchen and then knelt on the tile floor to clean up the puddle, her ample backside threatening to split the seam of her pants. Other dogs went out twice a day, but this one must have a bladder the size of a peanut, she thought. Estelle hadn't known its history, or so she said, and Julia suspected the previous owner found the dog too demanding.

Julia's life had been filled with demands: her kindergarten students—make her stop touching me!—her children—I'm hungry!—and her husband—did you wash my blue shirt? During Sam's funeral last year, strands of joyful liberation laced her sadness. Now it was her time, a time when she could stay in bed all day, eat ice cream for dinner, and let the laundry pile up if that's what she wanted to do.

Taking care of Bitty was like starting all over with a baby, one that mutilated impeccant shoes resting on the floor and flunked House Training 101. More than once during the past two months, Julia considered taking him back to the shelter...pictured the needle slipping into his vein, eyes closing, body cremated.

When she finished cleaning up the puddle, she opened the door and glared at the mutt, waiting patiently, its snake-like tail waving back and forth. "Are you still here? Why don't you run away and find some other sucker to keep you?"

Julia bent down to put Bitty's leash on, and they followed the sidewalk, the dog strutting past small gardens fronting the pale-yellow stucco buildings, his short legs beating out a rhythm. He held his head high as if to say, "Look! This is my territory, my home!" to unseen eyes watching from behind the window blinds. A small green lizard scampered across their path, and Bitty threw his entire twelve-pound body into dashing off after it.

The unexpected movement jerked the leash out of Julia's hand. "Get back here, you damn dog!"

Seconds later, the lizard climbed four feet up a tree trunk, stopped, turned around, and looked down. Julia swore she could hear it chuckling.

Bitty stopped at the base of the tree, sniffing, and Julia picked up the leash. She took a deep breath, inhaling the smell of cut grass and budding azaleas. Ragged-edged clouds highlighted feathery palm fronds, and she marveled at the spiky shapes pointing in all directions like myriad compass needles gone awry. In a flash of red, a cardinal settled on a nearby live oak branch and issued a loud sweet-sweet-sweet call answered, more softly, by another bird at a distance. While Julia stood, waiting, she wondered if she'd become so inured to the mundane she'd forgotten to notice the magnificent moments nature offered.

Of course, it was all well and good walking Bitty in warm, dry weather. Northeast Florida had its own version of winter, though, and taking Bitty out four times a day when it was cold or wet—or worse, both cold and wet—made for a thoroughly miserable experience.

When they returned home, Julia measured out dry kibbles while Bitty jumped up and down in anticipation, raising his front legs, then his back legs, looking like a miniature bucking bronco. Day after day, his enthusiasm for this ritual never wavered, and Julia grudgingly acknowledged the appreciation he showed, more than she'd ever gotten from her late husband or the now-middle-aged sons who seldom called her.

She put a frozen dinner in the microwave and, after she'd eaten, settled on the couch to watch Jeopardy. Bitty trotted over, stood with his paws on the seat cushion, and huffed: a sound somewhere between a yip and a whine.

"Go away. I don't want your hair all over the furniture."

The dog cocked his head as if he understood what she said and huffed again.

"No, you can't come up here," Julia said. They'd played this game before, and she knew he'd eventually sit at her feet.

Two round cinnamon-colored eyes stared up at her, pleading, reminding Julia of the contentment she'd once known holding a small, warm body in her arms, caressing soft, silky skin. But this wasn't a baby it was a dog, and not a well-behaved one at that. Still, she felt her resolve weakening.

***

Dr. Connor's burly presence filled the room, his bald head gleaming in the florescent light. "How are you feeling?"

"Not too bad," Julia said.

He settled himself on a wheeled stool. "You've lost five pounds, your blood pressure is down, and your sugar level is good. You must have taken my advice and gotten some exercise."

Julia's eyes narrowed as she said, "Don't be ridiculous, I wouldn't be caught dead in one of those places where grown people wear clothes that show every bulge."

The doctor turned his head, presumably to look at the computer screen, but Julia caught a glimpse of his smile. Images of Bitty floated to her mind, and she saw herself hurrying to keep up with him on their walks, bending over to put his leash on or clean up a mess, lifting him onto the couch. That wasn't exercise, though, she was just taking care of a stupid dog—nothing worth mentioning to the doctor; nope, nothing worth mentioning at all.

Damn dog.

Pat Rakowski

Pat Rakowski's commentary articles have been published in The Philadelphia Inquirer and Beaches Leader newspapers. She's had three short stories published in previous FWA Collection books and others in the FWA magazine. Her book about cultural and social changes during the past fifty years is available ww.patrakowski.com.

Seven-Eighths

Her breasts billowed above his face as she set the coffee cup on the table in front of him. The heady aroma of her patchouli perfume brought back the sixties in New York as she bent over and kissed the top of his balding head. His eyes followed her bottom as she walked back into the restaurant. For the umpteenth time he reminded himself that she was fifty years younger than he. The view still moved him. With all the choices the city offered this was how he started each day. Black coffee at twenty-third and Madison.

Some days this was the only thing that made breathing worth the effort.

He sipped his coffee and gazed across the street into Madison Square Park. The children were still swinging, the nannies gossiping and the old guys playing chess. But it was cold and empty without Ralph complaining about everything over their daily chess game. He died at sixty-three. A heart attack. Just like that. The bastard.

He materialized across Madison and stood beside the concrete table they had played chess on every day for the last six years. He could have teleported for all he remembered. One minute he was drinking coffee outside A Voce, the next he was standing in the park holding his cup to his mouth absently looking for Ralph.

"Hey old man, you losin it?" A very slight boy of about twelve called from the street.

"You can't lose something you don't have, smart ass."

"I have a name ya know!" The boy said cheerfully as he walked up to the table and threw his messenger bag down on the ground.

"Yeah and you probably have a phone number too. I don't want that either!"

"I had a cell but I traded it for a couple a j's." The boy said as he leaned over the table on his elbows. He may have been twelve but his chubby, round face looked even younger.

"So, you gonna stand there all day in that ratty old field jacket or are you gonna sit and play some chess?"

"With you? You don't know the first thing about chess. Why aren't you in school?"

"I graduated. Even you bought this clever disguise! I'm really a twenty something grad student at NYU. My name is Francis."

"That might explain your winning personality. So, all this schooling and the game of chess never came up?"

"I was too busy with serious stuff. Like finding food and a place to sleep."

He stared at the boy for a moment. It seemed like this boy had been at the periphery of his consciousness for weeks. He may have even talked with him before but he just wasn't sure. A big part of him just wanted to sit on this concrete bench and feel the cold.

"Why don't you ever pay for your coffee?" Francis said tilting his head.

"You been watching me, smartass?"

"It's Francis, if you don't mind."

"I mind especially if you are stalking me."

"So, you don't pay for your coffee. Do you know her?"

"My son works there. The coffee is his contribution to my welfare. Happy now? Francis."

"Yeah for a minute there I was afraid your memory was shot and you couldn't remember my name for two minutes."

"You make it so much easier to remember smartass."

"Then aside from the coffee it looks like you've got lots of time on your hands. Perfect situation to teach me how to play chess."

"I was just thinking about that this morning. No, not teaching you how to play chess. About how much time I have. If I'm 69 now and they say the average lifespan for a man that age is 79, that would mean seven-eighths of my life is gone. All I have, at most, is an eighth of my total life. Do I really want to spend my whole life or what's left of it teaching chess to a smartass?"

"That could be a problem if it meant lowering the bar on the quality of your life. But since Ralph isn't coming back, you don't seem to have much going on. I guess being bored out of your mind for the last days of your life could make it seem longer. But that has nothing to do with quality does it? And you might be teaching chess to the next Einstein!"

"Or Jeffrey Dahmer."

"Impossible, I'm a vegan."

"Really?"

"Jeez, you're easy. No, I really want you to teach me how to play chess. You looked so strong and full of juice when you played chess with Ralph. Of course, it did look like you two were going to have a fistfight about half the time."

"That was a big part of the fun. We did fight once but that was years ago. Ralph always had to be right."

"Yeah, I bet you've never harbored a strong opinion about anything."

"I'm getting one now about teaching someone chess."

"Listen, if something better comes up you can ditch me."

"I'm sure that'sgonna happen."

"So, can we start?"

"Not today, I don't have my chess set."

"Not a problem!" Francis turned his bag over dumping the chess pieces on the table. He stood there smiling broadly.

The old man looked at the table and slowly shook his head while suppressing a smile. He picked up a white and a black piece and put one in each hand offering them to Francis to choose. He picked white.

They quietly went about setting the pieces in their places until Francis was sure he had them in their right places and he looked up, smiling.

"So it's on, you're going to do it?"

"Yeah, I guess so."

"Gee, could you control your enthusiasm a little."

"Don't forget the time factor."

"I wouldn't worry about that if I were you. That spot on your wrist looks like melanoma to me."

"Med school, too? Impressive! It's your move. Francis."

The old man smiled softly and looked around the park. Even though it was early March the maples and oaks were beginning to bud out. A pale green mist hung in the air tempering the late winter sun. He hunched over watching Francis move a pawn and eagerly look up at him.

"Ah, now you're screwed smartass!"

Dale Simpson

Dale lives on the Treasure Coast and is the author of Sober and Miserable, a memoir focused on an unscheduled coming of age. He was also a contributor to FWA's Collection, Volume 5, and has an upcoming novel titled Enchantment.

Immolation

"Remember, no one can know the truth."

Derek rolled his eyes. "I know, Mom, I know."

Lacking barstools, they stood side by side at the breakfast bar eating cereal from polystyrene bowls with plastic spoons. Derek drank the last of the milk from his bowl. He had her gray-blue eyes and his father's curly brown hair. When had he grown taller than she?

Jo picked at her Raisin Bran. "The delivery truck will be here any minute."

"Fine."

"Get some shoes on."

"Yeah, yeah." He dropped his empty bowl into the brown paper bag serving as wastebasket and then padded down the hall toward his bedroom.

She dumped the last of her cereal into the disposal and tossed her bowl in with his.

The nook that would hold their table stood empty, like every room in this cold, white-walled house. Next week, she'd paint. Then the place might start to feel like home.

The power was supposed to be turned on sometime that day. A flick of the kitchen light switch produced nothing, so she left the candles and matches on the counter.

The truck, promised at nine, arrived at nearly ten o'clock. Jo stood on the pristine carpet of the living room and directed the men where to put everything.

The burly foreman approached with a clipboard. "Mrs. Sheffield?"

"Ms."

"Oh. Sorry." He turned to his paperwork. "Says here we're doing assembly for you, too."

"That's right."

"Okay." He shoved his sweat-stained ball cap back on his head. "We'll get everything inside first, and then start puttin' it together."

"Perfect. Would you do my son's room first?"

"You bet."

She went ahead to make sure he hadn't started unpacking.

Derek sat cross-legged on the mattress, though it was still wrapped in plastic, playing a game on his new cell phone. "Mom, this is pretty cool. Look."

She stepped close enough to peep over his shoulder. Spaceships rocketed about on the screen, exchanging laser blasts. How that was any cooler than the devices she'd made him leave behind, she couldn't guess. "So, you like it?"

"Yeah, it's all right."

"Good." She patted his shoulder.

The workmen came in and put his bed together.

Jo reached into the closet and pulled out the giant bag that held his new bedding. He'd picked a green-and-blue plaid almost identical to his old comforter.

A noise like a crackling campfire filled the room as the foreman crumpled the plastic mattress cover into a giant ball. "Never seen anyone with so much brand-new stuff."

Jo's heart rattled like an alarm bell against her ribs, but she held her face placid. "Yeah. We lost everything. In a fire.Had to buy all new."

"That's awful." He frowned. "Hope insurance paid for all that."

"Yep." No such luck. She'd had to liquidate Alex's retirement fund.

The deliverymen finished by midafternoon and drove off, leaving Jo with a furnished house, a surly teenager, and an empty heart. She walked to the doorway of his room. "You want to go down to the mall and pick up some new clothes?"

He shrugged. His suitcase lay atop the brand-new bedspread. A dresser drawer sat open, and he carelessly tossed things from the suitcase into it.

When they fled, she had allowed only one suitcase each. "We could do it tomorrow, if you want."

"Whenever.Doesn't matter." He slapped the suitcase closed, and turned to the drawer, intent on the precise arrangement of everything therein. He looked at her, then the drawer, then slammed it shut. Hiding something. "You wanna go now? I got shoes on and everything."

She pushed past him and opened the drawer. Socks, boxers, T-shirts…the glint of brass. Her hand dove down to the bottom and came up with a picture frame no bigger than her hand. Alex.

"Mom, please…" Derek's voice cracked.

She shook her head, studying one last time those keen, dark eyes and his sweet face. Tears spilled down her cheeks and onto the glass. "I'm sorry." She rushed down the hallway toward the kitchen.

"Mom, no. Please!"

She pulled the back off the frame, removed the photo, and grabbed the matchbox.

All pretense of adulthood fell away as Derek leaned on the counter and wept like a little boy.

Holding the photo in one trembling hand and a lit match in the other, Jo set the photo on fire. The paper curled and blackened and popped, and she dropped it into the stainless steel sink. Flames ravaged Alex's image—real flames, not the false fire she'd invented as a cover story.

Derek pounded the countertop. "It's not fair!"

"I know. I know, sweetie. It's not. None of it's fair. But no one can know. We can't have any evidence." Nothing of the old life could remain, not one bit. Nothing that might connect her and her son to the men who murdered her husband.

Kristen Stieffel

Kristen Stieffel is a writer and freelance editor specializing in speculative fiction. She has edited a variety of projects, including business nonfiction and Bible studies but is a novelist at heart and edits both general and Christian fiction. Her website features articles about writing and editing: kristenstieffel.com

Twelve Steps Forward

Alyssa, my petite fourteen-year-old daughter, was fighting me again. Friday morning chores were the worst. I wasn't a harsh parent but it ticked me off when Alyssa sneered whenever I gave her instructions.

"I already cleaned my room, Dad." Alyssa bit her words and shut her bedroom door behind her.

"If you don't change your sheets and make your bed, I promise I'll ground you," I said from the hallway.

Before my wife died eighteen months ago, Alyssa and I were best buddies. She was grieving, I got it. So was I. Now, with just the two of us, she picked on my drinking, I ragged on her sloppiness.

Being angry at Alyssa wasn't the best way to start my Fridays. I struggled through lunches Monday through Wednesday without wine. Thursdays I had a glass or two with my mid-day meal before returning to my law office.

Fridays I'd have vodka at noon and throughout the afternoon. I usually had no appointments on Fridays, but occasionally Barbara, my secretary, thought someone was so important she scheduled an appointment in spite of my drinking.

Today, Barb really pulled a doozey. I came back to the office about two o'clock. Using the back entrance I slid into my personal suite without being seen. I sat in my chair and got comfortable. My phone buzzed.

"Mr. Black, your appointment is here."

"I'm not expecting anyone."

"Mr. Cahill said he couldn't wait 'til Monday."

"See if I can meet him tomorrow for lunch." I didn't need another embarrassing time with my biggest client and oldest friend.

"I need you today," Dan Cahill bellowed into Barb's phone. "I don't care if you've been drinking. Sober up." Dan burst through the door and stood over my desk, face flushed, tears cascading down his cheeks.

"Marie is leaving me. She said she's had it with all my so-called business trips and bar escapades."

Dan shoved the chair in front of my desk, dropped his bulk into the overstuffed cushion and slammed his hands on its arms

I stood, eased the door shut, and returned to my seat.

"What's going on, Dan?"

"She just called me at the bar for God's sake."

Years ago Dan started a brake shop in a small garage and built it into a chain worth millions. Dan also owned Cahill's Perch, the most popular bar in town. It served as his unofficial office.

"You're at the bar a lot. Besides, she's threatened you before. What's the big deal now?"

"The big deal is – she called from Gloria's apartment."

Dan pulled out a handkerchief from his back pocket and wiped his raspberry-colored eyelids and sweaty forehead. His fingers trembled.

"Putting my girlfriend in the apartment above the restaurant wasn't my smartest idea."

The sun sent shards of light through my office window and streaked bright lines across Dan's bulbous face. He blew his nose and wiped away more tears. We had been through too many legal battles and had become too close as friends for him to be ashamed of showing his emotions.

"What do you want from me? You really don't want to lose Marie. But you don't want to lose Gloria?"

"I don't want to lose Marie, period. I'll do anything to keep her."

Dan put his face in his hands.

"Please, talk some sense into her. She likes you. At least she used to before you became a freakin' drunk."

"What? I don't drink anymore than you do, and I don't see clients when I'm drinking."

I reached for a cigarette, but didn't light it.

"I've always been nice to Marie. She doesn't think I'm a drunk."

"Right, no more than she thinks I am."

I pulled my tie down and unbuttoned my shirt collar.

"Last year I talked to Marie. I convinced her to stay if you agreed to marriage counseling. We got along just fine then."

"Yeah, you did a great job. She said you were half the problem with our constant meetings over a bottle."

"We meet over a bottle because we meet at his bar, I said. If she thinks that of me, and I see her now, it will only prove her point. I'll go see her in the morning and straighten this out."

"I can't wait 'til morning. She's moving her things out of our house tonight."

Dan stood and leaned his large frame over my desk, glowering.

"Take a shower, change your stinking clothes, and go begging for me. My future depends on it, and maybe yours, too.

I hadn't built a half-million-dollar law practice by letting people push me around. Then again, Dan and I had become like brothers...and he annually paid my firm six figures. I stood up from my chair, grabbed my suit jacket and smoothed my hair. Dan was right. My jacket smelled like booze. So did I.

"I'm going home and take a shower. I'll call you after I see Marie." Dan left by the front door, I stumbled out the back and drove home.

My shower was hot and steamy. I dried myself off and looked in the bathroom mirror. An out-of-shape, wine-soaked, middle-aged man stared back. Funny how you can slide up to a mirror and if you take just the right angle, you look pretty good. Today I saw all the wrong angles, and not in only my face. I saw how I'd let my life's standards slide lower and lower.

Later, outside Marie's door, I hesitated before pushing the button. Marie was a decent person, a good mother, and a help building Dan's businesses in the early days. She also was kind to me and my daughter when my wife died. Had our relationship gone wrong?

Could I convince Marie to give Dan another chance? Could I redeem myself in her eyes as well? Would she even let me try? I worked up my courage and rang the bell.

She opened the door and stared at me.

"Hi Marie, may I speak to you for a moment?" Tears glistened in my eyes but didn't fall. I shuffled my feet and looked down while an old friend greeted me with kindness and grace. We spoke for over an hour.

***

The next morning, I stood in my laundry room watching Alyssa load the washer. I spoke to the back of my daughter's head. "Alyssa, come here, honey. I need to tell you something."

Half in surprise, Alyssa turned to me. She held her dirty clothes in her hands like she used to hold her baby dolls. "What? I'm cleaning my clothes."

"Please? Come here a second."

"Dad, I'm busy." She spun around to face me.

I reached for her, hugged her tight and kissed her strawberry blonde hair.

"I love you, you know, even if you are a mess." I chuckled.

Alyssa softened in my arms.

"I love you too, Dad." She nuzzled her head on my shoulder.

"Starting today, my friend Dan and I are going to our first AA meeting. You clean up your room; I'll clean up my act." Tears filled my eyes for the second time in two days.

"You okay, Dad?"

"Couldn't be better baby, couldn't be better."

Tom Swartz

Tom Swartz lives in Casselberry Florida with his wife, Pearl. He is on the Board of Directors of the FWA and is a member of the Seminole County Writers Group and a Novel Group of Writers. Tom's stories have appeared in volumes five and six of the Collection contest.

Let Him Go

Instinctively, I knew the hour was almost up although I refused to look at the clock on the wall, as if time would freeze if nobody was monitoring it. The door to the room opened slowly, the person behind it clearly reluctant to enter. The peaceful feeling emanating from my soul—the feeling my newborn son evoked in me—evaporated, replaced by the weight of dread, pressing me down into the mattress, slowing my movements, dulling my senses. My social worker, Nancy, who smelled of cigarettes masked with a flowery body spray, tiptoed over to the hospital bed where I sat clutching my baby to my chest, shaking my head, no.

"Jacob."

I whispered his name to him like a secret, wanting desperately to have something sacred between us. I picked the name Jacob not to be cute, naming the boy after his father, Jake. After all, this boy would never get to meet his father. It was more that, although Jake wasn't interested in laying eyes on his perfect, handsome

or not.

What I couldn't understand was this: how would I make it through tomorrow? How would I wake up, my body void of the baby I was so used to sharing myself with, and start over without him? I had spent the last two hundred and sixty-eight days with Jacob. I talked to him. I held my hand over my belly constantly, hoping that he could feel love through my touch. I sang to him and played classical music for him each day simply because I had read somewhere that it could increase intelligence. I ate all the right foods and gave up caffeine and exercised every day just to make sure I was doing everything I could to send him into the world armed with a healthy body and mind. After all, it was the only contribution I could make to his future. It would be up to his adoptive parents to take him the rest of the way.

Without Jacob, it would be as if arctic water was thrown over everything I knew to be true in life, dousing colors and smells, diluting emotions, distorting time. It would change not only the way the world looked and operated, but the way I processed things in my mind. Emotions such as happy or excited, surprise or love even—reactions I used to take for granted every day—would all blur into one monotone feeling of sedation where I knew I would reside for quite some time.

"Miss Warren?" Nancy spoke softly, as if she knew that anything louder than a whisper would shatter the fragile façade I was clinging to like a shield.

I didn't answer. Maybe ignoring her would make her go away, or buy me some more time. Every second with my baby was precious.

"Bella? I'm so sorry but, it's time."

Nothing.

"Miss Warren? The adoptive parents have been waiting for hours. They came when you were in labor. It's time, sweetheart. I'm so sorry dear. I need to take him now."

The social worker reached for him, hesitantly, as if I may bite her arm if she moved too quickly. I may have actually considered it if I thought it would help. I wasn't ready. True, I wouldn't sign the consent to adopt until the next day, upon my discharge from the hospital, but that was irrelevant. This moment, the moment my son was physically removed from my arms, was the end for Jacob and me.

"Please? No. I need longer. I don't want to do this." I could hardly see through the tears streaming down my face, distorting my vision of Jacob, falling onto his swaddled body. I brought him up to my face, nuzzled his tiny neck, stroked his soft skin with my cheek, filled my lungs with his sweet scent. I listened to his grunts and squeaks with delight, savoring his voice, talking back to him in our own sweet language.

Nancy granted me this gift, a few more precious moments, without protest. She moved to the other side of the room, allowing me to have space and privacy in these final moments. I whispered again to Jacob, not wanting her to hear me pouring my heart out to him; if she had heard me, it would somehow make this time less special.

Because I too was adopted, I knew the questions that would plague him as time wore on. The ones that would keep him up at night and surface in his mind over and over with age. I wanted to answer those uncertainties for him. "Jacob. I am your mother and I love you more than life. In fact, the word love seems too short and simple to explain the way I feel about you. I adore you. I cherish you. I treasure you; and because of that, I must do what's best for you." I ran my finger along the perimeter of his face, tracing every inch, reading his bones like brail, burning his image into my brain.

"One day you will wonder why I didn't keep you, why I chose to give you up instead of struggling through, like many teenaged parents do. The word, 'enough' will circle through your mind. You weren't good enough. I didn't love you enough. You weren't important enough. But please Jacob, know this: it is me who isn't enough for you."

Those were the last words I would ever speak to my son. I was unable to suppress the sadness flowing though me, thick as oil. I had more I needed to tell him but the words were lodged in my throat, solidifying into a mass too heavy to move.

Nancy instinctively knew it was time. I was letting go in the only way I could. She placed a hand on the top of my hand, a kind gesture that said she understood how difficult it must be to hand over my baby to a stranger, to another family, to another life, apart from me.

She asked if she should send my mom in to be with me, but I shook my head, no. I wanted to fall apart all on my own, in private, unguarded and unjudged until the tears had all been shed and this feeling had completely drained me. I wanted to be left alone with the punishment of my thoughts, without anyone trying to comfort me or rationalize my decision.

And so, I squeezed Jacob to my chest once more and did what I had to do.

I let him go.

And tomorrow, one way or another, I would start over without him.

Aimee Taylor

Aimee Taylor has a B.S. Degree in Criminal Justice and a lengthy career in the field of child welfare. She is now an author of two novels woven together with threads of experience as a case manager for abused children and her own family history as a fostered and adopted child.

A Soul Revised

I'd managed to obtain most of my life's dreams by the age of thirty-two. I'd become a respected adult with two children and a husband, a great job, a house, two cars, and lots of toys, feeling in charge, feeling invincible. I had no idea that this was the year I would become an orphan. Death left no hidden clues, gave no notice, just silently slid into my mother's heart and stopped it in the dark of night.

My world imploded and the pieces scattered out to the universe, each holding a fragment of memory, an image of my mother, and the light of my life. I was thrust into an alternate reality. It was now gone, the light that once warmed my heart. My world no longer held the same meaning. It crumbled. I crumbled. I wanted this sphere to stop; just stop and let me catch up to the spinning in my head. But it did not. I was forced to walk in the shadows of this thing I called life. I became robotic, smiling at the appropriate times, cooking, cleaning, driving kids to school, picking them up, doing groceries, and everything else that resembled normality.

No one knew; no one saw the apocalypse that exploded within my soul leaving it in the dominion of perdition. My mother was gone. Time wasn't healing me like everyone said it would. I died and my corpse was rotting from the inside out, yet I'd been cursed to walk among the living. My mother was gone. And no one knew, no one saw. My pain was mine alone.

Days turned into weeks, into months, and closed in on a year. Still I existed in the ashen grayness of my smoldering realm. My subconscious would speak now and again. It would tell me that this isn't the life my mother would have wanted for me. It would say that I needed to let go and move on. It would say a lot of things. I would yell back, "This isn't a choice! Do you think I want to exist like this? In this devastation?In this darkened despair?" But there was light outside the walls I had built. I could see its faint glow rise in the distance through the vibrations of my children's laughter…and I wanted to touch it.

I pulled up a rock from the cracked pavement in my soul and stared around at the remnants of the earthquake that happened so long ago and made a choice. I would rebuild. I would not be able to rebuild what I had, my mother was gone and that would not change. But with some revisions I felt I could come close. And so I began to practice. I started small at first, a smile that I let reach my eyes or a genuine wish for someone's good day, and I worked my way up to a laugh. It startled me at first; I didn't even believe it came from me. And so I did it again. It made me feel warm. And so I did it again.

With my head down I did something I hadn't done in quite a while. I prayed. I prayed to God to give me strength. I prayed to my mother to stand by me and guide me. And then I went to work clearing a pathway through the shards of my life, and when I finally stopped and looked up there it was. I'd made it to the boundary I'd so carefully built. These walls were sturdy, my workmanship that to be proud of. They wouldn't come down easily. I looked back and knew I had to try.

It took another several months before I was able to break a hole through that wall. How I knew I'd broken through was the morning my daughter kissed me…and I felt it. I felt her tiny arms around my neck, her soft lips upon my cheek, and her giggle in my heart. I'd made it.

The revisions I'd made set a strong foundation for the new life I would lead. Instead of anger I chose understanding; instead of emptiness I chose to be Spirit filled; instead of sadness I chose to be happy.

The death of my mother turned out to be a precursor to other heartache that was right around the corner. It came in the form of a divorce. But the revisions I'd made to my life gave me the strength to stand strong. My heart broke once again, but this time I didn't crumble. I allowed myself an appropriate amount of time to grieve, but I did it in the light. My new found philosophy - told to me by a dear friend, told to her by her dear mother - is: I will not let anything or anyone steal my joy.

I pray to meet my low points with courage and strength of heart. I pray that I never again step out of the light. But mostly, I pray.

Dee Ann Waite

Dee Ann Waite shares with her audience an intense interest in psychology that has led to her third psychological thriller. As a former private investigator with military and FBI ties, the military and law have been strong influences and play out heavily in her writing.

Kitchen Magic

It's all over – my marriage and my job! I could care less about him, but I'm grieving the loss of my dream job.

When Sid Diamond and I met in college, he pursued me and I let myself fall for him. I now see that it wasn't me he loved, but the challenge I presented and the skills I brought to his family business.

We worked together at their upscale restaurant, the "Blue Diamond". His business skills and my culinary talents were the real marriage made-in-heaven. When he dumped me, his daddy told me my services were "no longer required."

The end of the partnership was inevitable. I was smart enough to save my money for the proverbial rainy day. It was now pouring and I opened my umbrella.

I decided to take a long cruise, not caring where it went, having no interest in men or romance. I needed time and space to decide what was next for me.

Splurging on a balcony cabin, I soon discovered this was my favorite respite every afternoon as I looked out over the water, relaxing and just enjoying the present.

One evening I was invited to the prestigious Captain's Table. Captain Basetti was much younger than I expected, probably no more than forty. He was quite handsome, but I avoided eye contact. No men for me!

"Mrs. Diamond, you are a true culinary goddess," the Captain said. "I had the privilege of dining on your elegant cuisine when I was in Miami last year."

"Thank you. However, I am not affiliated with the Blue Diamond any longer."

"I was under the impression that it was a family run establishment."

"It is. I'm not family anymore."

Well, that was embarrassing and I was pretty snippy. I guess I was still raw inside. After dinner, he followed me to the Lounge.

"Mrs. Diamond, I'm sorry if I embarrassed you."

I turned and looked into his emerald green eyes. "It's all right. My husband and I are divorced and I no longer have any connection to the restaurant."

"What a shame. You truly are a genius in the kitchen. My meal was outstanding; creative and delicious." His smile was warm and friendly.

KITCHEN MAGIC

"I hope you are enjoying your cruise," he continued.

"It's great. I love the feeling of peacefulness the ocean gives me."

"Do you enjoy eating great food as much as cooking it?" he asked with a smile.

I was anxious to try their gourmet restaurant. "Actually I do. I'm going to Nicola's tomorrow."

"Wonderful! She's a fabulous chef." He paused for a moment. "I know this is rather awkward, but would you mind if I join you tomorrow evening? I would be happy to have Nicola take you on a tour of her kitchen."

I had to consider the implications. It's not a date. It's just sharing a meal and I have been leading the life of a loner. The best part is that I would get to see inside the kitchen.

Why not? "I would enjoy having your company, Captain."

"It's Sam. What time is your reservation?"

"It's 8:30pm. And, it's not Mrs. Diamond anymore. I'm Olivia Ellis now."

He lifted my hand and kissed it. "Tomorrow it is, Olivia."

Later, I sat on my balcony watching the foam create intricate patterns on the surface of the water, deep in thought. Little did I know that tomorrow would trigger the first of several life changing events.

Sam was waiting for me outside Nicola's. He was so handsome I knew I had to be on my guard. Once we entered Nicola's I almost moaned in delight. It was elegant and her food was divine.

Sam was attentive and entertaining as we enjoyed an expensive wine. Nicola came over to our table and kissed him on the cheek.

"Absolutely wonderful as usual," he said as he hugged Nicola. "This is my friend Olivia Ellis, the Executive Chef form Miami."

"Former Chef," I corrected, still feeling a little bitterness.

"It's a pleasure Olivia. Would you like to explore my kitchen?"

This was too good an opportunity to pass up. "I would love to!"

Nicola's kitchen was an absolute dream. "I absolutely love it! I'm ready to don my chef's jacket and start cooking my Chicken Ellis."

I returned to our table to finish the wine with Sam. "So, what do you think of my sister's kitchen?"

I was startled. "Nicola is your sister?"

"That she is."

"Why it's a dream in there," I said like a star-struck teenager.

"Nicola is getting married this fall and is looking for someone to take over and manage the kitchen."

I didn't know what to say. Was it a statement or a job offer?

"Is there any way you would consider coming to live on the ship and manage Nicola's?"

Here it was, the opportunity of a lifetime! Living on a luxury ship and cooking in an elegant kitchen.

My eyes filled with tears. "Yes, I think that would be a wonderful idea. It's like starting over."

Sam and I spoke with Nicola. I hugged them both and plans were made for me to start in the fall. There was nothing keeping me in Miami so I packed my bags and sublet my apartment.

It soon felt like I had run the kitchen for years. Life was pure bliss. I saw Sam almost daily and we occasionally enjoyed a late dinner in Nicola's. I lived for those evenings where we could talk, laugh and relax.

Nicola and her husband cruised with us during Christmas week. She was delighted with how things were going. I was comfortable in my new life and very fulfilled, well almost. I was falling for Sam. I know he cared for me, but he never led me to believe he wanted a relationship.

On Christmas Eve, I was invited to dinner with Sam, Nicola and Peter. "I absolutely love how you have made Nicola's your own. I have to say I didn't think it could get even better, but it has."

"Why don't we go down to Nicola's for a nightcap?" Sam suggested with a sly smile on his face.

"Sounds like a great idea," Nicola agreed conspiratorially.

The restaurant was dark as we entered. The lights flashed on as the staff yelled surprise!

I was confused. Sam put his arms on my shoulders and turned me so I could look at the banner over the door. I saw that it was no longer Nicola's – it was Olivia's.

I couldn't speak or even see clearly though my tears. Peter and Nicola discretely walked into the kitchen.

"You deserve this. It was Nicola's idea and I whole heartily agreed. This is yours now."

Sam took my hand and kissed it as he had done the first night we met. "I hope there is an opportunity for us as well."

I could feel a crack in the ice that surrounded and protected my heart as I looked up into his eyes. I tilted my head and kissed him softly on the lips.

"I believe anything is possible now."

Sharon K. Weatherhead

Sharon Weatherhead has had articles published in national and local publications. She has been a sports writer and currently is a freelance writer and photographer for a regional newspaper group. She is also an accomplished musician and feels that both areas of art complement each other in her writing.

The Forgiveness Test

Here I am, approaching the office of my psychologist, my court-ordered psychologist, hopefully for the last time. Dr. Davis is a nice enough guy, if a little bland, who takes his work very seriously. So I can't really blame him for my distaste at these forced visits. After all, I'm the one who tried to commit suicide; I'm the one who, after a short stint in a regular hospital, was sent to a mental hospital for "treatment". Upon my release, Dr. Davis became my weekly penance, as though he were a homework assignment for school.

Has he helped me? I wonder about that again as I climb the flight of stairs to his office and ring the little bell outside his door. I prefer to think that I've helped myself. Now at age twenty-two, I have matured a lot since I came out of the closet when I was just seventeen.

A buzzer unlocks the door and I step into his empty waiting room. Yes, I've come a long way since leaving my childhood home, a place made unbearable by my father's inability to accept my being "different". For not wanting to go out with boys on dates where the night was supposed to end with sweaty, fumbling sex in the backseat of their father's cars. Several of those boys were sons of men my father worked with, dates that I know he set up. Pretty bad to think of your father as your 'pimp', isn't it?

Dr. Davis opens the door to his office and invites me in with his usual half-smile.

"Good afternoon Darla. Is everything good today?"

I paste on my own fake smile. "I'm feeling very good today Doctor. Isn't this supposed to be our last appointment?"

"This is the end of our mandatory visits, yes, but if you feel you should extend our therapy, that can be accommodated." He sits behind his oversized desk, arranging some pens and a notepad off to the side, a show that this is a casual meeting. I've wondered several times though, whether these sessions were recorded. I've tried to surreptitiously glance around for signs of a microphone, not spotting one and then thinking perhaps the whole room was wired for sound.

"Because this may be our last conference, I'd like to review your past depression, to make sure you recognize the danger signs and can move past them without ever considering doing anything drastic again."

I shift uncomfortably in my seat, and try to encapsulate my thoughts into something brief. "Well, you know about the two girlfriends I had, one that I moved in with right after I left home. Carolyn and her friends were into drugs that I didn't want any part of. There were parties all the time and it got hard to avoid it. So, when I met Tansy at the burger place, I knew right away she was gay, and soon we were dating. She hated drugs too, so I felt I'd be safe moving in with her."

I look across at Dr. Davis, and he's following through my file, I guess making sure his notes are complete. I continue, "Shortly after that, my mom was diagnosed with Alzheimers and my father said he needed me at home to help with her. But I couldn't. That was my weakness I guess, a real character fault, that I couldn't be around him. I blame myself for that."

The doctor raises a finger to stop me. "That's where the issue of forgiveness comes in. You would have felt much better at the time if you had been able to forgive him for his actions towards you."

"You have talked about forgiveness in every session we've had. I don't think it helps me at all."

"Ah, but it does. You know that Alcoholics Anonymous has a 12 step process that helps people beat their addiction?" I nod. "Well, helping people overcome depression and desperation has a path to follow as well. The steps involved are all of my own creation, but I firmly believe that a mandatory beginning is to forgive the people that have hurt you. In your father's case, for example, he didn't do those things to cause you any harm; he thought he was helping you, as misguided as his methods were. It's especially important to be able to forgive people whom you love, and who have hurt you." He pauses to let that concept sink in. "Have you also tried to forgive Carolyn and Tansy?"

"I guess I could forgive Carolyn, 'cause she just didn't know any better. But Tansy caused me to lose my job, put the blame on me for stealing when she was the thief. Then right around that time, my mother was put into an assisted living place and got much worse. I'd go visit her and she wouldn't even know who I was. She had become helpless and I didn't know who to blame. But the breaking point came when I found out that Tansy had a boy friend. She was sleeping with a guy! That's when I thought there was no future for me – a lonely lesbian with no family for support. No job – no money – no real friends."

Dr. Davis puts down the file and looks at me. "That summarizes it well for me. But I still say that forgiving the people who have hurt you will cleanse you as well. Will help to keep you from having such hopelessness about your future."

I rise from my chair and begin to wander around the room, touching the edge of his desk, the green shaded lamp, the chair where I had been seated. His eyes follow me as though wondering if this is a changed person, or still an unstable one.

I turn quickly to face him. "Well, I'm not worried, doctor. I've met someone; a woman older than me. She's helped me to see the possibilities in my life. I have a job; I've enrolled in the community college and with her help, I've found a small studio apartment that I'm decorating. I'm learning to cook; I got a small stereo and bought some CDs of stuff I like. This is the new me you're looking at. I'm starting over, and with her help, the sky's the limit. As a matter of fact, this past weekend we went down to Boca to this luxury spa and spent some wonderful romantic time together."

"How coincidental," the doctor says. "Which spa did you go to? My wife was at a spa in Boca this past weekend also."

"I know, doctor. She was with me."

Judy Weber

After years in marketing and advertising where her writing skills were devoted to work projects, Judy began writing fiction. Not just fiction, but murder mysteries, one of which was a multiple award winner. Following that came short stories, several of which have been published in FWA Collections and other anthologies.

Florida Youth Writers Program

Starting Over:

Florida Writers Association Youth Collection,

Volume 2

FWA Youth Writers Age Group 10-13

1st Place: Remembrance

I remember the days when the bluebirds would fly,
I'd listen to their melody as they soared by.
In the heat of the midday sun; we joked around—
It was great fun.
We would spend the days slipping through your house,
Jumping, playing video games, moving quiet as a mouse.
We laughed while the sunshine splashed upon the trees,
And the beach waves washed away our sorrows
With an easy ocean breeze.
Life was wonderful and nothing was hurried,
If not for the accident I would've never worried.
One day, I looked over my shoulder
In the screaming winds, pounding rain, and
Hail the size of boulders.
You excused yourself too early, you always tried too hard.
While I sheltered from the storm,
Your life was literally falling apart.

When the storm cleared, I looked around.
There was not a peep from you…not a wink from you…
Not a single sound.
Just like that! You were robbed from me!
Oh, you vanished so quick!
You were gone…you were gone.
The thought made me sick.

After that, my life became as barren as a bone.
Rain clung to my freezing skin as I shivered all alone.
I was shackled in chains! Trapped in this

Great, big, awfully frightening world!

Confounded, dazed and lost.
My voice grew icy with grief; smeared with frost.
Mourning can be bitter—terribly so!
But you shouldn't litter your life with regret, you know.

Make a fresh start and purify your heart.
Get out there! Go anywhere!
Pick up the pieces of the puzzle!
You never know what opportunities
Will come your way!
In time, you'll learn to cope,
Until then, try not to mope.
Always remember the following,
When you're through with sorrow and doddering:
Love can thaw the cold harshness of an icy heart,
Clear the clouds in the thicket of the storm.

Love can erase the pain, the blueness of your day,
So open up your heart to compassion warm.
In remembrance, sweet remembrance of you.

Sarina Patel

Sarina Patel lives in Tampa, FL. With her passion for writing and her dedication to detail, she is always looking to pursue writing books. When she is not writing, you can find Sarina curled up reading, acting, playing the piano. She loves traveling, is an unapologetic foodie, and enjoys performing.

Youth Writers Program
Florida Writers Association

2nd Place: The Wise Cherry

Berry was a cherry who went to the wide open plain where the elders told him never to go. They said he would get eaten or stepped on. But he did anyhow. He ran out to the plain, skipped and hopped around the green grassy area, and ran back home. Every single day he ran back and forth. All of the elders had no idea what he was doing. When he came home out of breath, the elders figured he had been playing tag in the village with his friends since it was the kids' favorite game.

One day, a cherry named Eddie the Tattle-Tale hid in a tree and spied on Berry running out to the plains. Eddie told the elders and by the time Berry returned, he was in trouble. Berry very mad at Eddie. Plus, he felt bad because nobody trusted him anymore. His parents were so ashamed of him. The elders were very disappointed. What on Earth could he do?

He begged and begged the elders and his parents for a second chance, but nobody believed that he was trustworthy anymore.

A week later, he went for a walk in the village to clear his troubled head when came across a house that he had never noticed before. Berry approached the front door, but he felt he was being watched. He slowed and looked around to see if anyone was there. There was no one. He knocked on the door twice then backed away. The door made a creaking noise and opened.

An old overripe cherry stood in front of him. He sounded cranky. "What do you want?"

Berry's eyes widened and he gulped. "M-m-my name is Berry."

"Are you that youngster that ran off into the forest?"

Berry nodded. "Yes."

"Well. Don't just stand there. Come on in."

Berry followed the old cherry into a tidy living room with future made from scraps humans had left behind, like thimbles and bottle caps. The old cherry waved to a cotton ball. "Sit."

Berry sat on the cotton ball.

The old cherry sat across from Berry on a second cotton ball, a torn one. "I know you're looking for something."

"You do? How?"

"I can tell from your expression."

Berry paused and said, "I want to know how to get other cherries to trust me."

The old cherry said, "When I was young, I was very adventurous and I too left the forest just like you." He inhaled and exhaled deeply before starting again. "If you be kind to others, they will be kind to you."

"How do you know?"

"Well," the old cherry said, "it happened to me as well. Just try."

Berry did what the old cherry said. He left the old cherry's cottage with a wave goodbye and strolled down the dirt road to his house. There, he helped his mother set the table and helped his father by cooking dinner.

His parents were very pleased to see that their son had changed. His father asked, "What made you want to be more kind?"

Berry replied, "I met a hermit that told me to be kind to others and they would be kind to me back."

His father told him that what he said was called the golden rule. "But why," he asked, "did you talk to a hermit?"

"I was just walking along and I wanted to know who lived in the broken-down house."

The father said that he knew who lived there.

Berry looked puzzled. "How do you know?"

The father replied, "Well, the old cherry is related to you. He's my Uncle Adventure. So he is your Great Uncle Adventure."

"How come you've never told me about him?"

Dad said, "We were afraid that you would ask more about him. So we never told you that he went out of the woods and got away with it. The elders told us never to tell the children about this incident so that they won't get any ideas of going into the meadows."

The next day, Berry and his parents visited the elders.

Berry told them about how his Great Uncle Adventure did the same thing as he did, but changed his life into being kind and understanding. He explained how the old cherry taught him the golden rule.

Berry's father said, "Everything he said–"

"Was true," his mother finished.

The parents explained how Berry helped them the night before.

They were astonished that Berry found Adventure and learned a very valuable lesson. They immediately scheduled a town meeting that afternoon to tell the town how Berry changed so quickly. And they wanted to make Adventure a very important guy in the history archives.

Some people thought this was nonsense and others thought it was grand. And some didn't know what to say.

The Elders said, "Let's take a vote whether we should let Adventure return to life and no longer ignore him."

The town voted the next day. It was decided that Adventure would no longer be ignored and join into town functions.

That afternoon, Adventure got an invitation to go to a town party for that night. Later that night, everyone was waiting for Adventure to arrive. Adventure came slowly but steadily because he thought it was a trick. When everyone cheered for him he realized it was not a trick but a friendly greeting.

Berry ran up to Adventure and told him, "The town had voted for you to come back into civilized life."

Adventure was stunned. He asked, "Is this true, Berry?"

Others, who heard what Adventure asked, said, "Yes. Yes, it is."

As the night went by everyone was enjoying the party. Soon, Berry got sleepy and had to go to bed. He waved goodbye to Adventure and told him that he would meet him again soon.

The very next day, Berry was out with his family buying food in the market and saw Adventure telling stories to the children. Berry asked, "Are you our new storyteller?"

Adventure replied, "Why yes. The mayor asked me. And I couldn't refuse." Then he said, "I told the children that you were very curious what was out of the forest to the meadow, where I had gone when I was child."

Years later the Elders got some workers to put out a sightseeing tour for children on field trips. The main thing the guides say is, "Two different people ran out to the meadows and risked their life. Their names are Berry and Adventure." This sightseeing tour place was maintained for years to come.

Jaina Hope

Jaina is a central Floridian, attending The Masters Academy in Oviedo. She is a motivated leader among her fellow students, participating in student council functions, volunteering in charity events, and running a successful babysitting business. She is also is an accomplished dancer in both jazz dancing and tap.

Youth Writers Program
Florida Writers Association

3rd Place: Emotion Chaos

Mr. Liam Romain stood in the room of his luxurious Paris house, playing an enticing song on the violin. He was a tall Frenchman with hazel eyes, tufted brown hair, and a curled handlebar mustache. He let out a hiss of frustration as he did a half-note vibrato, instead of a full note. Starting again at the full-note vibrato, E string of Ravel's Tzigane, he had to stop as he forgot to shift to third position.

He sighed as he perched on the jumble of unorganized belongings, the memory of failing the solo performance at St. Ephrem flooding back to him like rainwater after a drought. He shook his head, trying to clear his mind, but a whirl of emotions clouded his thoughts. Fear pricked his heart, as the absence of an audience filled him with nausea. A surge of overwhelm made his head dizzy with sadness.

Standing up again, Liam felt a wave of strong determination flooding his heart. Sucking in a deep breath, he exhaled and began the forte, allegretto, slurs on F major, then mounted the music to C on A, rested, and shifted to third position, in staccato, full-note vibrato metso forte, then switched to pizzicato on A on E, switched, back to arco. At the thirty-first measure, he accidentally changed his strings.

Liam tried again at the pizzicato, but his position was incorrect. He began once more, distracted by the ticking of a grandfather clock and the swish of curtains. The calm beating of his heart slowed his mind, relaxing him and making him long for the brush of people or the bustling crowds of shoppers in Paris.

He let his instincts take over, free and roaming the loud, packed city full of people. Relief swooped over his heart. But as he stared at his beloved violin, a feeling of affection flooded his heart and he felt nothing but the sweet feeling of passion for music, just like the taste of butter cakes. Encouraged, he started from the beginning, and the sound of music thrummed beneath his fingers, filling the air with beautiful tunes, a flow of ringing melody carrying his heart.

The joy of playing, the sensation of doing what he loved, the emotion inside of him rung out in the majestic tune, and a warm feeling spread through his body. But a low murmur of voices outside came to him, almost as if tempting him, and they rang in his head like ghosts, until it was impossible to ignore. It felt like the crowd outside and the crowd at St. Ephrem was hurting his feelings.

He sat down, a sudden whirl of possibilities spinning in his mind, as fear flooded his heart.

Pushing the thought away, he stood up, trying to ignore the frantic fluttering of his heart. "I can do this," his heart seemed to say, and the other part seemed to say. "I can't do this!"

He staggered, confused at the well of emotions, unsure of which to follow. His mind brimming with dark thoughts, his heart over flooded with a mix of emotions that jumbled like a tornado of feelings.

Liam fell, scraping the neck of his violin on his sofa, feeling like his head was about to explode. His heart was thumping allegretto. Like a timer waiting for an nuclear explosion. Thoughts swam hazily through his mind like hostile sharks. He tried to locate his violin, but it was a blurry outline in the midst of his mind.

Forcing himself to focus on the violin, he breathed heavily as the familiar sensations of affection and calmness entered his heart and mind. A clamor of raised voices distracted him as emotions and thoughts began brewing darkly as if a thunderstorm was coming. Shutting his eyes, he clutched his violin and breathed in and out. His thoughts brewed in turmoil and his heart fluttered frantically, like a bluebird's wings. As his emotions swirled in chaos, and his thoughts twisted and turned in a dizzying storm, the voices outside grew louder and more troubled. Liam swiftly clogged his ears with cotton balls and named the fingerings of Ravel's Tzigane to block out the sound outside and his own troubled thoughts and mixed emotions, now so jumbled he could barely describe one from the other.

Inhaling and exhaling deeply, he stood up to play to help him focus, his thoughts buzzing so powerfully now they almost knocked him off his feet. The noise was building outside, and so were his thoughts. They churned hungrily like a thunderstorm, booming sinisterly. His heart lurched sickly, every time he caught a word of the conversation. He closed his eyes, breathing deeply while he weaved through the music, playing quickly and emotionally, trying to ignore the rumbling thoughts and chaotic emotions.

He passed the second page, and relief nearly smothered the chaotic emotion lurking there, but the buzzing thoughts surged over his heart until he felt breathless with fear. A wave of emotions spiraled uncontrollably until his chest started to ache, but he kept going, forcing his mind to concentrate as a sweet sound filled the air in a high-pitched noise

A possibility filled his mind: what if there weren't enough people at the performance? He shook his head to clear his thoughts as fear swallowed his heart and he imagined hundreds of thousands of people seated there, watching in awe. His heart unclenched and he breathed deeply. Stringing his bow dramatically on a low-pitched string, he danced beautifully through a series of quarter notes while the boiling emotion seemed to simmer down and the roaring thoughts dulled to a slow beat.

He breathed in quick shallow breaths, closing his eyes and leaping through the music in swift high-pitched strokes, and the lovely melody rung in the air. His thoughts burned like fire, twisting achingly slow through his mind, while his emotions jumbled together like a pile of disorganized papers. He exhaled, relaxing as tension left his sore muscles, and he successfully reached the third page.

By now his thoughts were clearing, like fog after a sunny day, and his heart thumped slower. Fresh determination surged in his heart. He raced through a series of complex notes, paddling through a soaring rhythm, as he played swift, high-pitched strokes a sweet melody ringing the air and passion flooding his heart. Joy lifted his heart, and enthusiasm showered him in delight as he reached the last page.

Beginning at a steady rhythm, he played deep, slow, low-pitched notes. The graceful tune and majestic melody rung in the air. He felt completely in soothing relaxation as he played quiet, rhythmic notes at a slow tempo, joy carrying his heart on golden wings. Affection for music motivated him as he imagined thousands upon thousands of people gazing at him in wide-eyed astonishment. His thoughts were as clear as pure crystal water and his emotions thumped steadily.

His heart soared.

Yasmin Vuong

Yasmin loved reading since she was in her second grade. She had a very good teacher who supported and encouraged her to develop her reading and writing skills. She's 5th Grade student and she also plays the violin.

Youth Writers Program
Florida Writers Association

FWA Youth Writers Age Group 14-17

1st Place: Terminated

"Your existence has been terminated."

The two Temps seize me and drag me away from the dead lamplighter and into the nearest dank alley Victorian London has to offer. They throw me against the brick wall, and I wince at the rhythmic pulsing in my head.

"He had it comin' for him," I slur.

The man on the right trades a look with his partner. "He's intoxicated, Richards."

Richards narrows his eyes. "You have broken one of the highest rules of the Time Academy."

I blink, the world spinning as I begin to list off the rules ingrained into my head. "I can't marry anyone. I can't give spoilers. And I can't kill anyone." I hold up my hands, palms facing them. "Like I said, he had it comin' for him."

Their mouths are pressed into a firm line, and they regard me coldly.

The nameless man punches something into his watch. "Your existence has been terminated. You are to be relocated in a new time," he says as he presses his watch to mine. The feeling of being sucked into a vacuum overcomes me, muddling my brain.

I'd fall when the world becomes solid once more, if it weren't for the two men holding onto me with a tight grip.

"Where did you take me?"

"Twenty ninety-four," Richards snaps. "There's an entrance to the Time Academy here in Prom. If you screw up again, we'll know sooner this time."

Their grip on me is released, and I fall to the wet metal ground where blue lights are imbedded inside that surge forward. They press their palms to the faces of their watches and are sucked back into the Time Stream.

I spit, rain running off the tip of my nose. The Time Academy. Full of those preppy Temps.

My parents weren't originally supposed to have died. Apparently I used to have a time line with them. The Temps brought my sister and me to the Academy when I was eight. Ten years later—at least I think ten—I've been being sent into the time stream to live out my life normally.

I snort and pull myself to my feet. Normally. If anyone can call it that.

I follow the lights in the ground around the block and to the nearest real estate office. The girl behind the desk looks at me warily, pushing her blue hair with black highlights out of her eyes so she can see me better. She knows I'm a Temp, or Time Traveler. She knows I could alter her potentially blessed time line.

"You look a little young to be working here," I comment.

"Well, my parents needed someone last minute."

From my pocket, I pull out papers that work as my identification for any point in time.

She looks them over. "Mason, correct?" She's probably around my age. Cute. But my existence will be terminated yet again if I involve myself with her.

"Yep."

"I have an apartment a block over available."

"I'll take it." I probably won't be there long anyways.

After I use the false information the Time Academy gave to me with her, I decide to pay them a visit. The Time Academy is always in the same place, but depending on the time period, the style changes. They made it to be located outside of time, or rather throughout time. If one Temp is escaping an angry knight and another Nero burning Rome, once they enter the Time Academy they're both in the Academy at the same time.

I look down at my watch, and search for the entrance on the map. According to this the entrance should be half a mile away. I look around at the crowded downtown district. Yeah, I'm not walking. I press my watch, and I'm sucked through the Time Stream, deposited in front of a white, cylinder skyscraper.

Smirking, I walk up the steps. Considering these people should know about Temps, I'd say that wasn't too much of a spoiler. Once I scan my watch I am allowed entrance. A tingling sensation prickles over my skin as I cross the threshold.

How long does it take for a Time Traveler to cause trouble?

"Mason, right?"

I nod, fist pumping a serf. "Jackson, bring any plagues back with you?"

He rolls his brown eyes. "Last time I saw you, you were in Italy, graffitiing the Sistine Chapel when Michelangelo wasn't looking, two weeks ago."

I smile. Those were some good times. "For me, that was a year ago."

"So are you staying here for a while?"

With a quick glance of the room I see five knights, an ancient Egyptian, some guy in a Toga, and a person dressed like a parrot. Looking back at Jackson, I tilt my head to the side and furrow my eyebrows. "I can't stand an hour with these people, let alone a day." I blink my eyes. Wait. Did I see a parrot? I stare at the parrot before glancing back at Jackson, now raising my eyebrows.

He shrugs. "I don't know."

"Anyways, I figured I'd see how much trouble I caused killing that bloke."

"You killed someone?"

TERMINATED

I roll my eyes. "He practically asked for it."

He looks at me horrified. "Keep your voice down. That's against the rules."

"You're speaking to the guy who was terminated at his wedding right before he said 'I do' to a very lovely princess, and who used the Coliseum to tell the Romans about how the Solar System works."

He rubs his face. "I don't know why they keep letting you out into the Time Stream."

"Mason!"

I grimace before plastering a smile on my face and turning around, holding my arms open wide. "Jessie."

She hugs me. "It's so good to see you here."

I pull back and look at my sister with her black hair pulled back in a low bun—not a hair out of place. Her uniform has not a wrinkle to be found, and her numerous badges and medals glisten in my face. My sister.The gem of the Time Academy.

"What are you doing here?" she asks smiling.

"You know, I thought I'd start—"

Her face drops. "You got terminated again, didn't you?"

I scratch my head. "Anything new with you?"

Her smile turns smug. "I was promoted Commanding Officer on missions."

I place my hands on her arms and squeeze. "That's amazing. I'm so, so happy for you."

She shakes her head, sighing at my falseness.

I glance at Jackson at my side who's brushing off his muddy tunic, not making eye contact with my sister.

"Mason," her voice is cold—disapproving. "Don't mess this up for me. Just try to be a decent Temp." Her blue eyes are unsympathetic as she gives me a final look and leaves.

A decent Temp...

"Mason, don't," Jackson warns.

I type my destination into my watch. "They should've saved my parents." I press down, and my body lands in the real estate office in front of the blue haired girl. "Hi."

She tilts her head to the side. "Hi?"

Let's see how long I last.

"How'd you like to go on a date?"

Mikaela Bender

A fan of fangirling, Mikaela decided to take her love of reading and characters and create her own stories. Currently a senior in High school, she is planning to study either English or Communications in college to prepare her for a job as an Acquisitions Editor.

Youth Writers Program
Florida Writers Association

2nd Place: Midnight

Mallory gritted her chattering teeth as she stepped across the snow-covered ground. Her whole body was numb, protected from the cold only by her pajamas, and all she could think was how thankful she was it wasn't snowing. The forest was uncomfortably empty around her, lit by the full moon. The trudge of her footsteps was the only sound she heard.

She checked her watch: 11:40. Only twenty minutes left. She should have left the house an hour ago, clad in proper snow gear, but she'd closed her eyes for just a moment and accidentally fallen asleep. Now she just had to hope luck was on her side.

It wasn't long till she saw what she was looking for, only a dozen yards in front of her: the figure of a young girl, her pink nightdress and copper hair standing out against the white and black of the woods.

Mallory's breath hitched and the girl began to slowly turn around—and then Mallory blinked and the girl was gone. But the sight galvanized her, and she continued her walk with renewed strength.

A few minutes later Mallory saw the girl again, stepping out from behind a tree only to disappear behind another a moment later. Nearly-formed tears stung at Mallory's eyes. She was so close.

Then Mallory saw the girl out of the corner of her eye, skipping along only just over an arm's length away. Pulse pounding, Mallory extended her hand to the girl—and the girl tumbled into a ditch, disappearing the moment she hit the ground.

Mallory stood there a moment, breathing heavy, feeling as if she'd just run a marathon. She checked her watch again: 11:51. She was running out of time.

She took a step forward and—

—The girl was standing in front of her, gazing up at Mallory with lifeless eyes.

A mass of emotion pressing at her throat, Mallory stared down at the face that had haunted her nightmares for so many years. She hadn't forgotten a single detail.

"Corinne?" she finally choked out.

The girl remained quiet, her body unnaturally still. Mallory hardly felt she could blink; the girl's dead stare was mesmerizing.

"I'm sorry, Corinne." Stray tears fell down Mallory's face as she crouched down to the girl's level. "I should have been there for you. I'm so sorry."

They stared at each other a moment longer and then, slowly, ever so slowly, the girl's eyes closed and she nodded her head.

Mallory's eyes gave out and she blinked and the girl was gone.

She let out her held breath in a ragged gasp. The forest felt empty around her, even emptier than it had been before she saw Corinne. The emptiness wasn't just in the forest: the burning weight that had lived inside her since Corinne's death was gone. Now a hollow resided there, exhilarating in its possibility.

Corinne. Thank God. Mallory had waited years for the meeting of the full moon and New Year's Eve, hoping for this chance to see her. Now she might finally feel at peace.

She checked her watch. It was 11:54; six minutes to get out of the forest.

The forest seemed darker on the way back, the shadows deeper and more foreboding. She was once again feeling the cold, too, its icy fingers reaching to her core. Shivering was quickly becoming a way of being for her, an immutable part of her existence.

She needed to go faster than she was if she were to make it out in time, but she was so cold that it was all she could do to keep her feet moving. She kept her arms crossed, vigorously rubbing them in a desperate attempt to stay warm. It would be midnight any moment now.

The air seemed to snap and Mallory froze in her tracks. She exhaled, wide eyes scanning the forest around her, and she noticed her breath made no cloud. When she breathed in, the air burned colder than it had been.

Faint whispers entered her ears, worming their way into her head. She stood there, listening as they grew louder until finally she could make out the words.

Stay with us. Don't leave us. Don't go.

She caught movement out of the corner of her eye, but when she turned her head nothing was there. The whispers just kept repeating, crawling under her skin.

Movement again, and this time when Mallory turned to look she saw a face, inches away from hers.

She yelped and fell back onto her rear. A figure stood in front of her, human-shaped but formed of sticks and bark wrapped tightly together. Its face was a plate of bark standing on top of a twig neck, its features carved on just deep enough to be visible.

Mallory stared up at the creature, fear wrenching her gut. The creature's bark head tilted to the side and the whispers grew louder still, filling Mallory's ears, overlapping one another.

We want you/Stay in the forest/Don't leave us/Stay with us

"No!" Mallory scrambled backward, gasping at the snow's cold. The creature moved forward each time she blinked, keeping an unchanging distance between them.

Don't go/We want you/Stay with us/Stay in the forest

Mallory's back thudded against a tree and she pushed herself to her feet, forcing herself to stare the creature in its carved eyes. "Just let me go!"

Its head tilted again and the whispers entered Mallory's thoughts, drowning out her protests. She screamed, squeezing her eyes shut, trying desperately to block out the now-screaming whispers. They rushed through her body, filling the newfound hollow inside her—and an instinct within it triggered and she punched out, connecting with the creature's head.

Instantly, all was silent. She let out a sobbing gasp and cracked her eyes open. The creature was nowhere to be found; Mallory was once again alone in the forest.

Achingly she pushed herself off the tree and regained her bearings. After ensuring she was indeed alone, she checked her watch once more. 12:05. New Year's Day.

Tyler Vest

Tyler has been writing since age 12, exploring unique fantasy and sci-fi themes through novels, short stories, and flash fiction.

Youth Writers Program
Florida Writers Association

3rd Place: Me, Myself and Time

I hid behind a tree and used the tech watch given by Arnold as she ran away from me. I caught up to her and with a flash of lights; I was paralyzed with fear on what I would open my eyes to see. While between time wrap I thought to myself, how did I get in this predicament? Is it a sign that I should try starting my life over? Before I could do anything, she ran quickly to ask for directions to the red door building. Just this morning, I would have never thought that this would ever happen. I better go and warn them. As I ran the usual route, I thought back to earlier. "Come on, when have my calculations ever been wrong?" "Well..." I told my twin brother Isadore. "Oh shut up, that was one time." My brother was across from me at the round cafe table we shared in the small bakery in New Zealand. "But hear me out Indigo! I found a way to make copies of ourselves. Imagine! We could be at the mall or the arcade while our copies are doing our school work at home. They have the same mind capacity and DNA genetics just like us! Just come into my lab and we can try it out." "If by lab you're referring to Arnold's parents' basement then no." "Come on! You always drag me out with your friends and do all of these social events, but you never come to any science expos or Mega Cons with me!" "Fine, I'll go, alright!" I'm older as you can tell. We walked to Arnold's house. Well, I was walking, and Isadore bolted to the red door. He's a red head with circular glasses with the perfect stereotype character of a nerd.

Our parents did not care where we go or how long we stayed out as long as they saw us physically twice a day. I know our parents are weird, they were hippies in the 70s, and they believed that we should go with our free will and all that folly. We soon arrived at the one-story building, and my brother just barged in. "Hi Mrs. Pandor and Mr. P, it's me and my sister," Isadore called out. "I haven't seen your sister in a long time. "Come in darling!" Mrs. Pandor told me. I took couple steps towards her. "You've grown so much, sweetie! Go on ahead with the boys! They've made so much progress." "Okay. Thank you for watching Isadore all those times and making him feel at home! Bye Mr. and Mrs. Pandor." My brother has dyslexia and

ADHD, and that's why he is such a whiz at science. He gets so excited by the many formulas he has to memorize and the different projects he can create.

We took the wooden old staircase to get down to the basement. Arnold was there, and his hair shot up like a porcupine. "I finally got the right amount of energy voltage tags for the time warp!" he blurted out. "Really!" My brother proclaimed. "Okay, Indi, we gotta do this now. Just walk through the metal portal and out will come two of you. It's painless; we tested it on Arnold's gerbil." "Umm. Okay." I went along with them. I knew this wasn't gonna work, but it's true what Isadore said, I do make him go along with me, but I never hang out with him doing activities he would enjoy.

I braced myself as I slowly walked through the circular 6-foot portal with my eyes closed. "Mom and Dad, come quickly!" Arnold hollered. "Oh my gosh! Indi!" I heard his voice faintly. I opened my eyes. All around me were crowds of people in pastel and white colors. Men dressed in old fashion sailor attire and women in old fashioned dresses. "Why are you just standing around?" asked a random sailor with two medals on his hat. "Huh?" His screaming in my ears was making me deaf. "Haven't you heard?! The wars' over! We defeated Japan!" he shouted as he ran off into the festive crowd. Hmmm! So my brothers' machine sent me to a Broadway play on V-J Day in New York? "Boo!" arms touched my shoulders in a shocking manner making me jump. I turned around and came face to face with me. "What...how..." I murmured. "It's me silly!" the fake Indigo said. "Don't you just love the 1940s? I never realized how exciting this V-J Day is!" "The real 1940s?" I questioned dumbfounded. "Duh! Well anyway, I have to go! Bye!" she said and skipped quickly away from me. "Wait!" I shouted, but she never heard me. I ran after the figure with the same face as mine. She stopped at the crosswalk, and I grabbed her hand. "That's not nice!" she said in an angry and aggressive voice. She kicked me and ran away. When I finally caught up with my clone, she was looking around before entering a mysterious car. I hid behind the tree hoping she wouldn't see me.

"Yes, year of 2015 at the red building. Remember I'm going to go to her universe, capture the scientists and make them do it. Then, I'll send word for you to send the force of Japan after them." in her hand was a watch. She was clicking buttons and soon I started seeing the light that separates the different years. I ran behind her so that I too can go back to where I came from and defeat my evil twin...triplet, cloned person. "Get away!" she said in a thunderous voice.

Soon, all went blank, and I neither heard nor felt anything. When I finally opened my eyes, my body was on the ground. Maybe the time watch can't transport two people at a time. I slowly got up, and my head was beating with pain, and my body was sore from the hard hit. Her figure slowly faded into focus as I saw the clone run to find out where the house is. "Gotta get there before" I muttered to myself. I ran the usual route I take for cross country. When I reached the Pandor's household, the door was wide open, and it was silent. I braced myself to what was awaiting my presence.

Jade Browne

Jade Browne is a high school student in Winter Garden. She enjoys writing, drawing, music, softball, and countless other activities. She lives with her parents, and her dog, Princess.

Youth Writers Program
Florida Writers Association

Honorable Mention: Hope for a New Year

"10!, 9!, 8!, 7!, 6!, 5!, 4!, 3!, 2!, 1!, HAPPY NEW YEARS!!!"The crowd went crazy and the famous New Year's ball dropped. Everyone smiled and chatted, forgetting their troubles of the past year in favor of the new year, and for many of them, a new start. George Winstel leaned forward in his dark blue robe, reached for the remote, and turned the TV off, silencing the cheerful crowd. He took a shaky sip of water before shutting the lights off and lying down.

George laid there for a long time, wide awake, remembering his last talk with Debbie. She had been lying there on the hospital bed, telling him she knew her time was almost up. He had been crying and denying her sickness and Debbie had ended up comforting him. George would always remember the last words Debbie had spoken to him. "George, I love you, and I know that you love me too. However, I need you to move on once I pass away. There are only a few weeks until Christmas and the New Year. I don't want to hold you back. I want you to have hope for the New Year."

Knock, knock, knock.George awoke to the sound of someone knocking at his apartment door, and sat up quite drowsily, debating whether or not he should answer the door. It was probably just another neighbor or old friend that had heard the devastating news, and was here to give their apologies for his loss. George didn't want to hear it, though. None of them could bring his beloved Debbie back.

A key turned in the doorknob, and a girl entered the apartment. "Dad?" Jenna called out meekly. George sat up and lazily walked into the main room, gladly accepting the coffee Jenna handed him.

"Happy New Years, Dad! What's your resolution?" Jenna questioned. George shook his head dismally, replying "I don't have one this year, Jenna. This is going to be a fairly quiet year for me, and I suspect I'm going to spend most of it here by myself."

"You're not going to be spending the year alone. Mom's driving Jason over later to visit, and of course, I'll stop by whenever I'm able to. I'm sorry I never gave Debbie a chance, I just wish you and mom hadn't broken up, although Debbie was a good person." George nodded solemnly, "One of the best."

Jenna walked over to the couch and sat down. "Dad, I have some pretty big news. I'm pregnant. It's a girl. Josh is coming over later, but I wanted to come and see you first." George's eyes filled with tears and a smile appeared on his face for the first time since Debbie passed away. He hugged Jenna and said enthusiastically "I'm going to be a grandfather." Jenna smiled and placed her hand on her stomach. "We think we're going to name her Hope."

More tears fell from George's eyes as he thought back to Debbie's last words to him, "I want you to have hope for the new year," and at that moment, George felt as if Debbie had come through for him after all. George's heart filled with love for the unborn child as he decided maybe it wouldn't be such a bitter year after all.

Kira Lieb

Kira Lieb is currently in eighth grade. She is a volunteer photographer for the annual FWA writers conferences, and enjoys writing, hanging out with friends, listening to music, and skateboarding. Kira was a member of the school news crew and beta club in sixth grade

Youth Writers Program
Florida Writers Association

Hide and Seek:
Florida Writers Association Collection, Volume 8 and
Florida Writers Association Youth Collection, Volume 3

The next book in FWA's Collection series is *Hide and Seek: Florida Writers Association Collection, Volume 8*, which will include the *Hide and Seek: Florida Writers Association Youth Collection, Volume 3*, to be published in the fall of 2016. It's all about hiding, and seeking. Our Person of Renown for this collection, John Gilstrap, describes the theme in this way: "For everyone who has something (or someone) to hide, there's someone else out there that wants to find it." Fiction, nonfiction, prose, and poetry are all acceptable. Watch our website for complete entry guidelines, www.FloridaWriters.net.

This short story contest, sponsored by the Board of Directors of Florida Writers Association, and by Black Oyster Publishing, who is our new Official FWA Publisher for Collections, was created to offer our members another opportunity to be published, and another way to grow their writing skills.

Each year, the contest has a theme. All writing must conform to that theme, and must be within the total word limitations as set forth in the guidelines.

The annual contests are fun—they give you the opportunity to submit two entries. They stretch you, giving you parameters and guidelines within which you previously may not have considered writing.

All judging is done on a blind basis. Stories are posted by title and number only. The number is assigned consecutively as stories are received. Judges read each entry entirely and vote according to whether or not it was well written, was strongly on theme, and struck a chord with them. As with any judging, there is some subjectivity to the process. However, the judges understand that each entry selected as a winner must be ready for printing, as no editing is done other than fixing minor typos that happen to be caught.

Our Person of Renown for this book is John Gilstrap, the New York Times bestselling author of eight thrillers. His books include *Hostage Zero, No Mercy, Six Minutes to Freedom, Scott Free, Even Steven, At All Costs,* and *Nathan's Run*. His novels have been translated into more than 20 languages.

John has also adapted his novel, *Nathan's Run*, along with three other novels, for the big screen. Currently, he is writing the screenplay for his book *Six Minutes to Freedom* for Sesso Entertainment. A former firefighter and EMT, John holds a master's degree in safety from the University of Southern California and a bachelor's degree in history from the College of William and Mary in Virginia.

As in the past, our Person of Renown will select his Top Ten Favorite entries out of the judges' top sixty…and we'll be off and running with another book for the Collection, and, another contest to look forward to for the following year.